EVERYBODY WANTS TO RULE THE WORLD

EVERYBODY WANTS TO RULE THE WORLD

MIMA

EVERYBODY WANTS TO RULE THE WORLD

iUniverse books may be ordered through booksellers or by contacting:

iUniverse
1663 Liberty Drive
Bloomington, IN 47403
www.iuniverse.com
844-349-9409

ISBN: 978-1-6632-5809-0 (sc)
ISBN: 978-1-6632-5808-3 (e)

Library of Congress Control Number: 2023922015

Print information available on the last page.

iUniverse rev. date: 11/20/2023

ACKNOWLEDGMENTS

I want to thank all the people who've bought or borrowed a copy of any of my books over the years. It means the world to me. I don't care if you buy a copy or find one at the library. I'm just thrilled you took a chance on an independent author.

I especially want to thank three of my biggest fans - Rita Hustler, Lisa Maillet, and my mother, Jean Arsenault. Thank you for your never-ending support. Every repost or like on social media, a kind word or praise, is always appreciated.

Also by Mima

The Fire Series
Fire
A Spark Before the Fire

The Vampire Series
The Rock Star of Vampires
Her Name is Mariah

Different Shades of the Same Color

The Hernandez Series
We're All Animals
Always be a Wolf
The Devil is Smooth Like Honey
A Devil Named Hernandez
And the Devil Will Laugh
The Devil Will Lie
The Devil and His Legacy
She Was His Angel
We're All Criminals
Psychopaths Rule the World
Loyalty Above All (there are no exceptions)
House of Hernandez

Learn more at **www.mimaonfire.com**

Also find Mima on Twitter, Facebook, and Instagram @mimaonfireZ

CHAPTER 1

Courage. When we look back in history, it is the courageous we admire. We don't celebrate holidays, produce documentaries, or write books about those who hid at the first sign of danger. We love heroes. We love the person who rushes into a burning building to save a life. We love the child who stands up to the bully. We love the woman who took the chance when she was afraid.

The thing about courageous people is that they're impossible to control, and for a demographic of society, that's a problem.

We all have moments of courage in our lives, times when we feel as powerful as a lion, fear nothing, and fight to the death. But there are also times when courage escapes us, deserting us when we need it the most. For some, this is the vast majority of their lives, but for someone like Jorge Hernandez, it is the dark night of the soul.

"I stayed away too long, *mi amor,*" Jorge observed as he drove through the Toronto streets. They were heading to the *Princesa Maria,* where he would meet the top people in his organization. Glancing at his wife, he immediately felt a moment of peace sweeping through him as he looked into her eyes. "Paige, I know they will wonder why. This here is not like me."

"Jorge, you were around for the election with Alec, and after that, you announced that you needed some time off," Paige gently reminded him. "I don't think anyone suspected that anything was wrong."

"If they see a weak leader," Jorge reminded her of what he had been saying for days. "Then everything crumbles underneath him."

"You aren't a weak leader," Paige quickly countered, with a strength in her voice that immediately put him on alert. "Jorge, you used to run one of the most powerful cartels in Mexico and survived. You came to Canada, started *Our House of Pot,* took over the entire cannabis industry in the country, started *Hernandez Productions,* and took control of the government from behind the scenes. You've slayed a lot of dragons along the way. I would hardly call you *weak*. No one in our family is weak."

Jorge grinned, thinking about his children and, of course, his wife. When he met Paige, she was an assassin who almost mistakenly killed him after the last-minute hotel room switch. Even more recently, she used these same skills to save his life after a miscalculation on his part.

"But again," Jorge reminded her as they inched closer to his bar where the group often held their meetings in the VIP room. "It was after that lady almost-

"*Almost* killed you," Paige cut him off. "But she didn't. And no one in the group knows about that. All they know is she pulled strings from the top, and she's dead. They don't know anything more, and we can keep it that way."

"People, Paige, they can smell weakness."

"Well, they won't smell it from you," She assured him as she leaned over, her hand touching his arm as their eyes met. "Just walk in there as if nothing changed. They don't have to know what you've gone through the last couple of months. It's January. A new year, and you can start fresh, leaving everything behind."

"I still do not understand why," Jorge started but couldn't finish his sentence. The words stuck in his throat.

"Does it matter?" Paige countered. "We all have low points in our lives. Even you. You're human."

"I like to think I'm more than human, Paige."

"I know you do," She teased. "I hate to break it to you, but you aren't. That's the problem because you had to face your mortality that night in the penthouse, and it was a rude awakening. But that doesn't make you powerless. It makes you aware. It makes you see the world differently."

"It makes me weak," Jorge insisted. "Once a man sees that he is mortal, every day may be his last."

"You can't focus on that," Paige insisted as she glanced at the *Princesa Maria* as they pulled into the back parking lot. "Because that's when you get into trouble. Trust me. Once you get in there, your old instincts will come back."

Jorge wasn't sure but knew it was something he had to do. A weak man was a dead man. He learned this as a boy growing up in Mexico, and it was a lesson that had served him well. It kept him alive during many situations where he should've died. Some would say it was a guardian angel, but he knew better than to think anything so holy was looking out for him.

After parking the SUV, the couple took a moment before getting out. Jorge could feel his wife's blue eyes watching him closely as they made their way to the back door of the bar, where he pulled out his key. Entering the VIP room, he walked in to find Marco Rodel Cruz sitting at the table. The middle-aged Filipino man was officially the IT Specialist for *House of Pot* but did more hacking than anything.

"Good morning, sir," Marco looked up from his open laptop on the boardroom table and smiled at Jorge and his wife. "How are you today, sir? Did you enjoy your time off?"

"It was good, Marco," Jorge replied as his strength grew. "But too much time with the kids over the holidays. Now I need a break from that, you know?"

To this, Marco laughed. He opened his mouth to say something when Diego Silva flew into the room from the other door. He was the CEO of *House of Pot* and a longtime friend of Jorge Hernandez.

"You're here!" Diego's eyes widened as he fixed his tie and stood up straighter before turning back toward the door, yelling into the bar. "Hey, the big boss is here."

Jorge exchanged looks with his wife before heading to the table while Diego sat at the head. The Colombian was a longtime friend and the person he often referred to as his *hermano,* which allowed certain privileges.

"Hey Jorge," Tom Makerson entered the room, followed by Andrew

Collin and Tony Allman, all from the *Hernandez Production Company* side of his business. "Nice to have you back."

"Nice to be back," Jorge moved his chair forward as the others took their seats. "How are things at *HPC?* My production house still standing?"

"Are you fucking kidding?" Andrew Collin gave Jorge a sideward glance as he headed for his chair. "We're taking over Canadian production. Those other motherfuckers are eating our dust."

"In fairness," Diego spoke bluntly at the end of the table. "There ain't much to take over."

Jorge grinned but didn't say anything.

"We've been more…aggressive in recent months," Makerson quickly jumped in. "With the cartel show, docuseries, and daily news show streaming, our subscriptions have soared, especially now, in the winter months."

"Yeah, no one wants to leave their house it's so cold," Tony quietly added as he ran a hand over his bald head. "We are gaining momentum."

"This shit is true," Andrew nodded as he removed his leather jacket, exposing a ripped t-shirt over a long-sleeved shirt.

"What? We do not pay you enough to buy new clothes?" Jorge pointed at Andrew.

"Hey, you guys can have your suit and ties," Andrew leaned back in his chair. "Me? I'm not into that."

Diego rolled his eyes while Makerson gave him a dirty look. Tony made a face.

"Where's Chase?" Jorge finally asked.

"Probably banging the fuck out of Jolene in his office," Andrew replied with a shrug.

"Can we not talk about my sister like that?" Diego made a face. "I got breakfast still sitting in my stomach."

"I thought that was over, sir?" Marco muttered toward Jorge.

"Me, I do not care about this here soap opera," Jorge shook his head and glanced at the door just in time to see Chase enter the room. The half-indigenous young man opened his mouth to say something, but Jorge quickly cut him off.

"No Jolene?"

"She didn't think you'd want her to join," Chase Jacobs awkwardly replied as he closed the door behind him. "So she left."

Jorge shrugged. He was just as happy to avoid the Colombian femme fatale. She did nothing more than irritate him most days.

"*Perfecto!*" Jorge replied and pushed his chair ahead. "Now, let us...

"Sir, I don't mean to cut you off," Marco hurriedly spoke as he pointed at his laptop. "But there is someone around your vehicle."

"What?"

"I was just about to close my laptop," Marco pointed at the screen as Jorge rose from his seat, and the others followed. "But I noticed on the security camera..."

"What the fuck!" Jorge headed toward the door. Abruptly swinging it open, he didn't see anything at first. Shaking his head, it took a moment to notice his slashed tires. When he saw a pair of feet on the other side of the vehicle, Andrew tore past him, almost knocking Jorge over in the process.

"Hey, motherfucker!" Andrew ran around the vehicle. A young man with blue hair rose and started to run, but he wasn't fast enough for the lanky kid to catch him. Grabbing the back of his coat with one hand, Andrew pulled him back, knocking him to the ground. "What the fuck do you think you're doing?"

Jorge rushed over and pulled out his gun. Easing around the side of his SUV, he pointed his gun at the blue-haired young man on the ground.

"What the fuck are you doing?" Jorge yelled at him. "You flatten my tires?"

The blue-haired kid raised his hands and shook his head.

"You know how much those fucking tires cost?" Jorge continued. "You dumb motherfucker?"

"Do you know whose tires you just flattened?" Andrew continued as the others crowded around.

"I..I didn't know you were a cop," The blue-haired boy stuttered.

"A cop?" Jorge snapped. "You'd be so fucking lucky."

"Get him inside," Paige said. "Let's take care of him in there."

"Take care of me?" The blue-haired kid started to shake. "What does that mean?"

"Let it be a surprise," Diego put both hands on his hips.

Chase approached the young man and grabbed his hoody with one hand, almost choking the kid as he pulled him inside the building, with no concern for the bumps along the way.

It's easy to be courageous when no one is looking, but a whole other thing when the world is watching.

CHAPTER 2

"I cannot wait to hear why you cut my tires," Jorge hovered over the blue-haired twenty-something, who sat in a chair in the middle of the VIP room, a gun still pointing at him. "This here, it should be good."

"You can't hold me here," He boldly replied. "I know my rights."

"Why does this dumb fuck keep talking like we're cops?" Andrew wondered as he stared down the vandal and he moved closer. "If we were, you'd already be out walking around, planning the next person you want to fuck over."

"Ok, let us just hear him out," Jorge attempted to reason but was quickly cut off by the young man.

"You have no right to hold me here."

"Then leave," Jorge pointed his gun toward the door while continuing to give the blue-haired kid a dark glare. "But first, you tell me why you slash my tires?"

"You had no right to force me in-"

"I said," Jorge started to yell. "Tell me why you slashed my tires! Do you have a fucking hearing problem? I asked you a question!"

"You infringed on my rights as a human being-"

"Look, you little useless fuck," Jorge grew impatient, this time smelling the fear of the young man. "Tell me why you slash my tires."

"Tell him," Diego moved forward with a menacing look. "'Cause right about now, you are pretty lucky he don't slash *you.*"

The blue-haired kid seemed to weigh his options as he glanced around the room, then back at Jorge's gun.

"Because," he paused before continuing. "You're a climate criminal."

To this, Jorge's head fell abruptly back in laughter, causing the vandal to jump, his body tensing.

"Me? I am a climate criminal?" Jorge mocked him before glancing back at the others. "I have been called many things in my life, and many were true, but never a *climate criminal.*"

"What the fuck?" Diego's face scrunched up. "What is he talking about?"

"It's a woke thing," Makerson attempted to explain but was cut off by Andrew.

"Yeah, usually pretentious fucks like this guy, who attacks people they think are hurting the environment."

"So, you slash my tires?" Jorge was confused. "So that I need to buy *more* tires. Tell me, is this *better* for the environment?"

"It's because of people like you," The blue-haired kid continued, "that our climate is going to hell, and we're all going to die."

"Well, I hate to break it to you, but we are all going to die," Jorge corrected him as his eyes grew dark. "some of us, sooner than others."

He gave the kid a cold stare, but a sense of strength rose in the stranger.

"It's a crime against humanity," he continued. "Because of people like you, my generation and those after us will suffer."

"Oh, for fuck sake," Andrew rolled his eyes. "Don't you got some art to throw soup on?"

"What?" Jorge was confused. "Throw soup?"

"You don't want to know," Tony assured Jorge as he shook his head. "But some of these activists do some pretty illogical things to make a point."

"Like glue themselves to walls and shit," Andrew shook his head. "Because that's going to make a whole lot of difference."

"Is this here a joke?" Jorge asked as he put his gun away. "People, they do these things?"

"Yes, sadly, this isn't a joke," Tony replied. "These climate protesters do radical things to make a point. It's all this woke stuff."

"Or dye their hair blue and declare themselves a different gender or species or some shit like that," Andrew reminded. "These kids today!"

"You, you are not much older than him," Jorge pointed at the blue-haired young man.

"There's a definite line in the sand," Andrew reminded him.

"How old are you?" Jorge directed his attention back to the kid as he fidgeted in the chair.

"Twenty."

"Do you have a job?"

"No."

"Why does this not surprise me?"

"Saving the environment is my job."

"Is that so? Does this here pay well?" Jorge spoke in a mocking tone. "And what does the day of an environmental savior look like? Please tell me. This I must hear."

"It depends."

"On what?"

"I dunno."

"Who is telling you to do these things?"

"No one," He insisted.

"So you just woke up this morning and decided to slash my tires."

"No, not exactly."

"Then tell me," Jorge grew angry. "How did you get this here idea?"

"I'm part of a group," he attempted to explain. "And we decided that there are a lot of expensive SUVs in Toronto, and they are gas guzzlers, so maybe if we slashed their tires…"

"We would all give up our vehicles and walk?" Jorge cut him off.

"No, but you'd open your eyes to your impact on the environment."

"Is this so?"

"You should have an electric car."

"And you should have a fucking job," Andrew jumped in.

"Ok, this is enough," Jorge shook his head. "I do not have all day for this shit."

"What do we do with him?" Chase stepped forward as he watched the blue-haired kid.

"*You* should be most offended," The blue-haired kid directed his comment at Chase. "White man came along and fucked up the environment for your people."

"Save the woke shit for someone else," Chase snapped back as he glared at the kid, then awkwardly stepped back.

"In case you did not notice," Jorge gestured at his brown skin. "Not everyone here is white."

"Yeah, but you're rich," he looked at Jorge. "You people are the *worst.* Flying on your private jets, multiple cars, big houses...."

"Jets?" Paige spoke up. "We don't have a jet."

"Or multiple cars," Jorge complained. "Paige, can you call the dealership? We need these tires replaced, and you," he turned his attention to the blue-haired young man, "I must figure out how you will pay."

"I don't have any money."

"I can find a way for you to pay that does not involve money," Jorge insisted. "And it will discourage you from ever doing this shit again."

"Good luck with that," he countered. "I plan to dedicate my life to..."

Before he finished his sentence, Jorge raised his arm and backhanded the environmentalist, almost knocking him off the chair.

"You can't do..." He protested, only causing Jorge's rage to rise as he grabbed the kid off the chair and threw him on the floor.

"What is it I cannot do!" Jorge yelled at the kid, who finally seemed to understand the situation. "You! You think I'm ignorant about the environment, but you are ignorant about *life.* And more specifically, how the real fucking world works. Do you understand me?"

There were signs of fear in the young man's eyes as he slowly nodded.

"I have done much *worse* to people who have done much *less* to me," Jorge continued, his eyes glaring as his heart pounded in rage. "Do you understand?"

"Yes," he nervously replied.

"Now, if I ever see you around here again," Jorge spoke in a low voice as he challenged the kid's eyes. "Or any of your friends, around my vehicle or anyone else's, for the climate or whatever fucking excuse you make, there will be consequences."

"I understand."

"Because you can call me a climate criminal all you want," Jorge attempted to control his anger as he leaned closer to the kid. "But you, *you* are a criminal too. You are just looking for an excuse to justify the crimes you commit. But you know what? We can all attempt to justify what we do. It does not mean there are no consequences, and believe me, as a man who has lived a lot of years and seen a lot of things, there are *always* consequences, and most would make you much more uncomfortable than climate change."

The kid nodded as he nervously swallowed.

"Now, you will leave here today, thankful that this *climate criminal* let you off easy," Jorge continued. "Consider it the luckiest day of your pathetic life."

With that, Jorge let him stand up. Without saying a word and with his head down, the blue-haired kid ran toward the door and slid out, letting in the brisk January air.

"You let him go," Diego observed. "I did not expect that."

"I let him go for a reason," Jorge insisted without giving further details.

"I am watching, sir," Marco said as he stared at his laptop. "He ran out of here like he feared for his life."

"This here is not such a stretch," Jorge replied as he glanced around the room. "Now, we have a meeting to continue unless there is something else?"

"Tow truck is on the way," Paige gently commented as she touched his arm. "They'll text me when they're here."

"Well, if this is the case," Jorge paused. "We may as well continue with our meeting."

CHAPTER 3

"I'm telling you," Diego said as he glanced into his rearview mirror to make eye contact with Jorge in the backseat. "Kids like that, they got nothing to feel good about, so they jump on some fucking cause like this climate change shit."

"You don't think it's real?" Paige asked from the passenger side as she glanced out the window. "The weather is bizarre."

"Who fucking knows?" Diego replied as his face tightened, and he shook his head. "There's different schools of thought on it."

"Must we talk about this?" Jorge asked as he let out a heavy sigh.

"Hey, you're the one who asked," Diego reminded him. "I'm just telling you what I think."

"It makes sense he still lives at home," Paige agreed. "Otherwise, he'd have to get a job to survive. Toronto isn't exactly a cheap place to live."

"He could live in a fucking gutter somewhere, who cares?" Jorge intervened, growing less interested in this conversation, his mind elsewhere.

"Nah, that kid's got money," Diego insisted. "Trust me, I watch stuff online, and I hear a lot in my support group. That kid, he comes from a rich family, was never made to work, has no sense of purpose, so he joins this group to feel like his life means something."

"That's still debatable," Jorge muttered as he glanced at his phone. "How long did they say it would take to get my new tires, Paige?"

"Later today," Paige replied. "They plan to drop your SUV off when they're done. You can use my car if you need to go anywhere."

"Maybe you gotta get a spare vehicle," Diego glanced at Jorge in the mirror. "Like one of those big ass trucks. The kind that you can drive over anyone in your way. That sounds like you."

"Like a hummer?" Paige laughed. "Or a tank?"

"Hey, either would work," Diego paused and twisted his lips together. "But if you gotta move *something,* a truck could come in handy."

"Ah, but Diego," Jorge found himself light up. "Then I would be a climate criminal because I have multiple vehicles."

Paige started to giggle.

"According to him," Diego shook his head. "You already are, so what difference? You've already crossed the fucking line."

"I've already crossed many lines," Jorge muttered as he heard a ringing. He glanced at his phone, but the screen was dark.

"Hello," Paige spoke, causing Jorge to glance her way and out the window.

He was himself, but not quite himself. He was strong during the meeting, but his battery was running low. He just wanted to go home.

His wife let out a frustrated sigh.

"We will be there as soon as possible," She ended the call and turned toward Diego. "Can you drive us to Maria's school?"

"Sure," Diego nodded.

"I hate to ask…"

"Paige, what is it this time," Jorge interrupted. "What the fuck is wrong with that school now?"

"Isn't it always something?" Paige shook her head. "I don't know. Maybe Maria expressed a politically incorrect statement like last week."

"Was that when she called the black kid….*black?"* Diego asked as he looked ahead, his face scrunched up.

"Just turn up there," Paige pointed toward the next intersection. "It will be easier to take the back route."

"Diego," Jorge jumped in. "Apparently, it is offensive to call a black person *black* now because it is…what is the word, Paige?"

"A microaggression," His wife nodded.

"What the fuck is microaggression?" Diego shot back.

"We looked it up on the way home and still don't really understand," Paige insisted. "But it was offensive, and Maria had to apologize to the other kid."

"Oh, for Christ's sake," Diego shook his head. "For that, you got a call?"

"Yeah, like my Maria," Jorge shook his head. "Her grades, they are good, and her attendance, it is good, but her mouth, it gets her in trouble. I know the feeling."

"She's not compliant and thinks for herself," Paige intervened. "apparently, that's the real issue here."

"They want the kids," Jorge complained. "to come out brainwashed."

"Sounds like they want a bunch of fucking sheep," Diego commented. "In this world, you need to be a wolf to survive, especially these days."

"This is true," Jorge said, turning his attention to Paige. "So, what is this about? They tell you nothing?"

"Nope," Paige shook her head. "Just that there was some kind of 'incident' with Maria, and we have to get her."

"What the fuck am I paying this school for if she's always sent home early?"

"That's a great question," Paige agreed. "But they didn't want to answer last time, so I doubt they will this time either."

Jorge ran a hand over his face and took a deep breath. He was not in the mood to deal with this problem. A situation like this used to fire him up, but now, Jorge didn't have any fire left in him. He closed his eyes.

"You might want to leave your gun out here," Diego sharply commented, causing Jorge to open his eyes. They were arriving at the school.

"That's debatable," Jorge muttered as he glanced around the vast yard surrounding the school.

"Might be one way to get your point across," Diego said as he parked his Lexus and turned it off.

Jorge's body felt heavy as he got out of the car. He shared a look with Paige, who seemed to be reading his eyes. She smiled, and his body relaxed as they approached the school. Paige reached for his hand and squeezed it.

"I can take care of this," She said as they headed toward the entrance. Jorge turned to see her blue eyes studying his face, a caring smile on her lips.

"Paige, I must be present because this school will never back down if I don't push back." Jorge reminded her. "And at this point, I've almost had enough of them."

Automatically knowing the way to the principal's office, neither said a thing as they made their way down the corridor. To Jorge's surprise, he felt his ire rising with each step. It was almost as if they looked for reasons to find fault with his Maria. There was simply no way any other parent was being called to the school this often. He felt anxious, angry, and unsettled as he glanced around the familiar surroundings. Paige squeezed his hand again, causing him to look back into her eyes as they approached the office.

"Mr. and Mrs. Hernandez?" The Asian lady behind the desk alerted their attention. "Mrs. Dundas is ready for you."

Neither said a word as they walked into the elegant office. Classical music flowed through the room while a middle-aged woman sat behind the desk, her face stern as she watched the couple enter her office. Jorge noted that his 15-year-old daughter sat to the principal's far left. She turned her head around to share a look with her father; her big brown eyes softened his heart, but only for a second.

"What the fuck is wrong this time?" Jorge suddenly snapped, letting his wife's hand go and stomping across the room. Behind him, he could hear the door being closed. "And remind me again how much money I pay this school to *teach* my daughter something?"

"Please, you will have to calm down, Mr. Hernandez," Mrs. Dundas insisted as she stood up and pointed toward the chair. "I'm starting to understand why your daughter's behavior is so erratic."

Jorge glanced at Maria again as he and Paige sat down.

"This is bullshit, *Papá,"*

"Miss Hernandez!" Mrs. Dundas snapped as she sat down. "If you can't control yourself, I will ask you to leave."

"Do we not have freedom of speech anymore in our country?" Maria snapped back. "Or are the rules different in this school?"

"This here is a good question," Jorge felt himself stumbling over his English as Paige sat beside him. "I am wondering the same thing."

"Miss Hernandez, you can wait outside," Mrs. Dundas spoke sternly, her dark eyes narrowing.

"But if this has to do with her," Paige attempted to reason. "Doesn't she have a right to be here?"

"Not if she can't act respectfully," Mrs. Dundas said as Maria abruptly stood up. "That was one of the stipulations I gave before allowing her in the meeting."

"Again, I pay you how much for my daughter to go to this here school?" Jorge asked, waving his hand as Maria left the room, slamming the door behind her. "Or are you going to throw me out because I cannot control myself?"

"What is this about?" Paige pushed. "I have to pick up my son at preschool."

Jorge knew this was an excuse. Their live-in nanny, Tala, would pick up Miguel, but he appreciated her quick thinking. He wanted to get the fuck out of there.

"We continue to have behavior issues with your daughter," Mrs. Dundas spoke toward Paige, occasionally glancing at Jorge. "Outbursts, like she had just now, are common occurrences."

"She's a fucking teenager," Jorge snapped. "What else you got lady?"

"I would prefer there be no profanity..."

"I don't give a fuck what you prefer, lady," Jorge cut her off. "I pay your school a lot of money, as I *keep* reminding you, and you call me over ridiculous things."

"Was there something *specific* that happened today?" Paige jumped in.

"There was something," Mrs. Dundas nodded. "We have a teacher who recently announced identifying as a woman, and Maria refuses to acknowledge this."

"What?" Jorge shook his head. "What are you talking about? Is this here a man or a woman?"

"You mean Mr. Kregas?" Paige asked. "Maria mentioned that last night-"

"No, please," Mrs. Dundas dramatically replied. "You are dead naming *Miss* Kregas and-"

"What?' Jorge cut her off. "What the fuck are you talking about, lady?"

"Mr. Kregas no longer exists," Mrs. Dundas shook her head. "We now have *Miss* Kregas on staff, and Maria refuses to refer to *her* with the proper pronouns."

"She means that this guy is a trans woman now," Paige attempted to explain to Jorge. "She's trying to be politically correct, so she's walking on eggshells. It's a whole thing..."

"Oh, for fuck sake," Jorge felt his anger rising. "So, you call us here today to complain because Maria, she called someone who *is* a man, a man?"

"No, because when someone identifies..."

"Lady, if he still got a dick, he's a man," Jorge yelled. "Is this some pervert who's just trying to change in the girl's change room or some shit, because if he is...."

"No, of course not," Mrs. Dundas said, her voice rising. "It's nothing like that at all."

"It better not be lady, Jorge jumped out of his chair. "Because I'm telling you now, I'm getting sick and tired of this school and all it's bullshit. My daughter, she is here to learn something, to be smart, not to learn all this politically correct, woke crap."

Jorge swung around and stomped out of the office, with Paige rushing behind him. He may have started the day off feeling like a helpless animal, but he ended it by being a lion. And no one fucked with a lion.

CHAPTER 4

"So, like, I've been a girl for 15 and a half years, but he decided like *yesterday* to be a woman, and he suddenly has more rights than me," Maria began to rant before they were even out of the parking lot. "What the *hell?*"

"Maria, I cannot do this right now," Jorge pulled on his sunglasses while loosening his tie. "I am feeling claustrophobic in this here little car. Can we talk about this when we get home?"

"What?" Diego jumped in as he pulled onto the street. "What do you mean, Maria?"

"It's a long story," Maria shook her head dramatically while turning her attention to her father. "You're right, *Papá.* I'm feeling claustrophobic too. Why *are* we in Diego's car? Are you guys carpooling now?"

"Yes, Maria," Jorge spoke sarcastically. "We are suddenly concerned about the environment."

"At least we can take the HOV lane," Diego observed while nodding. "Maybe we should do this more often."

"So why are we in Diego's car again?" Maria pushed, and Jorge felt it would take everything in him to answer, so he said nothing.

"Because some environmental kid decided to slash your father's tires," Diego blurted out, dramatically waving a hand.

"Why?" Maria scrunched up her nose. "Like, you caught him, and he said that?"

"Yeah, some blue-haired freak," Diego continued to rant. "Said your father was a climate criminal."

"Oh my!" Maria started to giggle, her girlish laughter quickly moving up a notch to explosive laughter. "*Papá,* does he not know who you *are?* Did you like...."

"Maria, is your phone off?" Jorge sharply cut her off.

"No."

"Then we don't talk about..." Jorge reminded his daughter of possible dangers. Although Marco went to great lengths to ensure apps on all their phones couldn't eavesdrop on them, one could never be too careful.

"I know, I know," She raised her hands in the air before sharing a look with Diego in the mirror and burst out in laughter again. "I mean, it's just so..."

"I know, *right*?" Diego replied with wide eyes.

Jorge glanced around to see that even Paige was laughing. It made him smile.

"Oh no," Maria suddenly stopped. "You don't think that he was only saying that...I mean, what are the chances that he just happened to pick your SUV? You know..."

"Marco is on it," Jorge replied.

"Let me," Maria suggested as she reached for her phone. "I can go on and find these environmental people for the local area and see what I can find out. Did you catch a name or anything? Did you save his ID after you..."

"Maria, I let him go," Jorge shook his head. "And I do not think he was up to anything other than just being a useless fuck."

"He did have blue hair," Paige spoke up. "He was twenty."

"You've just described half the people his age in Toronto," Maria shrugged. "I will see what I can learn."

"Maria, focus on your schoolwork first," Jorge insisted.

"My marks are perfect," Maria shook her head. "No one can complain about *that,* at least."

"So, why were you in trouble today?" Diego asked, looking in the rearview mirror. "What happened?"

"It was something I said," Maria shook her head. "Or *didn't* say."

"This I gotta hear," Diego said as he zoomed through traffic.

"One of my teachers, like *five* minutes ago, decided he's a woman," Maria complained. "And I got in shit for addressing him with the wrong pronoun."

"Maria," Paige spoke up before Diego could reply. "You have to be sensitive to the fact that Diego..."

"Diego's gay," Maria rolled her eyes. "I obviously *know* that."

"Hey, I'm gay," Diego dramatically rolled his head around. "It don't mean I'm wearing a dress and asking to be called Deidra. It ain't the same."

"Who would *want* to be called Deidra?" Maria countered, wrinkling up her nose.

"Just...you know," Diego scrunched up his mouth. "The first name I thought of. If I were transgender, I would probably pick a better name than that."

"And why does it always have to be a name starting with the same letter?" Maria shrugged. "I don't understand."

"Right?" Diego waved his hand around. "I tried to ask someone that once and got the fucking third degree."

Jorge turned his head to look out the window, attempting to ignore the conversation, showing a calm exterior. Behind the sunglasses, he could feel himself breaking into a cold sweat, and the car suddenly sounded hollow, as if the voices were coming from behind a wall. He attempted to hide his symptoms, even as his heart raced uncontrollably. Jorge allowed himself to get caught up in the wave, knowing that fighting it would only cause him more grief.

"Jorge?" Paige was saying his name, but he didn't know what she was saying.

"*Papá?* Are you ok?"

He felt Maria's hand on his arm, a sense of panic flowing through her voice.

"*Si,*" He finally answered, taking a deep breath.

Glancing around, he saw fear in everyone's eyes, including Diego's. Jorge suddenly realized the car had stopped and was in his driveway. Wasting no time, he opened the door and jumped out, welcoming the cold air touching his face. He attempted to hide that his legs were weak, but when his head started to spin, he found himself leaning against the car.

"Jorge!" Paige was suddenly in front of him, her hand touching his arm. "Maria, call an..."

"No, no," Jorge shook his head. "I am fine."

"You're *not* fine."

"Paige, it was just a panic attack," Jorge insisted as he took a deep breath. "The car, it was too small, and I...today, it has been..."

"Are you sure," Maria was suddenly on his other side, followed by Diego. Studying their faces, Jorge realized he looked vulnerable and immediately stood taller.

"I'm fine," Jorge insisted. "I love you all for worrying so much, but I am fine."

"Are you sure it's just a panic attack?" Paige countered with fear in her voice. "You aren't having chest pain, are you?"

"No," Jorge spoke honestly. "I swear, Paige, I am fine."

"Ok," She seemed reluctant as she glanced at the others for assurance. "Maybe, just in case, we could call so they can check you out."

"Paige, by the time an ambulance arrived here," Jorge shook his head. "I would be dead and buried already."

"Jorge!"

"They are slow," Diego nodded. "He ain't wrong. Last week, I heard a guy had a heart attack and died an hour before they got someone there."

Maria gasped and grabbed her father's hand.

"Diego, you are scaring my daughter," Jorge gave him a look and watched him backpedal.

"But, you know," Diego quickly added. "It was probably a busy day, and, you know, the news exaggerates everything."

"Let's just go inside," Paige suggested. "See how you feel when we get in there."

Once in the house, Jorge loosened his tie again, removed his sunglasses, and walked into the kitchen.

"Can I get you something to eat?" Paige followed behind. "Some coffee? No, maybe coffee would be worse."

"Paige, I am fine," Jorge attempted to lighten the mood. "Although, maybe I will make a sandwich."

"You go sit," Paige pointed toward the living room, where Diego and Maria huddled together, talking. "I will bring you something."

"Paige, I don't..."

"Go!" She insisted, almost pushing him toward the living room.

Jorge headed into the next room, noticing Maria and Diego parting, abruptly ending their conversation.

"Yeah, so what's this?" Jorge jumped in.

"Nothing," Maria replied.

"You got something to say, you tell me," Jorge insisted. "I see you two talking."

"It was nothing," Diego shook his head, scrunching his lips. "Just, you know, life stuff."

"I was talking about school," Maria was lying to him, "not you."

Jorge gave her a skeptical look.

"Boy troubles," Diego insisted.

"Diego!" Maria's face turned red.

Jorge studied them both and shook his head.

"I'm fine," He insisted and turned toward the kitchen. "Paige, I'm going to be in my office. Do *not* call an ambulance. I feel fine."

"I wasn't..." His wife replied as she rushed into the room with a sandwich on a plate. "You haven't eaten in hours. Maybe this is what you need."

"*Gracias,"* Jorge dropped his defenses and took the food before turning to look at Diego and Maria. "You two, I am fine."

"You just seem....off," Maria spoke in a small voice, with fear in her eyes.

"I am fine, *princesa,"* Jorge insisted. "Do not worry about me."

She appeared skeptical.

They all did.

"I will be in my office," Jorge calmly added before taking a bite of the ham sandwich and turning around. "*Not* having a heart attack."

Once behind closed doors, he took a deep breath and finally relaxed. He had barely left the house in the last month, and today turned out to be more than he bargained for, but yet so much less than he used to deal with in everyday life. Would he ever be back to normal? Why did having a gun pointed toward his head affect him now when so much of his life had been far more dangerous?

Sitting behind his desk, he took another bite before setting the plate down. Looking at his bulletproof window, he found comfort in the quietness surrounding him.

And then the phone rang.

CHAPTER 5

"Well, isn't this the icing on the cake?" Jorge sarcastically commented as his words flowed through the room. "I am already having a shit day, and of course, this would be the day *you* call, but, of course!"

"Look, I wouldn't, but this is important," Alec Athas spoke in a low voice on the other end of the line as Jorge leaned back in his chair and listened. "Do you have me on speakerphone?"

"*Si,* but the door is closed, and I'm alone," Jorge insisted as he closed his eyes and listened to the Canadian prime minister. "Not that anyone cares what is going on in government anyway. The people they are too busy digging their heads in the sand."

"That's what worries me," Alec spoke frankly. "There's some stuff coming down the wire that affects children."

These words caused Jorge's eyes to spring open.

"What do you mean?"

"I mean, Big Pharma is trying to change laws that will end up with them profiting," Alec replied. "They're lobbying now, but I suspect they have a lot of my cabinet in their back pocket."

"Athas, how often do I tell you to stop being a pussy?" Jorge reminded him. "You're the fucking prime minister! Act like one! Tell your cabinet to play by your rules or get the fuck out. I do not understand why this is so difficult for you. You just got reelected, so the people will take whatever you say as God's word. And even if they don't, who gives a fuck?"

"If I push too hard," Alec said. "They'll try to have a non-confidence vote against me."

"As usual," Jorge reminded him. "If you have an issue, you know I'm happy to help if I can."

They both fell silent, knowing what that meant.

"Things were going so smoothly...."

"Athas, the honeymoon is over," Jorge bluntly reminded him. "It's time to get back to real life. Before the election, we had plans for you this time around. You can't be a pussycat anymore but a lion. This is *your* time."

"You're right," Athas sighed.

"So, what is Big Pharma trying to push down your throat now?"

"They said that all the erratic behavior in our youth is because of increasing mental health issues," Athas explained.

"Is that so?" Jorge nodded. "So, let me guess, they have a pill for that?"

"Well, they have several pills," Alec reminded him. "But they have one that's brand new that they claim is formulated for young people."

"Right...."

"And they want to change the definition of mental health issues specifically for youth to justify putting them on this pill," Athas continued. "This comes with a media campaign, where they pay off news corporations to create fear with parents, showing them worst-case scenarios to encourage them to put their kids on medication."

"It wouldn't be my fucking kids," Jorge replied. "So drug up an entire generation for profit because this makes them a lifetime customer."

"Essentially," Athas replied. "I worked in social work for years. There's no difference with kids today than 10 or 20 years ago, except that our culture has changed with the internet. But kids are kids. This is bullshit."

"Did you tell them this?"

"Yes," Athas said. "I was like a skunk at a yard party."

"I can imagine," Jorge said as he continued to look around his office. "There's too much money to be made. I'm sure any of your cabinet that's for this already has shares in the company doing this?"

"Their spouses or relatives do," Athas replied. "So, you see the issue?"

"I do," Jorge nodded. "Let me meet with my people this week. We will find a solution."

"They're already making their way through our universities," Athas continued. "They had one in particular, here in Ontario, that's insisting kids that show *concerning* behavior go on meds, or they can't go to school."

"Is this happening in other schools yet?" Jorge sat forward, moving his chair ahead. "Like, high schools?"

"I think it's coming," Athas admitted.

"I see," Jorge took a deep breath, thinking about his earlier meeting with Mrs. Dundas. "We must take care of this soon."

After their conversation ended, Jorge was left with his thoughts. The world was changing, but not necessarily for the better.

A knock at the door interrupted his thoughts, something he welcomed.

"Come in."

The door opened, and Paige stood on the other side. A toddler ran into the room, heading directly for Jorge.

"I thought you might like some company," Paige said as Miguel jumped up on his lap. "He just got home."

"Miguel!" Jorge pulled the little boy into a hug. "*Cómo estás?*"

"Buen, Papá."

"He was looking for you as soon as he walked in the door," Paige said as she crossed the room and sat across from Jorge. "He loves having you home more. We all do."

"I know, Paige," Jorge shook his head. "But I must get back to my old self someday soon."

"There's no rush."

"There is," Jorge insisted as the little boy curled up in his arms. "I spoke to Athas, and there's an issue."

"Oh…"

"Big Pharma," Jorge paused for a moment. "We will need to gather the troops for a meeting."

"Not today," Paige shook her head. "You need to take it easy."

"No," Jorge agreed, "maybe tomorrow."

"You need to take things slow."

"I cannot seem weak, Paige."

"No one is thinking that."

"No one that you know of," Jorge reminded her. "Do you not think that Diego went home today thinking I was powerful after he saw me have a panic attack?"

"He doesn't think you're weak," Paige insisted. "He was worried like we all are."

"A leader can never show weakness."

"You're human, Jorge," Paige spoke evenly. "And it was just Diego. He's been a friend for over 20 years. I don't think this will change how he sees you."

"You have to be careful, Paige," Jorge shook his head as he looked down at his son. "It is a, how you say? Slippery slope."

"What's going on with Big Pharma?" Paige asked.

"They want to get more kids on pills," Jorge replied. "Trying to say there's a rise in mental health issues."

"I've been seeing that in the news more lately."

"They all work together, Paige," Jorge said. "Athas cut the funds to broadcasting, so they're going to cut his throat."

"Everyone's scratching someone's back."

"That principal at Maria's school," Jorge said in a low voice. "She is one of them. That is why she is trying to make it seem like Maria is out of control."

"Do you think…."

"I do."

"But your daughter," Paige sat forward. "She tends to get mouthy."

"She's 15," Jorge raised an eyebrow. "Is that not what teenagers do?"

"True," She agreed. "But let's not jump the gun."

"Paige, this here is going on in universities," Jorge said as he glanced toward the door and back at his wife. "That is where it starts. It's where they test. Next, it will be Maria's school. They want these kids compliant because they are easier to control."

"Not to mention the money they could make."

"And trust me, Paige," Jorge nodded his head. "Everyone is making money on this."

"With kids as their guinea pigs."

"Well, someone has to be," Jorge sarcastically remarked. "After all, it works on many levels. Compliant kids, customers for life, this is all they care about."

"And those drugs," Paige said. "They aren't easy to get off once you're on."

"Ah! So this here, it is the *new* opiate."

"Yes, the ones they said *weren't* addictive," Paige narrowed her eyes and Jorge nodded.

"I worry about Maria."

"You shouldn't," Paige shook her head. "This isn't the Maria of last year. It's a different book and a completely different chapter. She is stronger than ever and isn't afraid to call people on their BS. That's why the school has issues with her. She's 100% your daughter, that's clear."

To this, Jorge laughed and looked down at his son, who was watching him with admiring eyes.

"And Miguel," Jorge gently said to his son. "You will be next. Just like your sister, you will be strong. You will carry on the Hernandez name one day. I will teach you how to be a man."

He looked back at his wife to see the concern in her eyes.

"Not that I'm going anywhere anytime soon, Paige," Jorge reminded her. "I'm here to fight these motherfuckers till the end. And I have no intentions of losing."

CHAPTER 6

"At least the school can't call you today," Maria quipped as she stuck a spoon in her yogurt and glanced around the table. "It's a long weekend."

"It seems like a strange time for teachers to have a meeting," Paige observed as she wiped Miguel's face, which he attempted to rebel against. "You barely got back to school from Christmas break, and they're off for another meeting."

"I don't know what they're doing," Maria said as she rolled her eyes. "And I don't particularly care."

"Well, for the money I pay them," Jorge began to rant as he reached for his coffee. "There should be more school, less meetings, and even less bullshit."

"It's the *woke* agenda, *Papá,"* Maria continued to speak dramatically. "They're supposed to teach us how to prepare for the world."

"Wonderful," Jorge sarcastically replied. "Instead of teaching my daughter life skills, they teach her not to offend anyone."

"And that goes against everything you believe in," Paige gently teased.

"Well, Paige," Jorge shrugged. "This here is the real world. We will not always like what people say, which is fine. Then you get the fuck over it and move on."

"*Papá,"* Maria glanced at Miguel, who was watching Jorge.

"Whatever, Maria, that ship, it has sailed," Jorge shook his head. "He swore last week. I told him no, do not do this."

"We don't need any issues at preschool again," Paige reminded him with a sigh. "Come on, Miguel! Let's go upstairs and clean you up so you look handsome when Tala comes upstairs."

Jorge smiled as his wife picked up their son and carried him upstairs. He glanced at the door that led to their nanny's basement apartment and back at his daughter.

"So, Maria, what is on the agenda today?" Jorge pulled out his phone and glanced at it. "Hanging out with your boyfriend? What's his face?"

"I told you we broke up," Maria reminded him. "Which is just as well since you never can remember his name."

"You know," Jorge looked at his daughter. "The guy you met at the rollerskating rink or whatever. Anyway, Maria, my memory isn't so great. I'm not good with names."

Maria shrugged and fell silent, and Jorge felt guilty for bringing it up.

"I am sorry," he gently added. "I did not mean to sound…insensitive."

"It's ok," she shook it off. "I don't care anymore."

He didn't believe her.

"I was thinking," Maria said and looked down at her food but stopped eating. "I hope yesterday, when you had that panic attack, it wasn't because of me because…"

"No," Jorge automatically cut her off. "Maria, do not say such a thing. It was a full day for me. Especially after sitting at home for so long."

"It's called taking a break," Maria reminded him. "You were burned out. You're always saving the day for everyone, but who saves the day for you?"

Without saying a word, Jorge smiled, reached over, and kissed his daughter on the head.

"I will be fine, Maria," Jorge assured her as he stood up. "But I do love you for worrying."

She smiled and gave a self-conscious giggle.

"Now," Jorge returned his phone to his pocket and fixed his tie. "I have a meeting to attend."

"Ok, *Papá.*"

"Enjoy your day off, *Princesa.*"

Once outside, he took a deep breath. He stopped to inspect his four new tires. Swearing under his breath, he jumped in behind the wheel, relieved not to be stuck in a little car again, and tore out of the driveway.

Random snowflakes drifted through the air as he drove. Jorge shivered and turned up the heat. He would never get used to these Canadian winters, although he heard they were much harsher in other provinces. Chase had horror stories from his days growing up in Alberta. Thinking of the group's youngest member, Jorge decided to call him.

"Hey," Chase answered right away. "What's going on?"

"I'm heading to the bar now," Jorge replied. "Are the others there yet? I think I'm running late."

"Just Marco," Chase referred to the IT Specialist. "But he's always early."

"Ok, "Jorge thought for a moment. "I will be there shortly. Any sign of that blue-haired fuck again?"

"Nah, I checked the cameras this morning to see if he was around last night," Chase replied. "And again this morning, but I didn't see anything. I think he knows better than to come back."

"I'm not so sure of this," Jorge replied. "He did not seem to get the message as quickly as most would."

"It's the arrogance of youth," Chase insisted. "The entitlement that they have."

"I will be there soon," Jorge said, ending the call.

His heart was racing, but he managed to contain it. There was too much traffic everywhere and too many people. He and Paige had talked a lot recently about getting out of Toronto, but he knew to do so would be like disconnecting from the world. He also knew that it was a move that would affect his whole family. However, when he considered the issues Maria had at school, it might be best to get out of the city. Then again, would that seem as if they were running away?

Jorge stopped for a coffee at *Taza de Sol* on his way to the bar. When he finally arrived at *Princesa Maria,* he hesitated to leave the SUV. Just as he started toward the backdoor to the VIP room of the bar, it swung open, and Marco stood in the doorway with a smile on his face.

"I have been keeping an eye on things, sir."

"Thank you, Marco," Jorge gave his employee an appreciative nod as he walked toward him. "If that fucker comes back here, it might be the last place he goes."

"Yes, sir," Marco giggled as Jorge entered the room to find the others coming in through the door from the main bar. Makerson, Andrew, and Tony sat in their usual places, as did Chase and Marco. Jorge felt his heart begin to race but chose to ignore it.

"So, I talked with Athas yesterday," Jorge got right to the point as he sat down. He directed his comments at Makerson, Tony, and Andrew. "We might have an issue, so you gotta find ways to counter this new narrative that's picking up steam."

"Is that the mental health thing?" Makerson guessed. "I was going to bring it up yesterday before we got interrupted, but then it slipped my mind."

"Yes," Jorge was impressed with the man who oversaw *Hernandez Production Company*. "How did you know?"

"The narrative has been getting stronger for weeks," Makerson observed. "I assumed it was because we were heading into a new year. It's winter, dark, and depressing, so they would take advantage of this time to launch new meds for the depressed kids. But yesterday, they started to talk about increases in mental health issues with children in schools, and an alarm went off for me."

"Yeah, and how teenagers are depressed," Andrew jumped in. "Because this is fucking news now?"

"The snow never stops," Jorge pointed toward the door. "Who wouldn't be depressed?"

"Well, they claim it's linked to something more serious," Makerson continued. "To deeper mental health issues, which they attempt to say is due to the problems in the world. I heard through some sources that the government is looking at laws to help *protect* youth in case they go off the deep end and go on a shooting spree or something. In their minds, every kid should be on meds as a preventative measure."

"Which is ridiculous," Tony jumped in. "It's not like Canada has a lot of school shootings, but they're still trying to create the fear narrative."

Jorge took a deep breath and said nothing while they watched him.

"It is concerning," he said, "what Athas told me yesterday."

"But he *is* the fucking government," Andrew complained. "Don't tell me he doesn't realize he has the power."

"No man has power until they see it to be true," Jorge reminded him. "He tell me yesterday that these companies want to push for laws forcing those who are not compliant to go on pills. They want kids to have a mental health problem. And even worse, they want to make it so that you cannot go to school unless you are on this new medication."

"That's fucked!" Andrew complained. "Who would believe this bullshit?"

"It's easy," Makerson countered. "You get them scared with never-ending stories of teenagers going crazy and killing their whole family, then at just the right time, the drug companies will swoop in and save the day."

"Yeah, but people aren't that dumb..." Andrew attempted to insist but stopped.

"Yeah," Chase cut him off. "They are. Scared parents will do anything for their kids, even if it makes no sense. My ex-wife wants to put one of my sons on a pill because he was hyper. He's a normal, energetic kid."

Jorge cringed and shared a look with Chase. It was a touchy subject. Over the years, Chase saw less and less of his children. They lived in Alberta with their mother and stepfather and, over time, seemed to ease Chase out of the picture.

"That happens a lot," Makerson assured him. "I'm telling you, if people get scared of these kids going over the edge, they'll go along with the government passing a bill making it law."

"Even if Athas is against it?" Tony asked then, turned his attention to Jorge. "He *is* against it, right?"

"He is," Jorge nodded. "But his cabinet is another story."

"Yeah, they get kickbacks if they go along," Makerson said. "Don't worry, it won't affect *their* kids."

"Ain't that illegal?" Andrew pushed.

"Like it fucking matters," Jorge reminded him. "Politicians are all crooks."

"I hadn't noticed," Chase quipped, causing them all to laugh.

"So, we gotta figure out a way to counter this narrative," Jorge continued. "With facts that destroy it."

"That all we doing?" Chase asked and made eye contact with Jorge, who paused.

"For now."

CHAPTER 7

"....which proves that teenagers are no more depressed now than they were 10, 20 years ago," Tom Makerson replied, his eyes appearing sincere as he spoke into the camera. *"The only difference is they're depressed for different reasons. Social media and online bullying are considered contributing factors. One of the doctors I spoke with said that kids and young adults often base too much of their self-esteem on what others think of them, which is a slippery slope, no matter what decade you're from."*

Paige and Jorge shared a look before returning their attention to the laptop. They were watching the most recent episode of *Raging Against the Machine* online while having breakfast. This episode tackled the topic of the mental health of children and young adults.

"*This is disturbing,*" Sonny McTea commented and shared a glance with his co-host, Andrew Collin, before looking back at the camera while the image of Makerson showed up on half the screen. "*But why are we suddenly hearing so much about young adults and depression? I watched a news report the other night that suggested it was detrimental that we get on top of this before anything serious happens.*"

"It's all about money," Andrew interjected. *"Big Pharma's gotta make some money to satisfy their shareholders. People haven't been trusting them since they made that pill for indigestion that was proven to cause stomach cancer."*

"*Consumer confidence has been down since....*

"You know, Paige," Jorge turned his attention back to his wife. "This here should show the people how terrible these companies are when they are willing to drug up our children to make a profit."

"Especially considering the side effects of this new medication," Paige shook her head. "It's not a short list."

"They do not care," Jorge sighed. "To them, we are only consumers, not people. Our only purpose is to buy their products. But who am I to talk? I once was the same. Back in Mexico, I only cared about selling cocaine and making money. I did not care who it killed."

"You also didn't force anyone to buy it," Paige reminded him. "They bought it with their own free will. This is completely different. Their goal is to get most kids on pharmaceuticals to have lifetime patients. And not because most kids need it either."

"No, because *they* need to make money," Jorge shook his head. "As bad as I am and as bad as I ever was, I understand that money cannot buy everything."

"This doesn't seem to be a lesson they learned yet," Paige muttered as she glanced back at the screen.

"*....again for sharing this information with us,*" Sonny commented to Makerson, who nodded. "*To learn more about this, people should watch your special tomorrow, when you take a deep dive into the side effects of this new medication. Thank you, Tom.*"

"Look at all the views so far. This should rattle some cages," Jorge said as he stopped the video and reached for his coffee. "This is just the beginning. We plan to keep pushing back."

"I somehow don't think it will be that easy to make them back down," Paige observed. "Even when they do, they come back again. Kids are an easy target because people may not care about their health but worry about their children."

"Big Pharma will fight back," Jorge predicted. "But we will fight harder. And another thing, if Maria's school think she will be on medication, they are in for an unpleasant surprise."

The propaganda machine would be silent for a few days as a winter storm blew through Toronto, closing most of the city. Jorge grumbled about the conditions, irritated with the snow, while Maria was in her glory because school was closed. On Thursday afternoon, Jorge was in his office when the secure line rang, causing him to jump. He had been enjoying the silence.

"Athas," Jorge sat back in his chair, glancing at the phone and then at the bulletproof window. Outside, Jorge caught a glimpse of the snowman that Maria and Miguel had worked on that morning. "What can I do for you today?"

"Did you see that video that went viral?" Athas sounded tired. "The one with the kid going crazy in the classroom?"

"No," Jorge replied and reached for his laptop. "Where is it?"

"I'll send you the link," Athas replied. "This is their latest attempt to convince people that our kids should be drugged to go to school."

"Wonderful," Jorge sarcastically replied as he found the link and hit the button. "Where is this from?"

"The Vancouver area," Athas replied as Jorge watched a young man screaming at his teacher in a classroom full of students. Jumping up from his desk, he grew more agitated as he pointed at the teacher, showing signs of aggression.

"I thought the kids weren't allowed to have their phones on during class time," Jorge commented. "Maria, she is not allowed."

"Well, this student was apparently concerned and recorded it."

"Oh yes, of course," Jorge sarcastically replied. "I can't see this kid's face. You got a name?"

"No," Athas replied. "For privacy reasons…"

"Yeah, yeah," Jorge cut him off. "I got it."

He watched the young man pick up a book and throw it at the teacher.

"Oh no!" Jorge mockingly replied. "Not a book!"

"In fairness, those books can be heavy," Athas reminded Jorge, who rolled his eyes. "But it gets worse."

Jorge watched as the kid approached the teacher and roughly grabbed her by the shoulders.

"That it?" Jorge wasn't impressed. "He grabbed her by the shoulders?"

"Well, yes, but…"

"But this here, this one kid, is why they should drug up every kid in Canada?" Jorge complained. "If you ask me this kid, he needs a slap across the fucking face."

"Well, obviously, the teacher can't slap him."

"This here is too bad," Jorge replied as the video ended. "In my world, disrespect is punished."

"In your world," Athas reminded him. "He would probably have a bullet in him for doing that."

"Well, you know, I come from a completely different time and place," Jorge reminded him. "Do we know what happened before this video?"

"No, but I mean..."

"No, well, this could be out of context."

"He can't physically attack his teacher," Athas firmly replied.

"I did not say he could," Jorge pushed back. "I am saying is that we only know what we see. It is very convenient after Makeson's report that shows proof that kids aren't more depressed and violent than they used to be. All this here shows me is kids are more entitled and spoiled."

"That is true," Athas seemed to back off. "I can't argue with that."

"I have said it a million times," Jorge continued. "People are too lazy to do their fucking work. That includes parenting."

"It's a busy world," Athas attempted to explain. "People are overwhelmed, and by the time they get home at the end of the day, they don't have much to give to their kids."

"Then they should not have them," Jorge countered.

"But, I...."

"Athas, I have a busy life," Jorge reminded him. "But if there is a concern with my daughter or son, I am there. I do not half-ass it. This here is one of my jobs. People have to learn to parent. Television and the internet were the old drugs when they didn't want to deal with their kids. Now they are moving on to an actual pill to keep them compliant."

"I agree," Athas jumped in. "I'm not saying you're wrong. But I can't go out there and lecture Canada about being shitty parents. I have to give them real solutions and calm their fears before my cabinet has justification for pushing this bill through."

"Athas, you were a social worker," Jorge reminded him. "I would think your word is stronger than any of these morons you work with, and why is it you keep them around if they don't listen to you. You're the boss. Fire them."

"I can't just..."

"You can push them out," Jorge reminded him. "Say that their values do not align with the party."

"I'm concerned that the whole party will go against me."

"And then what?" Jorge asked. "There's a non-confidence vote?"

"Yes."

"Then I will step in and do it right," Jorge replied. "You cannot do your job. You fear the public. You fear your cabinet. You let everyone walk on you. I will not. Do you think they would try this shit with me? You have to be fierce, Athas. I have told you that a million times."

"You've told me not to be a pussy a million times," Athas snapped.

"And that there," Jorge ignored any attitude he was hearing. "Is still true. Athas, stop being a pussy, and remind them you are the boss. You said you were going to be fierce this time around. I want to see it. They are doing this to you because they know they can."

Met by silence, for a moment, Jorge thought he hung up. Athas finally spoke.

"I hate to admit it," his voice was pathetic and weak. "But I think you're right."

"I hate to admit it," Jorge confirmed. "But I am."

"Should I have an interview with Makerson?"

"You can," Jorge thought for a moment. "But I have another idea."

CHAPTER 8

"There are times that I think bullying should make a comeback," Jorge ranted to Chase and Marco the following morning. The group met in the VIP room at the *Princesa Maria*. "It's easier if people know where they stand."

"I wasn't aware that you ever stopped, sir," Marco said as he started to laugh.

"Nah, Nah, you can't do that," Chase mocked the situation. "Words are violence."

"These people," Jorge complained as he reached for his cup of *Taza de Sol*. "They have not known real violence because words would be the last thing they'd worry about. Where I come from, mean words are much better than a bullet to your head or having a body part cut off."

"Oh, the good old days," Diego said as he stood in the doorway, causing the others to turn around. "This position as CEO makes it harder to get my hands dirty now, you know?"

"You don't gotta keep your hands clean," Chase reminded the Colombian as he entered the room and sat down. "You gotta keep it quiet."

Diego gave him a knowing look.

"Me," Jorge shook his head. "I wonder every day why I didn't run in the last election. None of this shit would be happening. No kids would have to take drugs in order to go to school. Sure as hell *not* my party."

"Yeah, that's the part I don't get," Chase shook his head. "Why is Athas' party against him?"

"Because clearly, he hasn't put the fear of God in them," Jorge replied and glanced around the table. "You got your phones turned off?"

Everyone either agreed or checked. Jorge said nothing as he waited. One could never be too careful.

"Sir, I will tell you," Marco shook his head. "My children will not take medication. I do not want them even taking something for a fever now that I've learned so much about these companies."

"Yeah, hacking them gives you a view that most do not have," Jorge reminded him. "But others, they believe anything you tell them. They think their children are fragile little creatures who always need to be saved. It is not that they will want their kid drugged up so much as they want *your* kid medicated. You know, just in case."

"The irony is that if these kids are pushed too hard about these new rules," Chase jumped in. "They *will* become mentally ill and do something crazy."

"When did kids *not* do crazy things?" Diego made a face and shook his head. "Why is this suddenly such an issue?"

"Because they got a pill to sell," Jorge reminded him. "So *we* gotta compete from *Our House of Pot* and introduce a more natural product to calm kids, that is safe. Use the argument that our products are not full of questionable chemicals."

"So, that's our public side," Chase nodded. "What are we doing behind the scenes? Anyone at Big Pharma we gotta deal with?"

"Not yet," Jorge replied. "The problem now is Athas' cabinet. We know they are being paid off or bribed, but we got no proof."

"Sir, I'm looking into it," Marco pointed toward his closed laptop. "So far, I found emails mentioning Athas not agreeing with them, and they don't understand."

"Of course, he doesn't agree with them," Jorge said. "They wanna drug our kids."

"They say or *suggest*," Marco commented. "That it will only be *some* kids that may have to be on this medication. But then they list all the reasons or situations that might require medication. And sir, these are things common to most kids."

"Like they wake up in the morning and are cranky?" Chase grinned. "I can't wait to hear this."

"Well, yes, this is the kind of thing I mean," Marco vigorously nodded. "Moodiness, irritableness, cannot get along with others, right up to violent tendencies."

Jorge shook his head, feeling a wave of anger surging within him. He shared a look with Chase.

"You've just described everyone in this *familia,"* Diego commented as he crossed his legs and sat back in the chair. "Jorge goes through all that in the run of a normal day."

Laughter filled the room, and Jorge grinned.

"Well, you know," he finally replied. "I am a complicated man."

"Sir, if you were 15-years-old, they would have you on medication," Marco laughed.

"Like fuck they would!" Jorge laughed.

"That's another thing," Chase said. "Even if you do give a kid medication, who's to say they are even taking it anyway? I sure as hell wouldn't have."

"They have addressed that," Marco replied. "They want it taken in front of the teacher."

"Has the whole world lost their fucking minds?" Diego sniffed. "Why would people believe this garbage? I don't got kids, and this wouldn't fly with me."

"Critical thinking," Jorge shook his head. "This is not popular anymore."

"Probably because the parents are on pills themselves," Chase pointed out.

"This here makes sense," Jorge agreed.

"So, what are we doing?" Chase pushed.

"It depends," Jorge thought for a moment. "Marco, do these people meet or just email each other?"

"So far, sir, I am only seeing emails," Marco replied. "But I am planning to hack their phones too."

Jorge nodded.

"Maybe we leak the emails?" Chase suggested.

"They do not mention the connection with Big Pharma," Marco replied. "Just their *concern* for kids and what they should do."

"Then how do we know about Big Pharma?" Chase asked.

"I talked to Athas about that part," Jorge replied.

"And why is it again that he isn't taking care of this himself?"

"Because he cannot fire everyone," Jorge reminded Chase. "Or we got a minority government, which is easy to take down. It is one thing to deal with a lone wolf but quite another to deal with a cabinet full of them. If the people are stronger than the leader, then everything collapses."

"But they know Athas got you behind the scenes," Chase reminded him. "I would think that's enough."

"We can break some kneecaps if we gotta," Diego moved closer, his dark eyes narrowing on Jorge's face. "You don't have to ask me twice. I got a new baseball bat that is light as a feather but can fuck someone up good."

Chase let out a snicker, and Marco's eyes widened.

"I will not say no yet," Jorge replied. "I suspect that this group will be meeting in secret. If they didn't yet, they will soon."

"Sir, when I hack the phones, I can send a text that looks like it's from one of their phones," Marco suggested. "And get them together at the same time."

"Find the ringleader and make the suggestion to that person," Jorge said. "We must get them all in the same room at once."

"But even if we do this," Chase said as he leaned back in the chair. "We know what Big Pharma is like. They're not going to back off. They'll work with the opposition and the media they buy off. Maybe throw in a few *scientists* or *doctors* for good measures. They aren't going to give up that easily."

"No," Jorge agreed. "But the government can stall anything, and if we plug up that hole, we can work on the others."

"What about schools?" Chase wondered. "Are they pushing this shit?"

"Well, at Maria's school," Jorge shook his head. "I think they are trying to do this, but I am not sure. They always contact me about her behavior issues, which often are *not* issues."

"Are other parents having this problem too?" Diego asked. "Maybe that's to target *you* more than Maria?"

"This here has crossed my mind," Jorge nodded and glanced at his cup of coffee. "I will look into it. I must contact my good friend Juan Perez to see if his daughter is dealing with the same problems. She's Maria's age."

"That the guy from *Taza de Sol?* Was it his daughter that had...issues with the last principal?" Diego asked. "I was a bit out of the loop then."

"*Si,"* Jorge nodded. "He and I worked well together. I must visit him and discuss this situation. I am wondering if his daughter has also had *behavior* issues."

"Maybe, sir," Marco jumped in. "I should also hack the school emails and the board that oversees them."

"Boards are useless," Jorge shook his head. "They sit through meetings and do nothing. Focus more on that principal, Mrs. Dundas. I got a feeling she is playing the game with Big Pharma, but I don't know for sure."

"If she is," Marco nodded. "We will find out."

"The fact that any of these people are willing to make guinea pigs out of kids is fucking sick," Chase complained.

"These people at the top," Jorge replied. "Believe me, they *are* sick. They are psychopaths. And psychopaths, they are smooth. They can convince anyone of anything, and they do, as we see."

"Psychopaths rule the world," Diego quipped.

"They can try," Jorge replied. "They can try."

CHAPTER 9

"Jorge Hernandez!" Juan Perez warmly welcomed him to *Taza de Sol's* head office. "It has been, what? A few months since we talked last?"

"*Si,* I've been keeping a low profile," Jorge commented as he followed the owner of the local coffee chain into his luxurious office. "You know, after the election campaign with Athas, the holidays, I decide it is good to spend time with my *familia.*"

"Is there anything more important?" Juan went behind his desk and sat down while Jorge found a seat across from him. "The kids, they grow up so fast!"

"That they do," Jorge nodded. "That they do."

"It is funny because my secretary had your name down to meet me today," Juan grinned as he pointed toward his desk. "And she told me that *Jorge* Hernandez, using the pronunciation we used in Mexico, was coming to see me. It took a minute to figure out who she meant."

Jorge laughed at his delicate dance around the topic. He hated the Spanish pronunciation of his name, which sounded more like *Horhey* when spoken. He hadn't used it in years.

"Yes, well, after spending so many years working in the US in my youth," Jorge attempted to explain. "It was just an easier transition, and I feel it comes across...stronger."

"I agree," Juan nodded his head and thoughtfully watched him. "So, tell me, what can I help you with today?"

"I was wondering if you've had any issues with your daughter at the school since..."

"No," Juan quickly answered. "After the incident with that old pervert, I take my daughter out and send her to another school. I didn't care that they fired him. I would never trust them again."

"For the money we pay..."

"For the money we pay," Juan cut in. "They should check the staff thoroughly, but they hire the filth they find under a rock. No, I send my daughter to another school, and no problems since."

"I may have to get the name of that school," Jorge said as he moved uncomfortably in his chair. "Because my Maria, I am about to take her out too."

"Oh?" Juan said with concern in his voice. "What is going on?"

"I am regularly being called to the principal's office because she's *misbehaving*," Jorge complained. "Last week it was because she misgendered a teacher who was formally a man, then *very* recently decided to transition."

Juan started to laugh. "Are you serious?"

"I am *very* serious," Jorge nodded. "And this is all the time. They think Maria is too mouthy, too strong. They want her to be compliant and quiet. And to that, I say no."

"This does not surprise me," Juan leaned back in his chair. "Unfortunately, it is a different world from when we grew up. In some ways, this is good. But in many other ways, it is not. They worry about offending someone more than teaching our children basic life skills. I got young people working at the cafes who can't count change for the customers. It's hard to find someone with common sense. Maybe your new principal needs to take a tumble down the stairs as the last one did?"

"Now, there is an idea," Jorge grinned when recalling how they took care of the previous principal after he attempted to assault Juan's daughter. "It is not easy knowing what to do. I try not to spoil my Maria. She works at my production house, and I tell them she better work or I'll fire her."

"Well, this is how kids learn," Juan nodded. "But hey, if she can count out change, Maria is always welcome to come work for me!"

The two men started to laugh, and Jorge nodded. "Do not think I would not send her your way if she didn't have a job already. My Maria has no problem counting money."

"So, you are looking at a new school for her?" Juan went back to their original topic. "I can assure you she would like this other school more."

"My concern," Jorge spoke honestly. "is that I might have the same issue no matter where she goes."

"Is this so?" Juan appeared puzzled.

"This is why I wanted to talk to you today," Jorge paused before continuing. "We have reason to believe Big Pharma is pushing a new drug for kids, supposedly for their mental health issues. However, their definition of *mental health* might be quite loose."

"I see," Juan appeared concerned.

"And they are attempting to pressure the government to make it law in order to go to school."

"Does your boy, Athas, does he not have a say?"

"That is a problem I'm working out now," Jorge replied. "We believe his cabinet has been infiltrated and working against him."

"He may have to get a handle on that," Juan raised an eyebrow.

"This here is the plan," Jorge nodded. "But I wanted to see if you had any issues with..."

"Not so far," Juan shook his head. "But I do welcome the warning. I will be talking to them. These things have a way of creeping in."

"This is what I am thinking," Jorge agreed. "Do be aware."

It was after he left the office and was on his way home that his cell rang. It was Marco.

"Sir, there is a meeting you might want to attend."

"Is this so?"

"Yes, I just found information on it," Marco hurriedly spoke. "I have the location and time."

"Today?"

"In an hour," Marco replied. "Here, in Toronto, which surprised me. I thought it would be in Ottawa."

"Can you send me the information and let Chase know?"

"I will, sir."

He ended the call and hit a button on his dashboard while sitting in traffic. Moments later, Athas' voice was echoing through the SUV.

"What's going on?"

"Athas, are you in Toronto today?"

"Yes, but I have to go back to Ottawa to…"

"Stay. There is a meeting you will want to attend."

"When?"

"In an hour," Jorge replied. "I am guessing the same time you're suppose to be leaving the city?"

"Well, yes, we had a cabinet meeting here earlier," Athas replied. "It's a long story, but we had to come to Toronto to…"

"I do not care why," Jorge cut him off. "They assume you are leaving, then they will have the *real* meeting. The one about how they are in bed with Big Pharma."

"I can't believe that…"

"Believe it," Jorge replied. "Because it is happening. I will send you the information shortly."

Taking a deep breath after the call ended, Jorge felt his heart race. These things that used to invigorate him, that he wouldn't think twice about doing, no longer had the same effect. He felt dispassionate but would still make it work.

Forty-five minutes later, he arrived at the government building where the meeting would take place to find Chase waiting. He got out of his truck and approached Jorge's SUV. Jorge opened the window.

"You ready?"

"Athas will be here in a minute."

"Is that necessary?" Chase wondered.

"It will have more of an effect," Jorge guessed.

"You can't take a gun in there," Chase spoke in a low voice as Jorge reached into his leather jacket. "Just in case you were planning on it. They got some kind of detector."

"Oh?" Jorge asked, suddenly feeling out of sorts.

Why hadn't he thought of that?

"Yeah, trust me on that one," Chase warned. "But I got a baseball bat that should get through."

"Would that not be more conspicuous?" Jorge asked.

"Marco turned the cameras off," Chase commented. "There's no security at the door, but they will show up if needed. The building itself is closed for the business day. That's why they're having the meeting here. So it don't matter."

Jorge said nothing as he saw Athas arriving in an SUV with only his driver.

"Where is his security?" Jorge asked, humored.

"*We're* his security, "Chase reminded him.

The prime minister got out and met the two men at the SUV as Jorge got out of the vehicle.

"I don't know if this is a good..."

"Shut up and follow us," Jorge cut him off and looked at Chase. "The baseball bat?"

"What?" Athas was alarmed. "What are..."

"Don't you worry about it," Chase interrupted. "We got this."

"That's what I'm scared of," Athas loosened his tie. "Should I..."

"Just shut up and follow us," Jorge grew irritated and started toward the door. Chase met them with the baseball bat in hand. "So, we got your cabinet secretly meeting because they think they *can.* Our job is to show them otherwise."

Athas used his security card to get in the door. Jorge and Chase followed him inside.

"I know where they will be," Athas said, showing them the way down the long hallway, stopping outside a door.

Jorge walked ahead and attempted to turn the doorknob, but it was locked. He knocked. No one answered.

"You sure about this?" Jorge asked him.

"That's where we had our meeting earlier," Athas nodded.

"There's people in there, I can hear them," Chase said. "You want in? Stand back."

Jorge and Athas followed his instructions, and Chase used all his force to kick the door open, causing the room of cabinet members to be shocked by the sudden action, one woman jumping from her chair.

"What is..." she started to shake. "Call security!"

"No one is calling security," Athas spoke in a firm voice, causing everyone to halt what they were doing, stunned to see their prime minister walk into the room. "But someone's going to be doing some explaining."

CHAPTER 10

"Well, we..." an older man at the other end of the table attempted to explain. Jorge recognized him. He recognized most of them from Question Period in the House of Commons. He didn't care about his name. They were all the same. "We just..."

"Let me guess," Jorge loudly said as he entered the room with Chase in tow, still holding the baseball bat as if it were the most natural thing to do in that setting. "You were planning a surprise party for Athas. Am I right?"

Everyone appeared shocked by his comment, many with fear in their eyes. Some looked at Athas in stunned disbelief, while others started to cry.

"I...this is highly unacceptable," a middle-aged blonde lady's voice cracked. "You can't..."

"Well, I fucking did," Jorge shot back as Chase closed the door behind them. "Now, you're taking out your phones and giving them to Athas because this here, is a private meeting. We want no interruptions."

"You can't take our phone," an older woman sitting close to Jorge spoke up. "They're government property."

"Oh, do not worry," Jorge insisted as Athas grabbed a nearby decorative bowl and started to go around the table. "I do not plan to keep them. This here is for privacy. You know, people hack phones, and people listen into our conversations. So, it is best to be safe than *sorry.*"

His eyes challenged her on the final word, causing the minister to look away. Jorge glanced up to see Athas was almost around the table now, most saying nothing but adding their phones to the pile.

"We do....we have added security to our phones," a younger man commented as he sat straight up, challenging Jorge's eyes.

"I'm glad you fucking think so," Jorge snapped back before addressing the group. "The truth is that people, they can get around everything. Just assume someone is always spying on you. People know what you're saying or doing when you're having a secret meeting away from the prime minister of Canada. Which is your boss."

"We work for the *people,"* the same young man said, challenging Jorge.

"Oh yeah," Jorge growled as he leaned forward, noting the man automatically pulled back. "Well, you can start *any fucking time."*

"What I want to know," Athas found his voice as he handed the bowl of phones to Chase, who immediately took them out of the room, leaving the baseball bat by the door on his way out. "What was this meeting about? It wasn't on the agenda."

No one said a word.

"He asked you a fucking question!" Jorge yelled, causing several members of the cabinet to jump. "*Answer* him!"

"We...we were having more discussion on an earlier topic..." the young woman close to him began to speak.

"Which was?" Jorge challenged, but she didn't reply. "Would it be a secret deal with Big Pharma?"

"It's not a secret deal," an older man attempted to explain. "We...we just don't agree with Alec on the details and wanted to discuss it more."

"Oh, is that right?" Jorge asked, his eyes glaring at the man. "You mean the one where Big Pharma drugs up everyone's kids to make money, that deal?"

"It's not like that," the younger woman attempted to explain. "You can't simplify it and make a blanket statement. That's not how it is."

"Then how *is* it?" Jorge countered. "Please tell me because I would love to hear."

"It's just...it's for kids with emotional problems."

Athas stepped forward. "Now, you're the one overly simplifying things. It's a broad range and an even more slippery slope. It's predicted this will affect most kids at some point in their childhood since the definition is very loose. I would hardly suggest that's a few random kids."

"Did they tip you off when to invest?" Jorge directed the question at the same woman who nervously watched him. "Tell me, *who* from Big Pharma approached you?"

"That's not how it happened," she insisted.

"We can't do that anyway," the young man added. "That's a conflict of interest-"

"So what?" Jorge cut him off. "You get your wife, your girlfriend... whoever to invest instead. Then you make sure there's a law passed enforcing it. Shares go up, and you walk away with a lot of money."

"We hardly want children taking this unless they need it," the young woman continued to deflate as she spoke.

"It doesn't hurt them anyway," an older woman added. "It's not permanent."

"It's an SSRI," Athas snapped. "Are you unaware of how hard it is for someone to get off those pills? When I was in social work..."

"Do we need to hear this?" The young man cut him off. "You bring your...*thug* friend, make us give up our phones, and now you're breaking into one of your 'when I was a social worker' stories again. No one cares. This is government. We aren't social workers. This is a different world altogether."

"What I mean to say," Athas sternly added. "Is that I've seen this many times, and these pills are much more serious than I think any of you realize."

"But children need them," the older woman jumped in again. "Have you noticed how out of control kids are now? School shootings? Gangs? We have to do something before they get out of control like they are in the US."

"Lady, when's the last time we had a school shooting in Canada?" Jorge snapped at her. "And how many fucking kids do you think are in gangs? And do you think those kids will take your fucking pills? Use your brain!"

"I think what she means," the younger woman started again. "We're heading in that direction. We viewed a study where-"

"A study created by Big Pharma," Athas cut her off. "Do you know how many of those studies they do and toss because they don't get the results they want?"

"Also, keep in mind," Jorge added. "They pay for a study that benefits themselves."

"But the numbers..."

"Don't look at fucking numbers," Jorge cut her off. "Look at the reality. Follow the money. Get out of your fucking Ottawa bubble! Look around you. How many of you even have kids?"

A few raised their hands, but not many.

"So, you people, that raise your hand," Jorge asked with interest. "Do you want your kids drugged up? Do you want your kids to take these pills? Being *forced* to take the pills to go to school? Maybe they should be the test study before the rest of Canada."

"That's different," the older lady attempted to explain. "My children are older and don't have behavior problems, so it wouldn't affect them."

"Oh yeah?" Jorge asked and glanced at Athas. "So, do you know what *behavior problem* my 15-year-old daughter recently had that caused the school to call me? The problem was that she *misgendered* a teacher who, five minutes before, decided he was a woman. Are you saying my daughter should be on medication for behavior problems because she called someone with a dick a man?"

"I'm sorry but this is crossing the line," the younger man started. "I've put up with enough of this conversation, but now you've gone too far. You're *clearly* a white supremacist and..."

"*I'm* a white supremacist?" Jorge pointed at his brown skin. "Did the definition of white supremacist change lately because the last time I dealt with these people, they looked more like *you* than me, or do you identify as being black, and I just do not see it?"

"He's right," the young woman anxiously commented as she started to stand. "You *are* going too far and clearly don't understand..."

"Lady, sit the fuck down," Jorge shouted, causing her face to turn pink as she followed instructions.

"You can't talk to her like..." the young man also started to stand, as something made a clunking noise as it hit the floor under the table.

"It's a phone!" Athas jumped ahead and grabbed it. "He was recording us."

"Oh, is that so?" Jorge turned his attention to the young man, who now had fear in his eyes as he sat down. Without saying a word, Jorge walked toward the door, grabbed the baseball bat, and nodded for Athas to put the phone on the end of the table.

"No!" The young man covered his face as if he couldn't look. "Please don't..."

Ignoring him, Jorge swiftly lifted the baseball bat, bringing it down hard on the phone. The entire table pulled back, aghast by his actions, as he furiously pounded the phone as pieces flew in every direction. Finally, he stopped and looked at Athas.

"Have Chase take care of this," Jorge turned his attention back to the group as he felt his anger rising. He continued to clutch the baseball bat. Athas said nothing but slid out the door. Furious, Jorge began to yell. "Anyone else? Has anyone else here got a phone? Does anyone else think that you will be recording this meeting? Anyone else got something to say?"

No one said a thing.

"Now, we are going to get a few fucking things straight," Jorge continued to yell as he pointed the baseball bat toward them. "Because none of you seem to get the rules here. Athas, *he* is running the country, and behind him is me. You stay in line, or you get the *fuck out*. I am not playing games with you people. Athas, he might be the nice one, but me? I play by a different set of rules, and you, do *not* want to be in a position to find out what those rules are. Do we understand each other?"

Fear was in the eyes of everyone around the table.

Athas and Chase returned to the room.

"Chase," Jorge turned around. "I need you to search each of these people. If you find a phone..."

"Oh, I got a pretty good idea of what you want me to do if that's the case," Chase replied as he started around the table.

"You're not searching me," the young man who had the phone smashed complained. His face was red as he glared at Chase. "This is..."

He didn't have time to finish his comment before Chase grabbed him by the shoulders, pulling him off the chair, twisting his arm behind his back, and bringing his upper body down hard onto the table. Everyone nervously backed away from the table.

"We can do this the hard way, too," Chase commented as he searched the man, who let out a whimper.

"You gotta be careful with these delicate boys," Jorge quipped, turning his attention to the stunned group. "Now, this here will be the *last* secret meeting you have without Athas, and if I must come back to speak to you…"

He didn't finish the comment but glanced down at the baseball bat before giving them all a dark glare.

CHAPTER 11

"At one time, I would've said you went too far," Athas hesitated before continuing. "But now, I think you did the right thing."

"Trust me," Jorge said as he leaned back in his office chair, briefly closing his eyes before they shot open again and pounced on the secure line on his desk. "People are people, Athas. It does not matter about their status or how much money they got in the bank. When a wolf walks in the door, the sheep knows they only have two options. And one of those options won't be too pleasant."

"I didn't think they'd buckle so easily."

"That's because they won't buckle for *you,*" Jorge reminded him as he leaned closer to the phone. "There is a big difference between you and me. But this here is fine. Now they know."

"I see a difference already," Athas admitted. "And it's only been a couple of days."

"And Marco, he has been watching them," Jorge reminded him. "Trust me. There are *no* secret meetings now. If anyone even suggested it, one of the sheep would come to you. Everyone in your cabinet no longer trusts the other. And they fear losing their status, money, and power. Or at least, the power they think they have."

"I was concerned they would all resign," Athas admitted. "That the next day I would receive resignation letters or worse, the cops would be at my door."

"Athas," Jorge began to laugh. "You are a funny man. Trust me, we both know that is not going to happen. These people are in politics for a reason. Politicians are the new celebrities, except they win elections, not awards."

"I have heard that before," Athas admitted. "It doesn't exactly make me ecstatic."

"It's an unfortunate reality," Jorge insisted. "Those with good intentions and truly want to make the world a better place are usually never allowed to get to the top."

"I did."

"That is because you had me," Jorge reminded him. "Otherwise, they never would've let you get this far. Trust me, *amigo,* politics are the same here, as in Mexico, the US, or any country."

"Corrupt?" Athas sniffed.

"Now, you are finally catching on," Jorge quietly replied. "You cannot change the game, but you can learn to play it."

Their call had barely ended when Jorge turned his iPhone back on to discover a vague message from Marco that indicated they should meet.

I will be there shortly.

Taking a deep breath, Jorge lazily stood up and walked around the desk and out of the office. He would jump in with both feet when needed, but the instinct wasn't as automatic as it used to be. Something in him was changing, and Jorge couldn't understand. He wanted to nap on the couch with his son more than solve everyone's problems. Unfortunately, his flock still needed guidance, and he would lead as long as they needed him.

Jorge could hear Tala upstairs, singing to Miguel as the toddler giggled. Maria and Paige were out shopping, leaving Jorge wondering why Marco was working on the weekend. Although he admired his IT Specialist's loyalty, Jorge knew he had children at home. Wouldn't he prefer to spend the day with them?

This question flowed through Jorge's mind as he drove to the *Princesa Maria* and was the first words out of his mouth when he walked into the VIP room, where the Filipino was working.

"Sir?" Marco appeared alarmed by his question.

"Marco, I was driving here and thinking it is Saturday morning," Jorge shrugged as he sat across from him. "Would you not prefer to be with your family? I do not mean to be working you..."

"Sir, this is fine," Marco insisted. "My schedule and where I work are both very flexible. I am home with my family plenty. Honestly, sir, I sometimes enjoy the break. The kids can be a little too much at times. Especially when they are fighting."

"Ok," Jorge nodded as he thought about that point. "I can understand that too. My two are such different ages that is usually not an issue."

"Be happy, sir," Marco said. "It can be difficult at times. My kids are also involved in activities, so it is not like they are always home anyway. I usually choose those times to work unless, of course, there is an emergency."

"Oh, Marco, please do not tell me there is an emergency this morning," Jorge heard the exhaustion in his voice. "Are these cabinet ministers being pricks again?"

"No, sir, actually quite the opposite," Marco shook his head, glancing toward his closed laptop. "So whatever you said...or *did* that day worked."

"You don't think they are not just being more careful," Jorge was curious. "They are probably smart enough *not* to be discovered."

"Sir," Marco shook his head. "I think you're giving them too much credit."

"So no?"

"No, I keep seeing them avoiding Big Pharma altogether," Marco insisted. "They avoid meeting requests or say they are too busy. One minister said he cannot help them at this time. So, I do not think this is a concern. They plan to remove the bill that Big Pharma wanted to push through."

"Well, this is good," Jorge nodded at the positive news. "Now, you must tell me what concerns you today."

"I continue to dig into the Big Pharma emails and that sort of thing," Marco reminded him. "As I said before, they're not smart about hiding information. I see notes from one of their meetings that suggest that Tom Makerson is making too much noise at HPC news regarding behavior issues in kids, countering their narrative."

"Do they say it like this?" Jorge was curious as a grin crept onto his lips. "That he is *countering the narrative.* And so openly in an email?"

"Sir, these people, much like the cabinet, are not clever about hiding information," Marco shook his head. "It was easy to find this. It just required time to read it."

"I would not have the patience," Jorge admitted.

"That is why you have me, sir," Marco smiled, and Jorge found himself doing the same.

"So, they are concerned about Tom," Jorge nodded. "What does this here mean? Do they plan to create propaganda against him? Try to suggest in their *new* narrative that he's a terrible journalist. Try to pay him off to stop? What is it they plan to do?"

"They talked about such things," Marco replied. "But Tom has been in the media too long and did not have a reputation of being bribed. And that if they attacked him publicly, they knew that you and your production company would come back against them in full force. They decided instead to threaten him...personally."

"And they did not think I would come back full force with this here too?" Jorge grew angry. "When has any threat ever worked with me?"

"They think if they go about it the right way," Marco continued. "That his fear will win They are talking about potentially attacking him. Not killing him but scaring him enough that he no longer feels safe covering this story. They plan to do it on his personal time, not at the production house, where he is protected."

Jorge took the news in stride and thought while he listened.

"We have a few days," Marco continued. "They are watching him now, trying to work out the details. My concern is if we put obvious security around him, we will not catch the person involved."

"And if we put him in hiding," Jorge nodded. "Same thing."

"But that might be what we must do," Marco said. "I am not sure, sir, but I cannot get the name of the person that does their dirty work. That is the one thing they are smart about because they refer to him as their 'guy'. He is not listed by name in the notes, so I cannot figure out who it is. And it does not sound like they give him an actual schedule about when or how the attack will happen, just general instructions. I do not know what to tell you, sir, but I knew you would know what to do."

"I do," Jorge replied as he started to nod. "I have an idea that I think will work."

He left the bar shortly after while he pondered the plan in his mind. It might work, but he had to check a few things first. He decided to make some calls while waiting in traffic.

"Hello?" Makerson's voice cheerfully answered the phone. "What's going on?"

"I got to come to see you," Jorge replied.

"Story tip?"

"Something like that," Jorge decided not to get into it. "Can I meet you at the production house?"

"Sure, I'm here now."

"See you soon."

He ended the call and thought for a minute longer before he made the next call.

"*Hola,*" A sleepy voice answered the phone.

"Jolene," Jorge spoke sharply. "Do you sleep all day?"

"It is the weekend."

"Where are you?"

"I am at my apartment," she replied. "I was out last night, dancing."

"Aren't you a little old to be partying at the bars, Jolene?"

"I'm *not old,*" She snapped back. "And I was not partying at the bars. I have a dance class on Friday evenings. Now that Chase and I…"

"Jolene, you know I do not care for this soap opera," he cut her off. "I have a job for you."

"Oh," She seemed to perk up. "Does this mean I'm back…"

"It means I have a job," Jorge cut her off again. "I cannot talk to you about it right now, but can you come by the production house? I must meet with Makerson. Maybe you can join us? Can you make it?"

"*Si,*" Jolene suddenly eluded confidence. "I will be right there."

"*Perfecto,*" Jorge replied before ending the call.

CHAPTER 12

"I do not know how any home can function without having an AR-15," Jorge shrugged as he looked across the table at a bewildered Tom Makerson. "But this here, it is a personal opinion. I can get you a handgun."

"I…I don't even know what to say," Makerson shook his head, stunned by everything Jorge had just told him. "First, you tell me that Big Pharma intends on attacking me because I'm going against their narrative, *then* you tell me the plan with Jolene, and *now* you're telling me you want me to own a gun? I've never even shot a one before, let alone…"

"This here, you do not have to worry about," Jorge shook his head. "It is…it is fine. Jolene can teach you. It is easy peasy. You will not have any issues."

"But I have to take the required firearms course and…"

"No," Jorge shook his head and shrugged. "This here, the government stuff, we do not deal with this here."

"You mean…." Makerson started but abruptly stopped. "Of course, you didn't take your firearms safety course, and you probably don't register your guns."

Jorge laughed. "You are the funny one today, Makerson."

"I guess….I mean, why would you?" Makerson thought for a moment. "But if I…"

"You, *you* are with me," Jorge reminded him. "And no one with me has to worry about this because I have it covered. You will get your gun, you will get your bullets, and Jolene, she will teach you how to shoot."

"The whole thing with Jolene," Makerson made a face. "I'm not sure about."

"Jolene is a perfect shot, but if you aren't comfortable having her teach you, I can…"

"No, not that part," Makerson cut him off. "I…I mean… I'm not sure if I want Jolene to teach me to shoot either, but what I was referring to is…."

The door flew open, and a frazzled Jolene Silvia rushed into the room. The Colombian femme fatale wore a modest pair of jeans and a heavy winter coat as her heels loudly clicked on the floor. She closed the door behind her and headed toward the table.

"I am sorry to be late," She stuttered through her English as she placed her purse on a chair before sitting down beside Jorge. "But I almost fall on my way outside my place. Why is it that building owners do not clean the ice well? I almost have a slip-fall on my way to the car."

"Jolene," Jorge pointed to her feet. "You are wearing those heeled shoes. What did you expect?"

"They are boots," Jolene insisted as she sat down her coffee and leaned sideways to pull up her jean leg to show him. "See, they are for winter."

"With heels, Jolene," Jorge complained. "You do not walk on ice wearing *heels*. I am a man, and I know this. Why is it you do not? This is not your first winter in Canada."

"But they are so pretty," Jolene gushed. "I just love!"

"Can we move on?" Jorge asked. "We must get to business. I know Makerson is busy. And me, I want to go home."

"Ok," Jolene followed orders as she pushed her chair in and unzipped her coat. "What is it you want me to do."

"I'm not sure if this is a good idea," Makerson started before Jorge could reply.

"What is a good idea?" Jolene innocently asked, looking between Makerson and Jorge. "Did you start this meeting without me?"

"Yes, well, I had to talk to Makerson about something," Jorge explained. "We have learned that Big Pharma plan to have someone attack him because he keeps going against the narrative."

"What narrative?" Jolene asked as she looked between the two men.

"Oh, I thought she knew?" Makerson hesitated and opened his mouth to continue, but Jolene was already cutting him off.

"Well, how would I know anything?" Jolene turned her attention toward Jorge. "You have meetings and never invite me. What would I know?"

"Jolene, I do not have time for this here," Jorge complained, growing irritated with her complaint.

"It's fine," Makerson said as he raised his hand to indicate they stop fighting. "I will explain."

"Please," Jorge sat back and let him take over.

"Jolene," Makerson turned toward the attentive woman across the table. "Big Pharma wants to introduce a new drug that they claim is for kids with mental health issues. The problem is that the range is pretty broad and honestly could include almost any kid at some time throughout their childhood. At the same time, they're pressuring schools and government to make it mandatory that kids with what they deem as mental health issues have to take this medication to go to school."

"What?" Jolene's eyes widened. "This here, that is terrible."

"It gets worse," Jorge threw in.

"Well, that's why Jorge has you here today," Makerson explained. "Because HPC news has been countering their misleading statistics and gaining attention. Jorge learned they plan to have someone attack me so I'm intimidated and stop reporting on this topic."

"They must see you as a threat," Jolene pointed out. "But how would they get to you here?"

"That's the problem," Makerson continued. "They don't want to get to me *here.*"

"Oh," Jolene continued to follow him.

"The problem," Jorge jumped in. "Is that he told the people the truth, so parents know. They don't like this."

"So, this is for sure true?" Jolene asked.

"Oh yes, it's true," Makerson confirmed. "We have the documentation. They were trying to push a bill through parliament, but Jorge stopped that, so now they want to change that bill while working on the parents."

"They think they can push it on school boards," Jorge added. "Over my dead fucking body, will my kids take their pills to go to school."

"So, if the children do not take these pills," Jolene scrunched her face up. "They won't be able to go to school. That is terrible."

"Well, if they have behavior issues," Makerson replied. "But let's face it, it's easy to say a kid has a behavior issue."

"My Maria, she got in trouble for misgendering a teacher the other day," Jorge informed Jolene. "That was considered a *behavioral* problem."

"I do not understand," Jolene shook her head. "What do you mean by *misgender?*"

"It doesn't matter," Makerson said and shook his head. "The point is that Big Pharma is desperate because we are getting a lot of traction on our stories about how they're misleading the public. They couldn't sneak it through parliament, so now they're attacking from this angle."

"And this is where I need you," Jorge turned his attention to Jolene.

"What do you need me to do?"

"I need you to teach Makerson how to shoot a gun," Jorge replied.

"Ok, I can do," Jolene nodded. "Whenever you wish."

"I also need you to stay at his house," Jorge continued.

"Stay at his house," Jolene repeated. "Like, a bodyguard?"

"Well," Makerson seemed hesitant to agree, but Jorge jumped in.

"Yes, as a bodyguard," Jorge replied. "Jolene, you can do this because you have done it before. No one will suspect that Makerson's new *girlfriend* is a dangerous killer."

"I can do," Jolene appeared to take it in stride. "I will go home and get my suitcases."

"You mean right away?" Makerson still didn't seem convinced of the idea. "I just don't know if..."

"Makerson, these people are not fucking around," Jorge insisted. "Trust me, I have dealt with them before, as has Jolene, so we know."

Jolene thought for a moment before nodding.

"It is either that, or I send....I don't know, Chase? But we need to seem unsuspecting. It will be obvious if you have an actual bodyguard standing at your door or with you all the time. If you go to a safe house, we won't catch him. If you are at one of our houses, they will not come near because they know. This is why you seem like the perfect target, and they do not know that Jolene works with us."

"This is true," Jolene loudly replied. "Since I am *never* invited to meetings."

Jorge gave her a dirty look.

"I guess that makes sense," Makerson reluctantly replied. "I feel weird needing a woman to look after me."

"Do not be sexiest," Jolene barked at him. "I can do!"

"She can," Jorge agreed. "Believe me, Jolene can."

"It's not that," Makerson immediately backed off. "I just meant…"

"You meant it is degrading that you need to have a woman look after you," Jolene complained. "I know that is what you mean, and…"

"Ok, go have your lover's quarrel," Jorge insisted as he stood up. "You two can work out the details, but please, keep it under the radar. Try to make it look like you're an actual couple."

"I do," Jolene nodded. "If I catch the person…"

"They will most likely try to get into Makerson's condo," Jorge replied as he headed to the door. "If you need help getting rid of a problem, call me. We will take care of it. But try not to kill him at his place. It is too hard to get him out without getting attention."

"Oh my God," Makerson shook his head. "Do you think…"

Jolene and Jorge shared a look.

"I will knock him out," Jolene replied. "We can make it look like we are taking to the hospital?"

"Let us cross that bridge when we come to it," Jorge replied, and raised an eyebrow before leaving the room.

CHAPTER 13

"Are you sure that's a good idea?" Paige skeptically asked as she sat beside her husband on the couch. "I mean, we're talking about Jolene."

"Paige, I do not know," Jorge confessed as he leaned closer to her. "But I could not have anyone there that was an obvious bodyguard, or it would tip them off that we know."

"Jolene is good, but…"

"I know," Jorge nodded. "believe me, I know, but she is eager to make me happy, so I know she will take good care of him. It was just a matter of time before Big Pharma came after Makerson."

"I guess that's their angle," Paige guessed. "Taking the media hostage?"

"More likely buying it," Jorge reminded her. "This ensures that they get the best representation on the mainstream news. The problem is that too many people were tuning into Makerson instead, so they decided that attacking him is the best way to intimidate and scare him."

"They might be in for a surprise when Jolene gets ahold of them," Paige predicted with a grin. "As long as they don't know she's associated with you."

"No, that is the great thing about Jolene," Jorge insisted. "She causes people to drop their guard at the worst possible time."

"Do we have any idea when this is going to take place?"

"Just that it will be on his own time," Jorge replied. "That is why Jolene is his new girlfriend."

Paige laughed and nodded.

"Which reminds me," Jorge glanced toward the stairs. "Are the kids..."

"They're both home."

"We must start keeping them close to home," Jorge reminded her. "Just in case..."

"I know," Paige nodded. "I was thinking the same."

"I might get some extra security."

"You think it's that bad?" Paige appeared concerned.

"Paige, normally, you and I could look after everything," Jorge replied, thinking for a moment before continuing. "But things seem to keep getting more dangerous, and I would rather be safe than sorry."

"I've been thinking about getting Maria into more intense self-defense training," Paige remarked. "I know she's been in and out of marital arts, but I have someone in mind that can train her to do...whatever she needs to do in a bad situation."

Jorge didn't reply but nodded.

"That would mean a lot of work," Paige continued. "And some more... intense training that might be more practical."

"Oh yeah, how intense are we talking?"

"Like, she could go into competitions when she's finished," Paige replied. "Or murder someone before they know she's in the room."

"Do it," Jorge agreed. "I would rather my daughter be prepared for anything because, as you know, *mi amor,* anything can happen."

The weekend rolled on, and for the most part, Jorge felt lazy. Other than hanging around with his family, he had no motivation. It was like an experiment. He stood back to see how much of his world could run without him solving problems. Sometimes it worked. Other times, it didn't.

It was on Sunday evening that his secure line rang. He had been sitting in the office having a drink, enjoying some quietness, while looking over emails, that Athas interrupted his short spell of solitude.

"Athas," Jorge answered. "And on a Sunday night, you call me. Wasn't the last time you did this here, I had to help you clean up a..."

"I can't believe you're still bringing that up," Athas interrupted him, while Jorge merely grinned to himself. "You won't let me forget."

"I think it is important that a man always knows where he fits into the world," Jorge reminded him again. "You and I, we are not so different. But from what I hear, you should have your weapon close at hand these days."

"What?" Athas hesitated. "What do you mean? I have a lot of security and..."

"Well, make sure you keep it," Jorge cut him off. "None of that driving around with just one of your guys like you did the day we interrupted the cabinet meeting. You might be getting in the wrong person's way, so best make sure you're driving a tank and not the bicycle."

"Is there a specific threat?"

"Not for you," Jorge replied. "Not yet, but I'm sure you're in a few crosshairs."

"Who's being threatened?" Athas asked. "It's not your family?"

"No," Jorge replied, somewhat appreciative that Athas could think beyond himself. "But Makerson, he is the one who they see as the threat at this time."

"Is he..."

"He is being taken care of," Jorge replied. "This here, it is not a problem. But it is good to keep our eyes open at all times."

"That's why I was calling you," Athas replied. "Big Pharma has completely backed off my cabinet, which is good. My concern is where their focus will be next because we both know they won't stay quiet for long."

"They never do," Jorge reminded him. "It is all about money for them. They see a vulnerable society and easy prey."

"I think our little conversation with the cabinet made a difference," Athas sounded surprised by his words. "I was skeptical, but they've backed off, and Big Pharma took the hint and left. My concern is they plan to work on provincial governments instead. That way, they can try one province as a test subject and use it as a reason the others should follow. Education is provincial."

"With slanted journalist, of course," Jorge nodded in agreement. "Let us see their next move and take it from there. Marco will continue to monitor. We will see what the *legal* cartel has planned next."

Jorge would learn the answer the following Monday morning when

Marco sent him a frantic message and showed up at his door shortly afterward.

"Sir, I am so sorry to come at this time," Marco was flustered as he glanced at a nearby clock as he walked into the house. "But I woke up early this morning and was monitoring things while I had my coffee and saw this…."

"I'm almost scared to ask what, Marco," Jorge said as he closed the door behind him. "But please, never apologize for showing up at my door, no matter the time. Can I get you a coffee?"

"Yes, please, sir," Marco appreciatively smiled as he stopped in the middle of the floor. "I was in such a rush I did not finish the one I had. I wanted to get here as soon as possible."

"What is it," Jorge asked as he poured the coffee. "that gets you here so early, Marco? How concerned should I be?"

"Let us talk in your office," Marco suggested as he glanced toward the stairs.

Jorge nodded as he handed Marco the coffee, and the two men headed toward his office. Once inside, everything would come out.

"Sir, do you remember that woman, the journalist Athas used to…."

"Oh, yes, Holly Anne Ryerson," Jorge nodded, putting his hand in the air. "Please, Marco, it is too early to put a visual in my head. My stomach is not so good in the morning."

"I found out that they fired her from the news channel she worked for," Marco sat in his usual spot while Jorge went behind the desk, taking a huge gulp of coffee on the way. "When Athas cut their funding, they fired her, so now, she is working for Big Pharma."

"Hopefully, she's a better salesperson than she was a news lady," Jorge laughed, "because…"

"No, sir, she's their media expert of some kind," Marco shook his head. "They hired her as their spokesperson because she is a familiar face and they believe the public trust her."

"And she has an ax to grind with us," Jorge predicted. "Since Athas cut the money for her network and they had a falling out…"

"That would be my assumption, sir," Marco nodded. "It seems like it happened fast. I didn't know they let her go until late Saturday night, but

I did not think it was a big deal. I would've brought it to your attention sooner, but I didn't know that things would happen this quickly."

"She was already working on a deal," Jorge guessed. "She probably had connections in Big Pharma."

"It looks like they sought her out," Marco observed. "I know they were scrambling ever since the doors to the cabinet closed, but I did not think they would get on their feet this fast."

"That's how psychopaths work, Marco," Jorge reminded him, "always thinking on their feet. They got her to spin things since that was her job before, *si?*"

"She knows the industry," Marco nodded. "Has the connections..."

"And as I already pointed out," Jorge finished his coffee. "An ax to grind with Athas and me, but she should know better than to pick me as an enemy."

"Some people, sir, they do not learn."

"So, what is next?"

"They plan to announce her as their...sir, I forget the exact title, but it's *long*," Marco shook his head. "And she is to make some kind of announcement later today."

Jorge didn't reply but nodded.

Holly Anne survived the first round, but the second wasn't looking so good.

CHAPTER 14

"Media Relations Liaison and Public Communicator," Paige leaned in to read the title on the screen as she and Jorge watched Holly Anne Ryerson approaching the podium to speak. "Isn't that title a little much?"

"Who fucking knows?" Jorge shook his head as he pulled his chair closer to the desk and turned up the volume for the press conference. "It is bullshit that means someone to spin their lies."

"Well, considering where she used to work," Paige muttered as she exchanged looks with her husband. "She certainly has experience with that."

"You mean the state-owned media?" Jorge replied as he turned the laptop slightly to see it better. "That there is just part of the job."

"Try *any* mainstream media," Paige raised an eyebrow as Holly Anne started to speak.

"*Good morning,*" Holly Anne faked a smile and began to speak. "*Many of you might know me from….*"

"I hope she gets on with it," Jorge complained. "After I listen to this bullshit, Athas will light up my phone. This woman knows the game and could be very dangerous for him."

"I thought his cabinet refused to work with Big Pharma to have these drugs mandated," Paige appeared concerned. "What else can she do?"

Jorge shared a look with her, and neither said a word, returning their attention to the screen.

"... saw *a cultural shift that was concerning,*" Holly Anne spoke, showing signs of worry in her expression. "*Psychologists believe this change is due to added stresses that our society has seen over the last few years. We hear more and more about school shootings, gangs on our streets, and financial problems in our homes. Crime rates in Canada, especially in the Toronto area, have steadily increased over the last few years, causing young people much deeper levels of anxiety and fears, many with psychological disorders like PTSD that used to plague adults. Add to that social media and its increasing influence....*"

"Is this woman for real?" Jorge shook his head. "If any kid would have PTSD, it would be my Maria, but she's fine! What bullshit!"

"Well, in truth, we don't know for sure she *doesn't* have PTSD," Paige gently reminded him. "With everything she saw and dealt with in the last few years, it wouldn't be hard to believe."

"She's fine," Jorge swung his hand in the air. "Paige, we have taught her how to deal with *life,* something most parents do not bother to do anymore. It's called *lazy* parenting, and this is all you see now. They put their kid in front of a television or a computer, and that's their parent. It's pathetic."

"I can't disagree with you there," Paige nodded. "But, you do have to realize that since..."

"She is getting someone else up to talk," Jorge cut off his wife, his eyes narrowing on the man walking across the stage to join Holly Anne. "Who the fuck is this guy?"

"It says child psychologist," Paige skeptically replied.

"A child psychologist *expert,*" Jorge corrected her, and they shared a look. "I wonder how much Big Pharma paid off this asshole to say what they want?"

"I think it's a safe assumption that he's compensated well," Paige replied. "He looks like an idiot."

"*....thank you again, Holly Anne. I appreciate this chance to speak on this concerning situation...*"

"What concerning situation?" Jorge spoke to the screen. "He talk like kids are running wild up and down Yonge Street, burning down the city."

"Ironically, if they're pushed too far with this nonsense," Paige pointed toward the screen. "They might do that, only justifying their argument more."

"That is what they want, Paige," Jorge ranted. "To....what is that called again?"

"Gaslight?"

"Yes, this is what I mean," Jorge nodded. "Gaslight the public."

"It's not exactly difficult."

"Maybe those people should be on medication."

"I assume they already are," Paige quietly replied.

"*....concerning, which is why it's detrimental that we address this situation now before things get further out of hand....*"

"I wish this asshole would get to the point," Jorge glanced at his cell phone. "I hope Marco can find something more so we can stay one step ahead of them."

Paige didn't reply but appeared concerned.

"Paige, if we have to," Jorge leaned forward to look into her eyes. "We will homeschool the children..."

"*We*?" Paige challenged.

"I...I will find someone..." Jorge corrected himself. "You know what I mean. I will not put up with this shit."

"What about the rest of the people?" Paige softly replied.

He looked away, unable to answer. The truth was that he was worried about what was taking place. Jorge wanted to believe that people would see through this insanity, but he wasn't so sure they would. As Diego often said, the world is full of sheep.

"*...and we will work with the opposition party to look after the best interest of our children,*" Holly Anne was speaking again, causing both Jorge and Paige to return their attention to the screen. "*Nothing matters more than our kid's health and safety. If this isn't something Prime Minister Athas feels is a concern, then it's our job to make him understand.*"

The press conference was barely over when Jorge's secure line rang. Athas was furious.

"I can't believe that fucking....."

"Wow, Athas, I have not heard you swear in a long time," Jorge cut him off, exchanging looks with his wife, who appeared stunned. "Do you not wish I had gotten rid of this woman last year when I had the chance?"

"It wouldn't matter," Athas was quick to reply. "They'd just get someone else to do the job."

"Yes, but," Jorge retorted. "That person probably would not have an ax to grind with you."

"And unfortunately," Paige jumped in. "Alec, I think she wants your head on the chopping block."

"Oh, hello, Paige," Athas seemed to change his tone, which irked Jorge. "You're right. She's mad at me because of our...disagreement last year, then I cut funding to her news channel, which had *nothing* to do with her, and here we are..."

"You cut funding because it's a sinking ship," Jorge reminded him. "You did not personally fire her. That was someone else."

"But that may not be the biggest problem," Paige added. "I'm sure Big Pharma is paying her well to navigate the situation and find a way to spin this story, justify adding medication as a requirement to go to school."

"I can't believe anyone would take *her* word over mine," Athas ranted. "I used to be a social worker for *years....*"

"But you know, Athas, they will say that you do not have children yourself," Jorge reminded him. "So, you don't understand."

"Neither does *she,*" Athas complained.

"Ah, but she does not have to," Jorge replied. "She has her *experts* to vouch for her."

"That *expert,* can be paid off by the highest bidder," Athas bitterly remarked. "He has a reputation."

"But not one the public knows about," Paige guessed. "We must find a way to beat them at their own game."

"That's the problem," Athas sighed. "How? She plans to get the opposition to table a bill, push hard, try to change public perception, and then the media will jump in with scare tactics."

"She already suggested that not only is it for *your* child's well-being," Paige said. "But for the well-being of the children that your kids are around all day. As if you can catch PTSD from someone else."

"I can't believe anyone would believe this shit," Athas complained.

"Do you not know people yet?" Jorge asked with humor in his voice. "They are not that smart, Athas. They believe whatever the media tells them. Critical thinking is long gone. People are *lazy and weak.* They want someone else to think for them."

"I'm not sure," Paige appeared skeptical. "I mean, yes, to a degree, but this is their kids we're talking about. Most people will be careful about casually giving them medication, and they certainly won't like it if it is required to go to school."

"Paige, you know I do not like disagreeing with you," Jorge laughed. "But on this here, I am telling you, Big Pharma is going to have them on their backs like a bitch so fast, you will not believe it."

Paige didn't reply but looked sad.

"I have to agree with Jorge," Athas spoke through the line. "I don't have a lot of confidence in people either. I want to believe parents will be more cautious, but I also know that parents get scared and don't know what to do. They make themselves vulnerable to these so-called experts. I've seen it in different situations when I was in social work. People are fallible."

"You call it fallible," Jorge replied. "But I call it being cowards. No one wants to stand up to anyone or anything."

"That, in part, is because society teaches them not to," Athas reminded them. "People who stand up are often punished and used as an example, so others don't do the same. It's in the corporation's best interest that no one challenges them."

"And governments," Jorge added.

"Yes, you're right," Athas replied. "But here we are…."

"Here we are," Paige repeated and shared a look with Jorge.

CHAPTER 15

"Maybe we need our *own* experts?" Tony Allman commented from further down the boardroom table, while beside him, Andrew sat back, nodding his head with his arms crossed over his chest. "If we have experts that counter Big Pharma, then people will have their attention diverted."

Jorge didn't say anything but felt the idea was flimsy at best. Glancing around the VIP room of the *Princesa Maria,* he wasn't feeling hopeful. The propaganda came at them from every corner since the press conference only two days earlier. Even Maria returned from school talking about rumors that they'd soon have to take medication if they *misbehaved.* He had gathered the troops together, and they were looking to him to figure it out.

"It won't work," Makerson reassured him from across the table. "All they'll do is discredit that person. Trust me. I've seen it before. Anyone who doesn't go with this bullshit will get thrown under the bus. It scares many professionals from saying anything. They're even changing the definition of misbehavior in children on the government website."

"What?" Marco suddenly spoke up as he looked toward Jorge and then at Makerson. "Can they do this?"

"Yes, apparently, they can do whatever they want," Makerson grimaced. "One of my staff discovered it yesterday while researching the story."

“Wait, why would this be on the government website anyway?” Jorge was confused. “What do definitions have to do with running the country?”

“They have a portion of their site dedicated to children and their well-being,” Makerson explained. “That’s *also* something new that someone tipped us off about.”

“Probably by someone on the inside,” Andrew suggested, sharing a look with Sonny, who pushed up his glasses and made a face. “How is that possible if Athas is still running the show?”

“That’s a good question,” Jorge nodded and turned toward Marco. “Can you find out who makes the decisions regarding the website?”

“Sir, that’s probably a whole team,” Marco replied. “But it is the government, so I am sure there is no organization with such things.”

“A bunch of fucking monkeys in a room,” Andrew muttered, causing Marco to laugh. “Why is it that Athas never has control over anything?”

“He should be in this meeting,” Makerson suggested.

“Then *he* would be accused of secretly working with the media,” Tony reminded him. “Different rules for him.”

“I do not understand,” Jolene suddenly spoke up as she leaned against a flustered Makerson to speak to Jorge. “Why are these people doing this? Is this *just* to sell these pills?”

“Yes,” Andrew sharply replied before Jorge could open his mouth. “Aren’t you paying attention to anything?”

“I am too paying attention,” Jolene snapped back, causing Andrew to look away. “But I do not understand why they are going to such lengths to push these pills on kids. Do they not have any kids, these people who work in these companies?”

“Do you seriously think their kids will be taking them?” Andrew shot back. “Come on, Jolene! It’s all about money, honey.”

“I am *not* your honey,” She snapped back. “I am just…”

“Jolene, this here, it is not complicated,” Jorge cut her off. “Big Pharma is no different from the cartels back in Mexico, except they do everything legally. No one gets arrested. At worse, they have some lawsuits.”

“Which usually is nothing compared to the money they’ve already made from the product in the first place,” Makerson added. “They weigh their options and go with the money.”

“Always go with the money,” Tony added. “But I gotta admit, I didn’t think they'd go this low, and why is the government so eager to jump on board?"

"Do we know if this medication is even safe?" Chase added, and Jorge glanced across the table and shrugged.

"This here is a good question."

"That is what I've been working on, sir," Marco said as he shook his head. "They are keeping this information guarded, or there is no data. Just a list of *potential* side effects."

"Doesn't there have to be proof to get it passed by Health Canada?" Tony asked. "I guess it doesn't matter if they're in on it."

"Yeah, but Athas is still running the country," Makerson commented. "Why isn't he having a press conference or making a statement? Is he too busy hiding under the desk?"

"Maybe he's hoping to find Holly Anne Ryerson under there again," Andrew quipped, causing everyone to laugh.

"Finally, a job she's good at," Jorge muttered.

"What?" Jolene jumped in. "This reporter from the other day?"

"She used to have a relationship with Athas," Makerson carefully answered. "Back during the election."

"It did not end well," Tony informed Jolene. "That's one of the reasons why she's trying to undermine Athas."

"Well, in fairness, she was fired," Makerson reminded him. "And that's because Athas cut the funding for her network."

"Oh," Jolene seemed to put it together. "So, if this is true, why can we not use this information against her?"

"Well, I…" Makerson started and stopped. "I don't think…"

"It might discredit her," Tony suggested.

"I think we keep this in our back pocket for now," Jorge suggested. "When the time is right, we use it against her. We must learn more about this drug they want to give the children. They claim it is *safe and effective,* but I do not believe this is true. I think, Marco, you should work with Makerson to learn more and maybe bring this up during HPC news, asking where the data is or why there isn't any?"

"It should have long-term studies because you don't get a drug through overnight," Makerson commented. "But I'm hitting a wall no matter where I look. This is highly unusual."

"Diego, he could not make it today," Jorge commented. "But *Our House of Pot* has been countering this narrative, suggesting some CBD oil specifically for children is beneficial to calm them without the bad side effects of medication. Maybe you should have someone from the company on your show?"

"That's the plan," Makerson nodded. "I had been planning to, but I've been on a wild goose chase trying to learn anything about this new pill. It seems like everyone is getting the same script. I've talked to doctors, pharmacists, and even schools, and they seem to repeat the same lines. No one has dug into it, just repeated the information on a pamphlet."

Jorge didn't say anything but thought about their words.

His anger exploded when he was on a call with Athas later that day.

"Why are you still letting everyone else run the country?" Jorge snapped through the secure line. "I thought we settled this with your cabinet last week? What the hell is going on there?"

"It's the opposition pushing this," Athas attempted to remind him. "Even Holly Anne said…"

"Then why does the Canadian government website have a section dedicated to children and their well-being?" Jorge continued to yell as he looked at his laptop screen. "I am looking at it right now. Why is there a definition of misbehavior that includes speaking out of turn or being too fidgety? Are we going to drug every kid who cannot sit still for hours?"

"I never saw…."

"You mean, you do not know what is on your own government website?" Jorge barked as he stood up and started to pace his office floor. "Athas, you need to get it together. You need to do it now! This is a weak position. This announcement by your old girlfriend happened two days ago. Where have you been? What are you doing?"

"I'm trying to find…"

"What? Trying to find what?" Jorge screamed. "Your balls? Because I will save you the trouble. You do not have any!"

"I'm trying to find where this is coming from," Athas ignored his remark. "I have people looking…."

"Do you?" Jorge snapped. "Well, they aren't looking too fast!"

"I can call a press conference…."

"Yes," Jorge continued to yell. "It does not have to be long. Just say that you have no plans to enforce medication on children. You are the government. Why isn't Health Canada releasing information on the pills? Why is this a secret? Shouldn't it be on their site? Ask some questions, Athas. Let them know that they can't sneak behind your back. Fire people if you have to! I do not care, but enough is enough."

With that, he ended the call. Feeling his heart pounding frantically, Jorge leaned against the desk and attempted to calm his breathing. A knock at the door caused him to jump, and he took another deep breath before answering.

"Come in!"

It was Paige.

"I could hear you yelling from upstairs."

Her statement was flat, with no accusation in her voice. As she moved across the room, Jorge could see the concern in her eyes.

"Paige, Athas, he has to go," Jorge shook his head. "I thought for sure that he would be tougher now. That he would have a voice this term, but he does not. I am so frustrated with his compliance and idiocy. This is an important issue, and he's playing dumb."

"I think he worries too much about what people think."

"He should worry about what *I* think," Jorge corrected her. "I cannot seem to get through to him."

"If you didn't with all that yelling," Paige touched his arm. "You never will."

As it turns out, Jorge had greatly underestimated Athas.

Things were about to explode.

CHAPTER 16

"There's a woman," Athas hurriedly spoke into the secure line the following afternoon. "Her name is Glennis Dumont Sparrow. I need her to have an accident."

"Is….is this so?" Jorge asked, slightly humored by the prime minister's demand. "Not that this will be an issue, but can I ask why?"

"She was pushing this from behind the scenes," Athas bitterly explained. "I had to….I had to get a bit *assertive* with people on my team yesterday, and that's the name I got. Her sister-in-law works for Big Pharma. She's linked to the new medication pushed on children."

"So you think," Jorge asked while grinning to himself. "That this person, and only this person, is responsible for all your problems?"

"No, of course not," Athas sharply replied. "But she's the ring leader on the opposition side. We need to use her as an example to..shake things up."

"Well, this here, it is not a problem," Jorge confirmed as he jotted down the name. "But how *shaken up* would you like things to be?"

"Use your discretion," Athas replied. "The less I know, the better."

"Are you sure of this fact?" Jorge asked. "Can you trust your staff?"

"I talked to several people," Athas said. "From both sides. They came back with the same name. When I had people one-on-one, they tended to say much more, including that they weren't behind this bill or the concept of getting involved with schools. There's a big push right now, and I guess this woman is just one of the problems, but let's start there for now."

"Do not think this is the end of the line?"

"No," Athas confirmed with some hesitation. "This is just the start, but we're going to work through it."

As it turns out, Marco was already familiar with the name Glennis Dumont Sparrow. It had appeared a lot in his research.

"But sir, I wasn't sure of her power with this issue," Marco explained from across the VIP room table the following morning. "Her name kept coming up in emails and a few documents, but I had no idea she was pushing things that hard."

"Her sister-in-law is helping promote this new pill," Jorge leaned back in his chair and took a drink from the *Taza de Sol* cup before continuing. "So, where are you seeing her name?"

"She has a lot of meetings," Marco replied as he pushed his closed laptop away. "That was what set off an alarm with me. The meetings were often on Zoom and marked as being with *constituents,* which I didn't believe. I now see there was more to this than I originally thought."

"See what else you can find," Jorge suggested. "I need to know how this woman's life looks. She has to have an accident, and I must figure out the best way to do so."

"A *fatal* accident, sir?" Marco wondered.

"No, but an accident that might knock her head around a bit," Jorge suggested. "It does not appear she is thinking very clearly these days. That might help to...correct her thoughts."

"It often does, sir."

"Tell me, has anything else caught your attention?" Jorge asked. "With the opposition, Big Pharma, the schools?"

"It would seem, sir, that Holly Anne Ryerson might have a very... *intimate* connection to someone on the board of the company that just hired her," Marco replied as he looked at some notes he had on the table. "She is making a big salary to convince people that children need medication."

"This here, it does not surprise me," Jorge said as he nodded. "Tell me, the schools, the school boards, where are they with this?"

"Some are for it, while others are conflicted," Marco replied. "There is a lot of fighting over the matter. Some are wondering why we are medicating children that only need discipline. Of course, teachers are not allowed to say that to parents. But at the same time, it sounds like some students make teacher's lives hell, so it is not hard to understand why they might want children medicated."

"Why do they not have rules for the classroom?" Jorge shook his head. "I do not understand."

"Because parents come after them for being mean to their children," Marco said. "Sir, I have seen it at my kid's school. Some kids are terrible to teachers, but the parents blame the teachers rather than their kids. Do not get me wrong, I don't think children should have to take medication, but at the same time, I can see why teachers might not object."

Jorge nodded and thought about it for a moment.

"I guess all we can do is keep monitoring things," he continued. "see what Holly Anne is up to because I think that's the key. She's the propaganda machine for Big Pharma."

"Oh, her, I watch closely, sir," Marco assured him. "So far, I am just seeing about her relationship with that man on the board, not much else. They seem to feel that her press conference came across as strong, and they are now polling parents to see their thoughts, then will proceed accordingly. They want to be careful not to push too hard or too fast. That's why we aren't seeing as much on the news. Just a few random stories about kids in trouble with the law."

"They plan it very carefully, Marco," Jorge said. "I am getting too old for this here."

"You and me both, sir."

A knock on the door interrupted their conversation. Knowing it was likely Chase, Jorge called for him to join them.

"Hey," Chase stuck his head inside the door. "I got a message on my phone. There's a press conference in ten minutes."

"Not Ryerson again," Jorge said as Marco grabbed the laptop and started tapping the keys.

"No, Athas," Chase said with wide eyes. "I dunno what it's about, but this ought to be good."

"I talk to him yesterday," Jorge said as Marco turned the laptop around to show an empty podium. "He didn't mention anything."

"Maybe something happened?" Chase shrugged. "I gotta go. I have a new bar....*beverage expert* I gotta train."

"What the fuck is a beverage expert?" Jorge laughed.

"The politically correct term for a bartender," Chase muttered as he started to close the door. "Keep me posted."

"I might have a job for you later," Jorge called out, and Chase gave him a thumbs up before closing the door.

Jorge and Marco exchanged looks.

Pulling his phone out of his pocket, Jorge turned it back on to see messages warning him about the press conference. None of them were from Athas, which made him nervous. One was from Paige.

Mi amor, do you know what this press conference is about?

No idea. I thought you talked to Alec today.

Yesterday.

Although a few minutes late, Athas eventually made his way to the podium, where he was to speak. The room had a slight buzz, and a quick message on Jorge's phone let him know that Tony was one of the reporters at the press conference. That gave him a small piece of comfort.

"*Good afternoon,*" Athas spoke into the microphone. "*I scheduled this short press conference today to bring up a matter brought to my attention this morning. As I said during my election campaign last fall, my government must always be open and transparent, which I continue to do.*"

He paused for a moment, taking a deep breath before continuing.

"Oh sir," Marco muttered. "I think I know what this might be about. It's all over *Twitter.* I mean, I guess it's called *X* now."

Jorge looked from the laptop to Marco, who had his phone turned around with an image of a naked breast on social media. Sitting forward in his chair, he continued to listen to Athas speaking.

"*Although I try to avoid talking about anything of a personal nature,*" Athas continued. "*When it somehow affects the reputation of the prime minister's office, I think it's important to be honest and direct. For that reason, I will confirm that images being shared on the internet, as suggested, are of myself and Holly Anne Ryerson, the current Media Relation Liaison and Public Communications director for....*"

"Woo!" Marco jumped in as his eyes widened, and his mouth fell open as he slid his finger over the screen. "Check this one out."

Turning his phone around, he showed Jorge an image of Holly Anne Ryerson in an intimate pose with an unidentified man.

"...in bad taste to have taken these photos, but...."

Jorge laughed and clapped his hands together.

"Sir, do you think that's him?" Marco asked as his face turned pink. "Would he release these pictures?"

"At the time," Jorge confirmed as he swooped in to take a better look. "I told him to take some photos in case, you know, he needed them. I see he followed my advice, but I didn't think he would hang on to them."

"...with great shame, and I apologize to..."

"But sir, maybe it was her and someone else," Marco shrugged. "Either way, this is going to make her look..."

"Not good!" Jorge confirmed. "I wonder if Big Pharma will want her as their Public Communicator, whatever the fuck she's called, now that this is out?"

"I am guessing, sir," Marco giggled. "She might have a few pictures of her own that might be her job security."

"If she's smart...."

"....please accept my sincere apologies. We can all learn from this indiscretion. This is embarrassing for me as I'm sure it is for Ms. Ryerson..."

"Sir, he does *not* look embarrassed."

"That's OK, Marco," Jorge grinned. "I suspect no one will be talking about his presentation in this matter."

Enjoying the moment, Jorge almost missed it when his phone rang. Glancing at the number, he grimaced and answered.

CHAPTER 17

"Now?" Jorge spoke into his phone. "*Right* now?"

"What do you want me to do?" Jolene's husky voice shot back. "Put him on ice until it is convenient?"

"Do you mean…."

"You must come!" Jolene shot back at him. "Now, this is important. We are at the production house."

"On my way," Jorge confirmed and ended the call. Glancing at his phone, he saw a string of text messages. All of which were in response to Athas and his big announcement. None were urgent.

"Another emergency, sir?" Marco gave him a sympathetic look. "It does not ever end."

"Unfortunately, you are right," Jorge said as he stood up, grabbing his cup of coffee and finished it. "This time it is Jolene. I think she caught something in a rat trap. I have to deal with."

"There are a lot of rats out there, sir," Marco muttered as Jorge headed to the side door. "And never enough traps."

"This is true, Marco," Jorge said as he reached for the doorknob. "We will touch base later."

The cold January air hit him like a brick as soon as he walked outside. Dark clouds hung overhead, causing him to cringe as he jumped into his SUV and took off. He called Paige while on his way.

"Hello."

"Hello, *mi amor,* did you see…"

"Yes," Paige confirmed. "I saw a little more than I wanted to see."

To this, Jorge laughed.

"What do you think this is about?" She asked. "Is it a diversion?"

"This could be," Jorge said as he looked ahead at the traffic. "But it may also be to undermine her."

"She's not commented so far," Paige replied. "She could always say they aren't her, it's hard to tell."

"It does not matter," Jorge guessed. "The damage is done."

"And Alec didn't mention anything to you when you talked last?"

"Paige, I was as surprised as you," Jorge confirmed. "So something must have happened quickly."

"It's like a soap opera," Paige commented. "Politics have become so dramatic."

"That they have."

"Are you on the way home?"

"No, I have to go by HPC for…a few minutes," Jorge muttered. "Something came up."

"Do you need me?"

"*Mi amor,*" Jorge spoke flirtatiously. "I always need you!"

"You know what I mean," Paige laughed.

"Not yet," Jorge said as he headed to his destination. "But if that changes, I will let you know."

"Sounds good."

"Are the kids home?"

"Yes," Paige confirmed. "Miguel is playing in the snow with Tala, and Maria is complaining about school."

He could hear laughter in the background.

"Tell her I will be home soon," Jorge wishfully said. "At least, I hope so."

"Please try," Paige said. "There's a storm coming tonight. Get home before it starts."

Jorge smiled.

"I will, *mi amor.* I will see you soon."

He ended the call. A few minutes later, he arrived at *Hernandez Production Company* and parked his SUV. Random snowflakes were floating through the air, which he chose to ignore. Going in the side door, Jorge glanced toward the board room to see Sonny sitting alone, looking at a phone. The two men made eye contact, and he pointed down to suggest the basement. Jorge nodded and made his way toward the back of the building. He hit numbers on the keypad for the door to unlock and headed downstairs.

The basement was dark and drab, with only a lone lightbulb hanging in the corner. Jorge used his iPhone to find his way downstairs. He saw Jolene, Makerson, and Andrew standing around a man who appeared to have his arms in the air. As he got closer, Jorge could see he had his hands clasped in chains, hanging from the wall. There was blood everywhere.

"This here," Jorge pointed toward the man. "Is this new? These here dungeon chains?"

"I found them last summer," Andrew shrugged. "I thought they might come in handy sometime. And here we are."

"Who the fuck is this?" Jorge pointed toward the middle-aged man with dark eyes who struggled with holding his arms in the air. Glancing down, he saw that his feet were tied together. A pool of blood was on his clothes and the floor. He appeared to be in shock but still alive.

"Oh, that there," Andrew nodded toward the rope-together feet. "Is from when he tried to jump up and kick us earlier. We were having none of that. The blood, that was Jolene."

"Who is he?" Jorge repeated. "And what happened?"

"He try to attack Tom!" Jolene's voice boomed through the room as she moved closer to Jorge. "I stop him."

"She did," Makerson jumped in. "I didn't even see him. We were leaving for the press conference, and he was waiting behind my car."

"I go there first," Jolene stood tall, hands on hips. "I put a gun on him and got him inside."

"Are you sure he wasn't just some random fuck, trying to steal his car?" Jorge asked.

"No, he has a gun," Jolene pointed toward him.

"*Had* a gun," Andrew corrected her. "We got it now."

"We get a confession out of him," Jolene continued as she held up a pair of pliers. "He did not want to talk at first, but I made him talk."

"What are you going to do with me?" The man suddenly spoke, his voice weak. "I have people who will..."

"I don't give a fuck about your people," Jorge yelled, causing the man to shut up. "What the fuck are you doing here?"

"He say," Jolene answered for him. "That they hired him to attack Tom. I say this isn't happening."

Jorge ignored her broken English and glanced at Makerson, who nervously nodded.

"So, what do you want me to do?" Jolene asked, her voice more vulnerable this time. "I can kill...."

"No, please, don't...." The man weakly spoke. "Please help me."

"So, he's sent by Big Pharma?" Jorge asked.

"Yes," Jolene replied. "He tell me this."

"Then maybe you should return him," Jorge said. "Find out who gave the orders and leave him on that person's doorstep."

"Yeah, but do we want to drag a body across town?" Andrew asked. "It could get messy. The fucker is already bleeding all over the place."

"How about," Jorge said and paused for a moment. "We just send his head."

"No!" The man started to respond. "Please let me go!"

"Why?" Jorge yelled at him. "So we throw you back out, only to catch you in another rat trap next week?"

"I will work for you."

"I'm not hiring," Jorge retorted.

"Please..."

Jorge stepped away, unable to think. He was getting too old for this shit. He exchanged looks with the others.

"Jolene?" Jorge asked. "What do you think?"

"Want me to call Chase?" Andrew asked.

"Yes," Jorge replied and turned his attention back to Jolene. "What are you thinking?"

"I think if we cut off his hands, he will have a hard time attacking people."

"No!" The man protested. "Please, my finger....you got my finger...."

"Oh yes, that is why all the blood," Jolene coldly replied. "His finger. I cut off the middle one."

To this, Jorge laughed.

"Maybe that's what we gotta send his buddy at Big Pharma," Andrew suggested. "It seems appropriate."

"I don't know," Jorge shook his head. "I do not feel right letting this one go."

"Please!" The man continued. "I have a family."

To this, Jorge shot him a look.

"You should not have told me this here."

"Please, no!"

"You know," Jorge thought for a moment. "Maybe this here we can work with. After all, this man will not do anything stupid that could jeopardize his family."

"No, please," the man spoke weakly. "Please, no."

"We send finger to Big Pharma," Jolene confirmed. "but to the house, not to the company."

Jorge nodded in agreement.

"This man, though," Jolene exchanged looks with Jorge as they moved away from the victim. "Maybe he learn his lesson?"

"I got his phone," Andrew called over. "I don't see no family photos."

Jorge turned and saw the terror in the man's eyes. A grin swept over his face as he turned back to Jolene.

"You know what to do."

CHAPTER 18

"Sir, what was Athas thinking?" Marco asked a few days after the press conference. The two men were sitting in the VIP room at *Princesa Maria.* "Did he seriously feel this was a good idea? He may have addressed the rumors and speculation, but I think there was a better way."

"As you know," Jorge reminded his IT Specialist. "He did not discuss this decision with me, or I may have encouraged him to...hesitate. However, he claims he had no choice since the pictures were online."

"But sir, wouldn't it make more sense if he had approached things differently?" Marco asked. "This seemed fast to jump the gun."

"Well, he must live with the consequences," Jorge sipped his coffee and loudly sighed. "Marco, I am *so* tired of all this drama, the constant problems with Athas. It takes up too much of my time."

"You keep trying to step back, sir," Marco agreed. "But there is always an issue."

"And right now, my only concern is this bill for the children's medication," Jorge confirmed and gestured to the closed laptop between them. "Not Athas and his drama or Jolene or any of her bullshit. Life isn't a *telenovela.*"

"Sir, I hate to say it, but as long as you're available," Marco tilted his head. "I think they will come to you with their problems."

"I know, Marco, I know."

"Not that I want to see you leave the city," Marco shook his head. "But I sometimes think that is the only way to escape all this."

Jorge considered his words and nodded.

"It is something to consider," Marco suggested. "And I wouldn't blame you if you did. It might also be safer if you're not in the center of everything."

"I am tired of always fighting," Jorge confirmed. "With everybody, I am tired. I did this here for my entire life. Now, I want to enjoy my family, sleep in sometimes, and not have a phone always ringing."

"You want to retire," Marco asked.

"This is true," Jorge took a deep breath and thought. "But for now, we must first resolve a few things. Did you learn anything more about this woman, Glennis Dumont Sparrow?"

"I hacked her recent Zoom meetings, and they were with Big Pharma reps."

"Even though she had them listed as meetings with constituents?" Jorge asked. "I think that is what you said before the shit hit the fan with Athas a few days ago?"

"Yes, that is correct," Marco confirmed. "Which, again, I thought was strange because, let's face it, most politicians do not care about their constituents."

"Not when the election is over," Jorge agreed. "And they have the majority."

"If the election were today," Marco shook his head. "I cannot see it, but then again, maybe?"

"Athas can figure out that mess himself," Jorge said. "I am not cleaning this one up. Did Ryerson end up getting fired?"

"No," Marco said. "But you must remember, she has a relationship with someone at that particular company, so it seems unlikely. She publicly stated she was embarrassed and claimed she didn't know about the pictures, so now it is a schoolyard fight. They both look stupid, sir."

"As they deserve," Jorge got back to their original topic. "This Glennis lady had a conversation with someone at Big Pharma?"

"Yes, the man she spoke with talked about how this would be helpful for children, *safe and effective.* I think that's the words he used."

"Yes, safe and effective until it's *not,*" Jorge grunted.

"The studies are only on mice," Marco shook his head. "So, that does not fill me with confidence."

"She believes them?"

"Yes, she seemed interested," Marco observed. "But not as interested as by their projections of how much it would sell."

"As she made a note to get some shares?"

"That is my guess," Marco nodded. "Sir, it is disturbing that people would try to make this look like it is to a child's benefit, only for profit. They're casual about this drug as if the kids need it. Some kids are hyper because they eat so much sugar, not because something is wrong with them."

"Even if there were," Jorge said. "Would you give it to your children?"

"Under no circumstances," Marco shook his head. "I am still looking into the studies, but considering they buried the ones they do not like, I am not confident, sir. This is the information that Makerson has to release once we get it."

"The sad part is, will it even matter?" Jorge asked. "If these companies can get it passed and market the right way, people will get it. They get scared when anything involves their children and, if mainstream media creates enough fear, you will be surprised what people will allow."

"Do you think so, sir?" Marco appeared skeptical. "I would like to think that people do their research."

"They won't," Jorge confirmed. "In the end, many are lazy. They take whatever they're spoon-fed."

"So, are you doing anything about this Sparrow lady?"

"I am about to talk to Chase about this," Jorge said as he stood up. "She might have car troubles when she leaves home one day."

Twenty minutes later, Jorge was relieved to get into his SUV and head home. Thinking about stepping away from his problems had given him some temporary relief.

He called home.

"Hello."

"*Mi amor,*" Jorge said as he sat in traffic. " Please tell me all is calm there."

"So far," Paige replied. "I thought I heard your secure line ring."

"Fucking Athas, can he not handle any situation by himself."

"He does rely on you a lot," Paige confirmed. "But I think he's afraid of doing something you don't like."

"You mean like having a press conference about pornographic pictures of himself than being surprised that they offend people?" Jorge quipped. "Did he think that was something I would like?"

"He was kind of in a bind," Paige attempted to reason. "They were out there anyway."

"He should've denied it was him," Jorge insisted.

"That's what I thought," Paige agreed. "But I think he was scared that if he lied, it would come back at him twice as hard."

"Paige, how did they even get out?"

"That's a good question."

"Meanwhile, I sorted out stuff at the club."

Paige knew why he went there and what he meant.

"That's good," she replied. "Was Marco there?"

"Yes, he was helpful," Jorge confirmed. "And Chase needs to take care of an issue today, but that is all."

She also knew what that meant.

"I saw Diego's interview with Makerson," Paige changed the topic. "It was online earlier. Well done."

"He talked about CBD oil for kids?"

"Yes, and he sold it well," Paige confirmed. "Maybe we should have Miguel on it."

"He crazy wild again today?"

"He runs all day," Paige giggled. "From one end of the house to the other."

"That boy," Jorge grinned as his voice softened. "He has a lot of energy."

"I wish I did!" Paige laughed. "Thank God for Tala."

"She is a good nanny," Jorge replied as he sat in traffic, his mind returning to the conversation with Marco. "Paige, I keep thinking of leaving the city."

"You are?"

"Well, you know, I am always sitting in traffic," He reminded her. "And I'm always helping solve problems. I am tired. I want to…as you always say, step away."

"I think that would be good," She confirmed. "I know you want to be…"

"But I cannot," Jorge shook his head. "Even this bullshit with Athas, I am tired of it. I am tired of holding him up and solving his problems. It is time he learns to stand on his own two feet."

"I thought he had plans to make some significant changes after this election," Paige said. "But so far, it's a lot of nothing."

"That is politics, *mi amor,"* Jorge confirmed. "A lot of nothing."

"I think I hear your secure line ring again."

"Let it fucking ring," Jorge said. "He can wait."

"Do you want me to answer it?"

"Do you *want* to answer it?"

They both laughed.

"That is what I thought."

"So, did Jolene move out yet?" Paige asked. "Or is she still…"

"She's out," Jorge replied. "But he is still nervous."

"Does he have a reason to be?"

"I do not think so," Jorge grinned. The man who had hired someone to attack Makerson was the recipient of an alarming gift the following day. He opened a box to discover a middle finger. There was no investigation. "But Marco is on it, just in case."

"It's good to prepare for anything," Paige confirmed. "These are dangerous times."

Jorge said nothing and glanced in the rearview mirror.

CHAPTER 19

"What is it you would like me to do?" Jorge bluntly asked as he turned away from the secure line. "I cannot turn back time, Athas. I also cannot erase these images from people's memories. If I could, I would be the first person to try."

Athas let out a loud sign that echoed throughout Jorge's office, causing him to swing his chair back around and glare at the phone.

"I will not hear *again* how taking these pictures was my idea," Jorge reminded him. "My question to you is, how did they get out?"

"That's what I was hoping you could help me with," Athas said. "That's what I'm trying to figure out."

"Well, Marco, he could not even find a way into this burner phone," Jorge reminded him. "So it would be someone who physically had the phone in their hand, or it was you."

"Why would I do something like that?" Athas rebutted.

"Don't know, don't care!" Jorge snapped back. "Athas, I am tired of this here soap opera. If this is too much for you, you can quit and become a drama teacher. I can give you a recommendation."

"People want me to step down."

"Athas, the opposition, they will find any reason to say this," Jorge reminded him. "Then get the ball rolling so that others feel the same. This is not news to you. What did you think would happen? You admitted those pictures were of you and Ryerson."

"I thought it would be better, to be honest."

"People, they cannot handle the truth," Jorge said. "No matter what they say."

"They need to get over it," Athas replied. "This isn't the end of the world."

"I would suggest you tell them this," Jorge leaned back in his chair. "Have someone spin it. Meanwhile, take a look at who is roaming around your house. Someone got their hands on your phone."

Jorge ended the call with a heavy sigh as he looked at the bulletproof window. A knock at the door interrupted his thoughts.

"*Si.*"

Paige stuck her head in.

"*Si, mi amor,*" Jorge's tone warmed. "You come to visit me…."

"Constable Hail is here," She cut him off, and they shared a look.

"Please, send him in," Jorge replied as he pulled his chair closer to the desk.

The door opened, and the young, black detective walked in. Wearing a leather jacket and jeans, Mark Hail reminded Jorge more of a 70s detective in a television series than someone who worked for the Toronto Police Department. The two had helped each other out on numerous occasions. Jorge wasn't expecting a visit from him.

"Mr. Hail," Jorge pointed toward the seat across from him. "Long time no see. What can I do for you today?"

Paige gave him a look before closing the door behind her.

"I didn't come for me this time," Hail confirmed. "I'm here 'cause I keep hearing about kids taking meds for school, and I'm not liking it much."

"You got kids?" Jorge was surprised. "I never knew."

"Nah, but I got nieces," Hail replied as he sat down. "And I got nephews and a nervous sister who's worried about this shit on the news about having to medicate kids to go to school."

"I'm working on it," Jorge nodded. "I share her concern."

"Big Pharma strikes again?"

"They strike a lot," Jorge reminded him.

"Yes, and if I recall correctly," Hail reminded him. "You tend to strike back."

Jorge smirked but didn't reply.

"You know people say the problem isn't the kids," Hail continued. "The problem is the parents. And I see it when I arrest kids for the shit they do, and the parents try to get them free with no consequences. I get that a lot. People think it's just the rich parents, but it's not. It's a whole different world out there."

"You got no argument here," Jorge confirmed. "This concerns me too."

"I do have some information for you," Hail continued. "I did a little research..."

"You did?"

"I know people," Hail replied. "And there's a rumor that a Toronto area school might be the test group for this new drug."

"Really?" Jorge sat up straighter. "This is the first I hear of this."

"I think they are aiming to keep it quiet," Hail said. "They're picking a public school in a low-income area. They want to focus on a difficult class, pay the parents to sign off on it, and probably manufacture the results that suit them. At least, that is what I assume."

"This sounds like a fair assumption," Jorge agreed. "Do you know what school? Where did you hear this?"

"Ah, I can't give away my sources," Hail replied. "But they are reliable, or I wouldn't be here. It's making people nervous, especially the parents with kids in this school. They expect to be coerced. They aren't exactly in a powerful position."

Jorge nodded.

"I suppose your boy Athas knows about this?"

"He is too busy worrying about his latest drama to notice," Jorge replied.

"Maybe that is why the drama happened so recently," Hail suggested. "Take your eye off the prize, and you don't see the real issues."

"I had not thought of that," Jorge nodded. "I will be looking into this, though. Can you give me the name of the school? I will take it from there."

After Mark Hail left, Jorge sat in thought before finally turning on his phone and sending Marco a message.

Can you meet me at Princesa Maria?

I'm already here.

See you soon.

Jorge slowly rose from his seat. A cramp in his foot caused him to stumble. He realized it was asleep. His body was telling him to slow down; if only he could.

Grabbing his jacket, Jorge headed toward the door. He was relieved Paige wasn't in the kitchen or living room as he passed them. He wasn't ready to share this distressing news with her yet. He didn't even want to deal with it himself. If Big Pharma took these steps, it showed they intended to creep into the schools any way they could. And it was up to Jorge to stop them.

Once outside, he shivered as the raw air hit his face. Jumping in his SUV, he tore out onto the street. His head began to throb, and his body felt heavy. This wasn't how he wanted to live. It was too much, and it never ended. Athas was powerless, and Big Pharma was relentless. The world was fucked.

Finally arriving at the bar, Jorge felt more like taking a nap than starting a fight, but he walked into the VIP room to find Marco furiously tapping on his keyboard while Chase stood nearby, looking over his shoulder.

"What's going on?" Jorge asked, feeling a heaviness in his chest. "Or do I want to know?"

"Sir, it looks like Big Pharma…."

"Is this about the test school?" Jorge cut him off as he sat down and sighed.

Marco observed him for a moment before answering.

"Yes, but how did you know…"

"I had a visitor who let me know," Jorge replied. "Do you know the school?"

"It is one in a poorer neighborhood," Marco confirmed what Hail told Jorge. "Sir, they want to bribe the parents with money. They insist the drug is safe, but I do not believe this. I'm just reading the documents. Sir, I am no doctor, but it sounds strange."

"The side effects are like ten pages," Chase grumbled. "You should see them."

"I have no doubt," Jorge nodded. "But people, they do not care."

"They should," Chase insisted. "It's their kids."

Jorge raised an eyebrow while Marco continued to type.

"The problem is," Chase continued. "Most people don't know a lot about this stuff. Science was hardly my top subject in school."

"We must find the information on the most concerning or likely side effects," Marco shook his head. "But my guess is it's hidden in this long list."

"Yeah, the longer the list, the less that people hear," Chase remarked. "Like those ads on television from American channels. After the first three potential side effects, who's listening?"

"Do not think that is not on purpose," Jorge replied. "We need to find out when this will happen and how Big Pharma managed to weasel themselves in. I would assume it was through the school board. Would it not have to pass their inspection first?"

"Yeah, and what are they getting out of this?"

"Follow the money," Jorge said. "Is that not usually what it is about?"

"The fact that people can do this to kids," Marco shook his head. "It makes me sick to think about."

"You are in the minority, Marco," Jorge gently reminded him. "The world, it is a different place now. Motivations and morality are two different monsters."

"They probably got someone into the school board ahead of time with this in mind," Chase said as he pointed toward the laptop. "It makes it easier. That person has to convince the others. Maybe more than one person to put the pressure on."

"I assume as much," Jorge said in a low voice as he's thoughts drifted off. "But what will we do? Attack the school board? The principal? Then what? They go to another school. They are like rats. They scatter to someplace else. The trick is to kill the rats, not just chase them out."

"How do we do that?" Chase asked.

"First, we must learn who the rats are," Jorge paused. "Then we catch them."

CHAPTER 20

"I was telling Maria," Paige said as she pointed at her stepdaughter while Jorge leaned back in his chair behind the desk. "This summer, she will have to do intense training. Our main focus will be self-defense and weapons, but I don't want to take over her summer either."

"Maria," Jorge said as he moved his chair forward. "You will be turning 16. This means you must know how to protect yourself if nothing else."

"Well, obviously, *Papá*, I'll use it for more than that," Maria nervously giggled.

"Yes, but if you were to change your mind," Jorge cautiously started. "I would not blame you, but I still want you to be able to protect yourself. You are a Hernandez, which means there is always a chance of danger because of who I am."

"I know," Maria nodded as her eyes grew in size. "But, *Papá,* I won't change my mind. I want to lead this family one day."

Jorge exchanged looks with Paige.

"I can do it!" Maria spoke with panic in her voice. "I know I'm a girl, but..."

"Maria," Jorge put his hand up in the air. "You know that this does not concern me. I *know* you can do this. I am not sure I want you in this world. I do not want to be in this world anymore."

"But it's not like when you were a narco," Maria said the last word quietly as if someone were listening. "Everything you do is legal."

"My business, Maria, is legal," Jorge reminded her. "My methods, sometimes, are not."

Maria nodded in understanding.

"Don't forget driving school," Paige quietly added.

"Yeah," Maria seemed less enthused. "I want to learn how to drive, but this city is crazy for traffic."

"Well, you do not have to stay in this city," Jorge reminded her. "I do not know if I want to be in this city anymore."

"Really?" Maria appeared surprised.

"Toronto, it is not the same as when we moved here," Jorge replied. "Now, everything is this woke shit."

"I think that's everywhere," Paige suggested.

"I do not think it is as prevalent in smaller places," Jorge suggested. "Some rural communities, they do not give a fuck how you identify or if you think you're a cat."

"It's like a whole thing in school now," Maria jumped in as she crossed her legs in a ladylike fashion. "They consider not knowing people's pronouns offensive. The teachers get mad because I question why it even matters."

Jorge grinned.

"They don't tend to like independent thinkers these days," Paige commented. "It is concerning."

"Maria," Jorge decided to change the topic. "Have you heard anything about teachers wanting to medicate children who are….how do you say?"

Exchanging looks with Paige, she nodded and continued.

"Have discipline issues."

"You mean, like me," Maria giggled. "They think *I* have discipline issues, but I am not taking medication. I've heard about that Ritalin shit and…"

"No, this is not Ritalin," Jorge shook his head. "This is a new drug, and they want to try to mandate it."

"Really?" Maria wrinkled her nose. "Can they do that?"

"Not if I can help it," Jorge insisted. "We know of one test school, but I'm worried there are others."

"Let us know if you hear of any," Paige told Maria, who nodded.

"I can ask around," Maria made a face. "What do these pills do?"

"That's what we're concerned about," Paige replied.

"Pills, they are not necessary," Jorge complained. "People need to teach their kids how not to be lazy assholes, but that is too much to ask."

Maria giggled. Paige gave him a look and grinned.

"It is true," Jorge shrugged.

"Can't Athas stop it?" Maria asked. "Aren't there laws or something?"

"The Greek God is useless," Jorge shook his head. "They are trying to weasel their way in, and he's too busy worrying about pictures of him and that reporter."

To this, Maria laughed.

"In reality," Paige intervened. "The pharmaceutical company can find their way around anything, regardless of laws. Plus, if they can find ways to convince people that it's needed, that their children are at risk or might get kicked out of school without it..."

"I don't know," Maria cut her off. "I don't think that would work. People would see that it doesn't make sense."

"Maria, you give people way too much credit," Jorge laughed but noted the concerned look on his daughter's face, causing the smile to fall from his lips.

It was later that night that he brought the topic up to Paige. They sat together on the couch, sharing a bottle of wine and looking at the falling snow on the nearby patio.

"Paige, I really do hate winter," Jorge announced. "Maybe we should go back to Mexico. At least we do not have to worry about what is happening in Maria's school there."

"Well, if you recall," Paige quietly reminded him. "She had issues at school there, and we might have bigger concerns if she's in Mexico."

Jorge nodded, remembering the legacy he left behind in his home country. She was right.

"So much has changed over the years," Jorge commented.

"I'm not sure if so much has changed," Paige commented as she sipped her wine. "We're just starting to notice what's behind the curtain."

"The problem is, Paige, even if we rip the curtain down and show people," Jorge wondered. "Will they even see?"

Paige didn't reply, but they shared a concerned look.

"Even on the news tonight," Jorge reminded her. "There was that story about the child in BC that attacked his classmates."

"I feel like we're missing something here," Paige said. "Was the story taken out of context?"

"It does not matter," Jorge shook his head. "The media take the story, chop it up, and spin it around."

"Yes, then they conveniently report how parents are concerned," Paige nodded. "Reminding those watching that *they* should be concerned too. I saw that report. It was incredibly biased, and online comments were concerning. People are talking about more incidents."

"My guess is these are fake accounts," Jorge said as he closed his eyes. "Paige, it never ends. I feel like for every dragon from Big Pharma that I slay, they have two more waiting on the sidelines. Greed is the motivator. Money? So they can buy what? How many yachts and cars and houses? Where does it end? It does not make sense to me. Even back in the day, it was never about money for me. It still isn't about money to me."

"But for you," Paige reminded him. "It's about power, and maybe that's the situation here too. These kids are easier to control if they are taking medication. That's what employers want. That's what the government wants. That's what Big Pharma wants to sell. Maybe this is even bigger than we originally thought. Maybe we have to dig a little bit deeper."

"I'm worried what we may find if we do."

"So am I," Paige confessed. "But this is our children's future. It doesn't affect Maria as much, but Miguel is just a baby. Plus, what does this say about the world we live in? Where does this take us? And who wants us there?"

Jorge didn't answer.

CHAPTER 21

"But what will we do without Clara?" Diego dramatically asked the group as they sat around the table in the VIP room. "She's been with us for *years,* Jorge. How can we find someone else who knows how to do this work and keep their mouth shut?"

"Diego, I have it under control," Jorge assured him. "Clara is currently training her nephew, who moved here from Mexico. I say that is fine as long as he does his work. I have met the boy. He is okay."

"I have researched him too," Marco jumped in. "He is clean. He needed to…get out of Mexico."

"We ain't gonna have problems, are we?" Diego asked as his face scrunched up. "We don't need problems from Mexico."

"No, they do not know he is here," Jorge assured him. "Diego, do you not think I have thought of this before? This here is fine. He will be fine. I tell him to stay off social media, to not talk to old friends and his family; they have disowned him."

"What exactly did he do in Mexico?" Chase wondered. "That sounds pretty extreme."

"Not really," Paige jumped in. "Families in Mexico are well aware of what it means to get involved with the cartels and don't want any association or, probably more importantly, no trouble from the cartels or the police."

"What did he do?" Diego asked the question again.

"He may have….killed someone high up in another cartel," Jorge said. "But again, we have covered all the bases. They think he is still in Mexico. I took care of it."

"He better stay under the fucking radar," Diego commented.

"Diego, relax, he will," Jorge promised. "Look, Clara, she has been with me for years, and this is the only favor she ever asks. It is the least I can do."

"He will be checking our offices…" Makerson started to ask, but Jorge was already nodding.

"Yes, he will check for listening devices, anything suspicious," Jorge said. "He will probably be better than Clara because he is more aware of new technology."

"What's his name?" Jolene innocently asked, but before Jorge could reply, Diego jumped in.

"His name is you don't fuck him," Diego snapped. "That's his name, Jolene."

"I just ask…"

"Ok, no fighting," Jorge said as he put his hands up in the air. "This is only a small portion of what we must speak about in this meeting, and we are already spending too much time on it."

Jolene sat back while Diego made a face.

"We are here to talk about other things," Jorge continued. "And his name is Pedro. Now, can we change the subject?"

He looked around the table, but for once, everyone was silent.

"Moving on, where are we with Big Pharma?" Jorge glanced around, his eyes falling on Makerson. "Any confirmation about the school they plan to take their poison to?"

"So far, nothing," Makerson shook his head. "Which I don't understand. They can't just decide one day that the kids need a pill and line them up. It has to go through the school board, and they must notify parents so they can share their opinion."

"Yes, but why the fuck would Big Pharma start following the rules now?" Andrew spoke up. "Those fuckers do what they want. So why not grab some kids and say, 'You're taking this drug', and do it? I mean, really?"

"It could be a class," Chase suggested. "Maybe not a whole school. There mightn't be as much red tape."

"Especially if they volunteer," Paige added. "If they wanted to keep low key, then they could."

"It is better to ask for forgiveness than permission," Jorge nodded. "And let's face it, the media is on their side to spin the story if it ever came out."

"And if they have a fine," Makerson shrugged. "So what? They're always paying legal bills. As long as the profits are higher than the bills, they don't care."

Jorge nodded.

"Sir, I've been hacking the principal's emails," Marco shook his head. "The board, Big Pharma, you name it, and I'm finding nothing."

"They know to be careful," Paige said.

"But they can only be so careful," Jorge reminded her. "Someone will eventually slip up."

"Isn't there someone who would be in charge of this project?" Chase asked. "In charge of research or something that we can track?"

"Sir, I see different people, but none are saying anything," Marco shook his head. "I do not understand."

"They know we are on to them," Chase replied. "We have to find a way in."

"I will get a job there," Jolene loudly said. "I will get a job and find out."

To this, everyone but Paige laughed.

"You're going to get a job there?" Diego rolled his eyes. "Doing what, Jolene? As CEO or something?"

More laughter around the table followed while Jolene's face grew flushed.

"I did not say that," Jolene snapped. "But why not? Why can I not get a job?"

"She is bilingual," Paige reminded them. "She could go in to be a sales rep. We could make up a fake resume to impress them."

"I can look in their HR to see what they want," Marco nodded. "We could do this."

Jorge thought for a moment and finally shrugged.

"Whatever, Jolene, if you can get in," he looked across the table at her. "Then do it."

"Maybe Paige would be better," Tony suggested. "I mean, she's..."

"White? Is it because she is white?" Jolene cut him off and sent a glare his way.

"No, if anything, *they'll hire you* because you're a minority, and companies want to represent diversity," Tony snapped at her. "I mean, she is more..."

"Ok, me, I do not want Paige anywhere near these fucks," Jorge said. "Plus, they may know that she is my wife. I do not see this working. Jolene, though, on the other hand, it may be different."

"We can work on this, sir," Marco nodded.

"It can't hurt," Makerson finally agreed. "It's worth a shot, but I don't think she'll find anything."

"Why not?" Jolene asked.

"Ok, this here, enough," Jorge cut them both off. "We must move on. You can try, Jolene, but I cannot see it working."

She sat back in her chair with anger in her eyes.

"Now, meanwhile, Marco, keep looking," Jorge instructed.

"I think the CEO is where to go," Paige suggested. "Does he not know everything going on in his company?"

"I'm sure he does," Makerson replied. "I think he's careful about what gets out. This is pretty controversial."

"I think they're still working on making parents scared," Tony suggested. "The traditional media is building a case. They're blaming video games and the problems in the world for kids being more anxious and angry. All these reasons, basically creating a problem, so they can, in turn, create a solution."

"They happen to have this magic pill that will solve your problems," Andrew quipped. "And make them fucking *billions*."

"They wonder why children are so hyper and out of control," Paige shook her head. "When you look at all the chemicals and sugar in processed food these days, that alone can affect children and their behavior."

"Yes, we cannot give Miguel any kind of juice, or he goes wild," Jorge said.

"Well, most of that so-called juice is sugar, water, and food coloring," Paige complained. "There's hardly any fruit involved."

"My children, too," Marco added. "Especially my youngest because it is so bad for them."

"That's what I mean," Paige nodded. "So, if you're feeding them highly processed food, full of sugar, kids will be hyper. Their emotions will be all over the map. Why doesn't anyone see that?"

"Especially once the sugar wears off," Tony nodded. "We did something about this in that series, *Eat the Rich Before the Rich Eat You.* Doctors told us that our modern, processed food is like poison to children, some more than others, depending on their sensitivities."

"And here we are," Jorge muttered. "The rich are still eating us."

"Or at least trying," Paige quietly added.

"There's a group of parents speaking up against these pills coming to the schools," Makerson added. "But people call them conspiracy theorists and discrediting them, dragging them through the mud. Even some professions speaking up against it, doctors, scientists, they're making them sound like lunatics for even suggesting that pills are ever bad."

"Yeah, and I also heard they're even making the pills for kids into gummies, so they seem more like a treat," Andrew said. "Like, that's some kind of fucked up."

"I am not surprised," Jorge shook his head.

"And Athas?" Makerson shrugged. "Does he still have his head up his ass?"

"Where else would it be?" Jorge retorted, causing everyone to laugh.

"So, what's the plan from here?" Diego asked. "Besides Jolene getting a job in Big Pharma?"

"I will, you see," Jolene assured him, to which Diego rolled his eyes.

Jorge thought for a moment.

"It is time to shake things up," he finally replied, "literally."

CHAPTER 22

"…Prime Minister Athas said in a statement that our children's health should be our top concern, not the profits of pharmaceutical companies…."

"Am I living in a dream world where Athas has a backbone?" Jorge asked as he twirled his chair around to look at his laptop before glancing at his daughter sitting across from him. "What is this? Is this real?"

Maria started to giggle as she returned her attention to the laptop.

"This bill is highly criticized by parents who say they should have the final say regarding their children's health…"

"You know, Maria, this here is a game," Jorge finally leaned forward and closed his laptop.

"What part?" Maria shrunk in her chair, her voice becoming small.

"All of it," Jorge leaned back and returned his full attention to Maria. "Athas, because he wants to get voted in. Big Pharma because they want to make money. The media because they want a story that catches attention. Everyone wants a piece of this, and no one cares about the kids."

"Even Athas?" Maria appeared skeptical. "I think he might be different."

"At the end of the day, Maria," Jorge shook his head. "No politician is different. Sure, Athas may be slightly more conscientious; this is true. But in the end, he will cave to whoever puts the most pressure on him. That is the way it is."

"Wouldn't that be you, *Papá?"* Maria innocently asked, causing Jorge to laugh.

"Well, Maria, yes, this is true," Jorge replied. "But do you now see why I have to put pressure on him? See how fast he bends for me? What if that were Big Pharma? What if that were Big Food? Big Oil? Any of them? Everyone has a master, whether they recognize it or not."

"Do you think this bill will go through?" Maria asked.

"I think Athas plans to ram it through if he can," Jorge replied. "But he is going to have a lot of resistance."

"Why can't they leave kids alone?" Maria asked. "I don't want to be forced to take pills. No kid does."

"You, Maria, will not be forced to do anything," Jorge assured her. "But these people at the top, they are psychopaths. And psychopaths rule the world. Remember that. And a psychopath, Maria, they have no conscience about anyone or anything. It is only about them and their interests, whether it's about money or power. This is how the world works."

"It's so depressing," Maria sighed. "Was it always like this?"

Jorge hesitated for a moment before answering.

"Yes, Maria, it was," Jorge nodded. "But things have changed to a degree. Now the psychopaths, they make less effort to hide it."

The sadness in her eyes pulled at his heartstrings, and he had to look away.

"Maria, I will be honest with you," Jorge finally continued. "I hate that this is the world I give to you, but at the same time, I would rather my daughter be strong and prepared than in a position of weakness."

"You say that all the time," Maria quietly replied.

"I would not be much of a father if I told you the world was rainbows and unicorns," Jorge reminded her. "You would end up being like Athas."

To this, Maria laughed.

"But Maria, it is not all bad either," Jorge reminded her. "You will have beautiful moments in your life. Look at me, with all the bad these eyes have seen. I was there when you were born, when Miguel was born. These are beautiful moments that make everything else bearable for me. Paige, my friends like Diego, these are the things that matter. It's what you come home to after you go out into the world and battle against the tyrants all day."

"It's battling against the tyrants that I don't like," Maria confessed. "I know I can, but it's not like a video game you can turn off. It never ends."

"Well, Maria, life is like that," Jorge reminded her. "It does not matter if you're the daughter of one of the most powerful men in Canada or the school janitor. It is just that your struggles are different."

Maria's eyes softened, and she nodded.

"Now, Maria, what did you want to tell me today?"

"Oh, I almost forgot," Maria shook her head as if she just woke up, causing Jorge to smile. "I asked around about this new pill they want kids to take, and I heard that it's only supposed to be voluntary."

To this, Jorge's head fell back in laughter, causing Maria to jump.

"Oh, Maria," Jorge continued to laugh, putting his hand up in the air. "I am sorry. I did not mean to scare you. It is, just what you said, is hilarious."

"But, isn't that good?" Maria appeared confused.

"It would be good," Jorge nodded and pulled his chair closer to the desk. "If that were what they meant, but I assure you, this is how it starts. They are trying to ease in, hoping most people volunteer, but I assure you, this will not last long. It will be volunteer first, volun*told* next."

"But, how?" Maria asked. "What do you mean?"

"It means that they won't force the pill down your throat," Jorge assured her as they nodded together. "But they will strongly recommend it, to the point that the pressure is on. Most people, Maria, cave to the pressure."

"Sheep," Maria complained. "Compliant people."

"And Maria," Jorge sat back again and studied his daughter's face. "We are taught from an early age to be compliant. Look at the schools. It is about following instructions. Jobs are a booklet of rules. They tell you when you can eat, go the bathroom, and who you must ask to do either. This here, it will be no different."

"And then, when people *still* don't go along," Jorge continued. "They will take things away until those people cave."

"But what if they don't?" Maria tilted her head. "What if they don't care about what they take away?"

"They will ostracize them," Jorge nodded. "Maria, I promise you, I know this game. It is the polite version of the cartel. Instead of cutting someone's fingers off because they won't talk, they cut them off from society until they cut their own fingers off."

Maria listened.

"The most dangerous games are the ones played with someone else's mind," Jorge continued. "People would rather you physically torture them, then what you can do to their brain or thoughts."

"I can see that," Maria softly replied. "It's hard to know who to trust."

"Never leave a stone unturned," Jorge suggested. "If there's something to hide, you will find it. You must be courageous."

The secure line interrupted their conversation, and Maria automatically stood up.

"I can go..."

"Nah, Maria, this here is fine," Jorge said. "Just do not talk. He will not know you are here."

Jorge leaned forward and answered the call as his daughter sat back down.

"Athas, I see you doing your press conference...."

"Did you see the questions afterward?" Athas asked. "I got reamed."

"Is this here new?"

"No, they were out for blood," Athas continued. "Especially the network where I cut their funds."

"Did you not see that happening?" Jorge asked as he pushed his chair ahead and exchanged looks with his daughter, who rolled her eyes. "You take away money, they won't give you favorable coverage."

"They talked about various attacks around the country by kids," Athas complained. "As if a magic pill is going to stop that."

"I hear they are talking about having people *volunteer* to try their pills," Jorge smiled at his daughter. "We know how that goes."

"It will start that way," Athas agreed. "They want to ease in, and after they convince everyone that they're getting positive responses to the pills, they think everyone else will jump in to take them."

"Yes, well, it's easier to invite the chicken into the fox's den than to chase them in," Jorge mused.

"The problem is that the media is focusing a lot on these 'sudden outbursts' by kids around the country," Athas continued. "They're trying to say that there's something different about this generation that was never an issue before, which is bullshit. Every generation has something to traumatize kids, but for some reason, they're now trying to imply that the world needs a magic pill to make it better."

"And people, they want things the easy way."

"Not only that," Athas continued. "But Big Pharma put a lot of pressure on schools, government, on the media, and I'm guessing gives them some hidden incentives too. That's where the problem lies. We can't fight against something we don't know. No one will admit to taking a bribe because it makes them look just as bad."

"Marco, he is looking into this, but it is hidden carefully."

"A lot of them are using this secure chatting site now," Athas said. "It's hard to break into. Did Marco look into it?"

"I know the one you mean," Jorge said. "And believe me, Marco, he can break into anything. That is not the issue."

"Then something else is," Athas insisted. "We know something more is going on here. It's just subtle."

"Or well hidden," Jorge said as he exchanged looks with his daughter. "But we will not leave a stone unturned."

Maria smiled, and he smiled back.

CHAPTER 23

"This job isn't worth a warm bucket of spit!" Athas complained on the other end of the line while Jorge glanced at his laptop screen. Protests were taking over the country, and what had started as a small group in Ottawa had spread throughout the provinces. "I make a sensible law, and people are fucking protesting! What would they rather, that their kids be drugged up zombies, a lifelong customer for Big Pharma."

"The problem is that Big Pharma is better at pushing its agenda than you are," Jorge mused as he watched the protest covered by his production house. Makerson was attempting to interview the irrational people. "You barely announced your new rules, and they had people complaining all over the internet, on social media and YouTube shows."

"I didn't think many people paid attention to that shit," Athas complained. "I also thought people had a functioning brain."

"But the mainstream news," Jorge shook his head. "They have been scaring them for months. It was a slow build, not to mention schools and their ridiculous rules. I have gotten called about Maria over stupid things. They want sheep, not freethinkers."

"They want conformity," Athas sighed. "How the fuck do I argue with that?"

"You have to be harsher," Jorge insisted. "You cannot be lightweight about it. You need experts to back you up..."

"*They* have their experts to back them up," Athas cut him off. "I saw it on the news again a few nights ago. This fucking idiot, who I've worked with before, suddenly thinks that kids need pills to calm them. He claims they should take them until their brain forms fully at age 25. He said then they *can easily* stop taking the pills at that time."

"It saddens me that people are so easily influenced," Jorge admitted. "The only thing we can do is push back and harder."

"That is starting to feel impossible," Athas said. "What are we supposed to do when common sense no longer prevails? If it even exists anymore at all."

"In the end," Jorge reminded him. "You have control. You cannot let them forget it."

"I might not have control," Athas said. "The provincial governments are starting to undermine me to make their constituents happy."

"Can they do that?" Jorge asked.

"They can fight me on it."

"You hold the federal money purse strings," Jorge reminded him. "Maybe it's time to tighten them up."

Marco showed up later that morning to discuss the situation. He looked upset before he even walked into Jorge's office.

"I am almost afraid to ask," Jorge admitted as the Filipino entered the room, his laptop bag swung over his shoulder. "What do you have for me now, Marco?"

"Sir, it is just more of the same," he said. "I found that Big Pharma has arranged for these people to protest. They started a small group and got it all over social media that the government wants to control whether or not we can give our children medications that they deem necessary. In turn, this caused others to join the protests and, well, you see what is going on now."

Jorge didn't respond but nodded as both men took their usual seats at the desk. Hopelessness was heavy in the room as Marco sat down his bag and exchanged looks with his boss.

"So, Marco, I do not like where this is going," Jorge admitted. "I have been thinking all morning. There are counter-protests now, but this here won't end well."

"No sir, you are right," Marco agreed. "I think what makes this difficult is that we both have children. This isn't just about a law we disagree with; this is much more serious. It is like I'm looking at a picture of a tree, and these other people think it is a mountain. I do not understand."

"It is like they are brainwashed," Jorge remarked. "The world has taught them to be compliant."

"They keep saying that these pills are safe and effective," Marco shook his head. "But the more I look, the more I see they are not. I just met Makerson at the production house. He said the people at the protest were crazy. One almost attacked him because they didn't like his questions. The person insinuated that the prime minister was wrong to create stricter rules around Big Pharma."

"Have you found anything?"

"As I said before," Marco reminded him. "I have seen the long list of potential side effects. I am doing more research in that area to find out the specifics. I think that is where our answer lies. If people see that they are more dangerous than they're worth, hopefully, this opens their eyes."

"I'm not very confident about that, Marco," Jorge admitted. "It almost seems like they have found their position and will continue to dig their heels in, even if they're proven wrong."

"They may not have a choice if the side effects are severe enough," Marco reminded him. "Some are very concerning."

"What stands out the most?"

"I am seeing a lot of suggestions that infertility could be a long-term side effect," Marco said. "I will admit, sir, that I do not know much about science, but I have found a man who does. He was a university professor who has spoken out against these pills and publicly said that they may hurt the development of children."

"And no one listens?" Jorge was curious.

"They forced him out, sir," Marco shared a look with Jorge. "They say he is spreading misinformation and therefore didn't represent their university's ideology."

"Is that a fact?"

"He had threats as well," Marco continued. "He shared this with me and said that it was just easier to retire, to step back because it wasn't worth his life."

Jorge nodded.

"I've found the documents, and he is going through them thoroughly," Marco said with a heavy sigh. "If what he sees is correct, this is not good."

"So, this here would cause fertility issues?" Jorge asked as he leaned back in his chair. "Marco, what is this really about? Is this about conforming, or is this about population control?"

"I am wondering the same, sir."

"If it is the latter," Jorge continued. "That is not Big Pharma. They may have created the pill, but if that is on purpose, maybe it's someone else's agenda."

"But maybe it is just a side effect they don't want to acknowledge," Marco suggested. "That is also possible."

"Yes, well, we do not want to be the conspiracy theorists they suggest our side is," Jorge laughed. "But at the same time, it depends on whether or not this is on purpose. I wonder if Big Pharma is working with someone else."

"Interesting," Marco thought for a moment. "I will look into this, sir. Up until now, I just assumed it was over profits."

"If this is the case," Jorge observed. "It is someone more powerful at the top of this issue. We fought Big Pharma before and won, so what makes this situation different?"

"We will find out what, sir," Marco replied. "I just do not understand."

"People are sheep," Jorge reminded him. "Although I must admit, this time, even I am surprised. I thought our children would be the breaking point in most situations, but maybe I was wrong."

"They're brainwashed, sir," Marco said. "They truly think that the government is trying to hurt their children by not allowing them this drug. It is like we are living in an alternate universe."

"If that is the case," Jorge replied. "I would like to go to another planet anytime."

"You and me both," Marco nodded. "and anytime, sir."

Jorge continued to monitor the situation throughout the day, noting that the protests grew more aggressive. Ironically, the same people complaining about their children becoming more violent and erratic were acting that way themselves. Meanwhile, the counter-protesters were less fired up. The police watched them more carefully. Jorge considered contacting Mark Hail to see if he had any information from the police department. Were they told to focus more on counter-protestors? Was this the usual procedure?

Opening his laptop, he went to a mainstream news source to see how they covered the story. As usual, their account was vastly different from that of HPC News. They sympathized with the parents, giving them a voice without showing a balanced report.

"Can you tell me why you're here today?"

"Because our prime minister has no idea what's happening in the schools. He has no children, but he's trying to tell us how to raise our kids. He doesn't care about the well-being of my children, and he doesn't care about the dangers my kids might be in if other kids aren't on this medication."

"Do you think your children are in danger?"

"My son had a classmate attack him one day after school," She gulped back her tears, causing Jorge to roll his eyes. *"He came home from school terrified. He didn't want to go back. He had a scratch on his face and...."*

"Oh, for fuck sake," Jorge slammed his laptop closed and was about to stand up when he heard a knock at the door. *"Si?"*

Paige apprehensively stuck her head in.

"Oh, *mi amor,* I need a break from this insanity," Jorge told Paige. "These people have lost their minds."

"I don't think I'm going to be much of a break," Paige confessed. "I just got a call from the school."

"Oh, not again," Jorge shook his head. "What did Maria do to offend them this time?"

"I think she had some colorful language to describe the protesters," Paige said as she entered the room. "I'm going to..."

"Just give me a minute, Paige," Jorge reached for his phone. "I'm coming with you."

"That's the problem," Paige showed some apprehension. "They told me to come alone."

"What!"

"Mrs. Dundas said she'd prefer I come alone since you demonstrate signs of...*word* violence."

Jorge felt the anger rising from his chest.

Enough was enough.

CHAPTER 24

"I thought I was clear on the phone," Mrs. Dundas sat behind the desk, across from Paige and Jorge. Her position was stiff, awkward. "This meeting was to be conducted between myself and Mrs. Hernandez."

"Hey, maybe I also identify as Mrs. Hernandez now," Jorge referred to their last meeting. "Or do you only accommodate teachers who do that?"

Mrs. Dundas gave him a dark glare and ignored his question.

"Why did you call us here today?" Paige bluntly asked. "And where is Maria?"

"Maria's at a school assembly downstairs," Mrs. Dundas replied. "Today, I called you here because your daughter continues to have outbursts in class, disagreeing with teachers, and refuses to follow our general guidelines regarding the expected procedure. She acts as if she's above the rules."

"Can you be a little more specific?" Paige pushed. "What *exactly* did she do wrong? I'm afraid you aren't giving me enough details."

"Today, for example," Mrs. Dundas directed her answer toward Paige, ignoring Jorge. "A teacher was attempting to explain how the government is looking at potentially giving students with behavioral issues medication that would enable them to feel more relaxed in class…."

"Drug them up," Jorge cut her off. "So they shut up?"

"That's not what I'm saying," Mrs. Dundas glared at Jorge, who showed no emotions. "Some students have more trouble concentrating and maybe are easily upset by events in the world. This new medication will make things more digestible, help them get over that hump."

Jorge and Paige exchanged looks.

"I'm assuming Maria spoke against it?" Paige calmly asked while Jorge seethed in the chair beside her.

"Yes, as she often does about many topics that come up in class."

"I think that's called critical thinking," Paige observed.

"Well, in Maria's case," Mrs. Dundas said. "It's more argumentative than it is to discuss. She told the class that they won't need these pills and that it was just a way to shut them up, so they were all zombies and for the pharmaceutical company to make money."

"So, she tells the truth? Is that what you mean?" Jorge found himself stumbling over his English as he grew frustrated. "You do not want that?"

"I would tend to disagree," Mrs. Dundas said. "We've received some information in a presentation, and everything seems to be on the up and up..."

"Is that the assembly that Maria's at now?" Jorge cut her off.

"No," Mrs. Dundas replied. "That has to do with the environment. Back to what I was saying..."

"So, who gave you this information?" Paige cut her off this time. "You mentioned a presentation."

"That would be the pharmaceutical company that's making this medication."

"Oh, yes, and they definitely would be unbiased," Jorge sarcastically commented. "It's not like they stand to make record profits if all the kids are required to take this here pill so they can come to school."

"My understanding is it's only for those with behavior issues," Mrs. Dundas corrected him. "And it's voluntary. We won't force anyone to take it."

"Or coerce?" Paige wondered.

"No, of course not," Mrs. Dundas replied. "There may be stipulations that if students have behavior issues and won't take the medication, they may not be allowed in certain activities like sports or music."

"Why not?" Paige pushed.

"Well, obviously, if they have behavior issues," Mrs. Dundas began to laugh. "We can't have them getting passionate about the game and potentially attacking other students, especially in more aggressive sports like hockey and football."

"And music?" Jorge innocently inquired. "Are you afraid they will break a guitar over someone's head?"

"Well, I admit that music is a little different..."

"Lady, what kind of kickbacks are you getting from Big Pharma to push this shit?" Jorge abruptly asked her. "This here is the real question."

"Of course, we aren't getting money!"

"So you don't got some shares in the company?" Jorge countered. "Maybe they throw you something to take the edge off?"

The principal glared at Jorge.

"I think the real concern here," Paige jumped in. "Is that Maria isn't allowed to express her opinions and counter...the narrative in this school, and this seems to be an ongoing issue. Are you not allowing the students to have a voice?"

"Of course, we want kids to have an opinion," Mrs. Dundas appeared offended.

"It just gotta be the right one, right?" Jorge shot back.

"That's not what I'm saying," Mrs. Dundas shook her head. "We can't allow misinformation. Maria was attempting to misinform the other kids. *This* is a problem."

"Are you sure it is misinformation?" Jorge asked. "Maybe *you're* misinformed, and my daughter, she knows what the real deal is?"

"I'm afraid she's wrong," Mrs. Dundas said. "And I can't allow her to upset the other students."

"You do not want students to think for themselves," Jorge corrected her. "That's what you're saying."

"That's not..."

"I think he's right," Paige cut in. "Critical thinking is still a right. Freedom of speech starts in the schools."

"As I said, freedom of speech is fine," Mrs. Dundas appeared defeated. "Misinformation is not."

"Yes, but how do you determine what is misinformation?" Paige shook her head. "Do you think that maybe rich pharmaceutical companies might have a motive other than making massive profits?"

"I am not saying that's not a factor," Mrs. Dundas insisted. "I'm saying is that the information they provided us is backed by science, not a 15-year-old's opinion."

Jorge and Paige exchanged looks.

"So, you have us here to tell Maria to keep her mouth shut in class?" Jorge asked. "Is that it?"

"I have you here because I'm afraid that this school may not be a great fit for Maria," Mrs. Dundas appeared nervous. "She might be better suited to…"

"Wait, you're kicking Maria out of school?" Paige grew angry. "Because she doesn't agree with your opinions?"

"We aren't kicking her out," Mrs. Dundas insisted. "We just think…"

"You better not be kicking her out for the fucking money I give you," Jorge snapped. "Think again, lady!"

"I think we agree that this isn't the ideal environment for her," Mrs. Dundas continued. "Although Maria can stay for the remainder of the year, I think it might be better that she consider another school in the fall."

Jorge looked at Paige, whose face was flustered.

"Let me get this straight, lady," Jorge's voice rose. "You are kicking my daughter out of your school at the end of the year because she won't be compliant? Because she's got a mouth? Because you do not agree with her opinions? Is this here true?"

"There have been some behavior issues," Mrs. Dundas continued. "And rumors that she attacks other girls in the bathroom."

"Attacks?" Paige grew upset. "What are you talking about?"

"There are rumors that she has physically attacked some students in the bathrooms," Mrs. Dundas appeared small in her chair. "But we have no proof because there are never any witnesses, and we don't have cameras in the washrooms."

"Maria? My daughter, who weighs about 90 lbs?" Jorge abruptly laughed, causing the principal to jump. "Are you serious? My *little* girl is attacking other kids? Does that mean that you think my daughter should be on this special medication?"

"It has been suggested," Mrs. Dundas nodded. "And I believe the complaints are legitimate. Despite the small stature of your daughter, she studies martial arts."

"My daughter, she is not taking your pills," Jorge raised his voice. "Over my dead fucking body, she will be medicated to go to this here school."

"We were hoping she would voluntarily take the...."

"Lady, what part of *over my dead fucking body* do you not understand?" Jorge yelled. "If you try to give my daughter any medication, lady, it would not be good for you!"

"Is that a threat?"

"Believe me, lady," Jorge jumped from his chair and leaned over her desk. "If I threatened you, you would know about it."

She shrank back in her chair while beside him, Paige stood and touched his arm. It had a calming effect on him, but barely.

"As I said," Mrs. Dundas appeared ill. "She can stay for the remainder of the year. It's only February, so you have time to look for another school in the fall."

"Let's go," Paige squeezed his arm this time. "This isn't worth it."

Jorge said nothing but stood tall, sharing a look with his wife.

It was on the way out when he started to calm down.

"Just leave it alone," Paige muttered. "It's time we get her out of here anyway."

"I am curious about this assembly she talked about," Jorge said. "What kind of bullshit are they teaching them."

"I know where they'll be," Paige stopped and glanced around. "Let's go see."

Jorge followed her down a long hallway, then down the stairs. A muffled voice drew them closer until they were outside the room where the assembly was taking place. Paige quietly opened the door, and Jorge looked at the stage. As soon as Jorge saw the person talking, he felt rage flowing through his veins.

CHAPTER 25

"Don't," Paige grabbed his arm before Jorge could tear into the room. He turned to see her shake her head. "Trust me, there's a better way."

"You bet there is," Jorge cringed as he turned his head back toward the stage. "A bullet would be my first choice."

"No," Paige continued to hold onto his arm. "We'll record some of this and send it to Makerson. He will know what to do."

"I'm going to talk to that fucking principal," Jorge attempted to calm down but was unsuccessful. "That is what I'm going to do."

"Ok," Paige finally let go of his arm. "You do that, *but* that's it because they have cameras everywhere. I'm going to record this and send it off to Makerson."

Jorge nodded, loosening his tie before turning on his heels and heading to the principal's office. Ignoring the secretary's attempts to stop him, he barged into the door to find Mrs. Dundas giggling through a phone conversation. When she saw Jorge, her demeanor changed as she ended the call.

"Can I help you…" She asked him, but Jorge slammed her door shut and rushed across the room.

"I want to know why you have that blue-haired freak preaching to our kids. That is what I want to know?" Jorge pointed toward the door. "That moron, he slashed my tires last month because he claims that anyone who drives an SUV is an environmental criminal."

"Climate criminal," Mrs. Dundas corrected him. "Yes, we're aware he takes extreme measures to get his point across, however..."

"Extreme measures?" Jorge cut her off. "He *slashed* my *fucking* tires. Last time I check, this here is illegal."

"Well, yes, but sometimes..."

"Please do not tell me that you're going to defend him, lady," Jorge snapped back. "If he's done it to me, he's done it to others. So, is he telling the kids this is ok? Will we have a bunch of fucking rich kids running around, slashing people's tires now? Is that what he is here to encourage? Is this why I pay all the money to this here school? For fucking trailer trash crackheads to lecture the students?"

"Sir, I think you are being unreasonable," Mrs. Dundas calmly replied. "He's a community leader, not a crackhead, as you call him. He's an environmentalist. Granted, he takes extreme measures to make a point, but he's passionate about his beliefs and knows a lot on the topic."

"So, if I go outside and slash your tires," Jorge took a deep breath. "Does this here make me an environmentalist? Would you be ok with this because I care so much about the environment?"

"Mr. Hernandez, I would rather not continue with this conversation if you're going to be erratic and unreasonable," Mrs. Dundas said. "And I certainly hope that is not a threat. I already felt..."

"Lady, if I threatened you," Jorge reminded her. "You would fucking know."

"I'm going to ask you to leave, or I'm calling security."

"You should be asking that moron you have in the assembly to leave," Jorge complained. "That there is the problem, not me. But that's not how this school works. You are too fucking woke for me, lady."

Jorge swung around, almost running into the same black man who stood outside, watching the door.

"Is there a problem?" He directed his question at Mrs. Dundas, but Jorge answered.

"Yes, there is a problem," Jorge complained. "That man giving the assembly slashed my tires last month."

The security guard appeared stunned by this news.

"So, you might want to watch yours when he leaves here today," Jorge continued before brushing past him and out the door. Fuming, he headed outside, where Paige was waiting by the SUV.

"I was hoping you'd be out soon," She gently said as he approached her. "I didn't want to have to figure out a way to get a bloody body out of there today."

"Paige, these people are unreasonable," Jorge shook his head. "It is like I'm on another planet. She did not even care that he slashed tires. She act like this here is normal."

"She isn't normal," Paige reached for his hand. "Let's go home."

"Should we get Maria," Jorge glanced back at the school.

"No, I texted her to watch things in there," Paige said. "I have her recording everything he says and sending it to Makerson. She's doing it in segments in case she's caught."

"If he is not saying anything bad," Jorge shook his head. "Why would it matter?"

"Who knows these days," Paige muttered as she headed toward the passenger side of the SUV. "Your daughter is crafty. She'll find a way."

Once in the vehicle and on the road, Jorge continued to fume while Paige called Makerson, explaining what had happened.

"I thought if you could find some kind of criminal record or something," Paige started. "This would make for a great story for HPC news. Maria will text you his name and is recording what she can of the assembly."

There was a pause, and then Paige said, "I will put you on speakerphone. Jorge is here with me."

"What's going on?" Jorge asked as he slowly made his way through traffic.

"The protests are getting bad," Paige replied, and seconds later, Makerson jumped in.

"I was telling Paige that the protesters and counter-protestors are getting into it outside a school where the drug is apparently to be introduced. Tony and Andrew are there, working on the story."

"I'm sure Andrew will piss someone off," Paige predicted. "He likes to get in people's faces."

"He might not be able to get near them," Makerson replied. "The police are there now, trying to pull protesters apart. One side says if you care about your kids, you'll drug them up. The other side says if you care about your kids, you leave them alone. Both are passionate about where they stand."

"In what world is giving your kids pills a good thing?" Paige questioned.

"The one where they lost their fucking minds," Jorge attempted to reason.

"Well, there is that," Makerson's voice echoed through the vehicle. "But also, they insist that these pills *help* kids so that they don't have any emotional overreactions to a situation and put themselves, or other kids, in danger."

"Why don't we just remove their hormones next," Jorge sarcastically replied.

"It almost sounds like this pill dulls them," Paige suggested.

"That's what it looks like," Makerson confirmed. "That's why Marco thinks they are linking infertility with it. I'm not a science guy, but it doesn't seem like much of a stretch."

"Does he still have that scientist to help him check the information?" Jorge asked.

"They're doing that right now," Makerson replied. "He's here, at HPC, working on it."

Jorge nodded, calming slightly. At least something was working in his favor.

"That and this environment dirtbag story should look good for tonight's live stream."

"I look forward to it," Paige replied.

The conversation ended shortly afterward. Jorge fell silent with his thoughts.

"Maria texted me and said the assembly is over," Paige said. "She said it was a lot of bullshit. Don't eat meat. Don't drive a gas car. Wear an extra sweater rather than turning up the heat."

"Yeah, well fuck him," Jorge muttered. "If we cross paths one more time, he won't have to worry about being cold when I throw him in the fucking crematorium."

"He'd probably complain that it uses too much power," Paige said with a straight face, causing Jorge to laugh. "But he'd probably approve of us only being ashes rather than taking up so much space and using too many resources."

"Well, he definitely falls into that category," Jorge muttered as he got closer to home. "Paige, I am tired of all of this. When did things get so weird? Where does this woke shit come from?"

"That's a good question," Paige mused. "I'm thinking you have to follow the money, like with most things."

"This is true," Jorge agreed. "Who stands to make money here?"

"It depends on what you're talking about," Paige replied. "But I'm certain that it leads back to people making money and their way of spinning things. You'd have to do a lot of spinning to suggest that kids should be drugged up to go to school or that someone who slashes tires for the environment is acceptable."

"Do you think someone paid that little shit to do this with the tires?"

"Possibly," Paige considered. "Someone had to help him get into a private school to talk."

"Remember, he says he didn't have a job," Jorge remembered when he caught the kid slashing his tires and interrogated him. "Probably rich parents, so he don't need one."

"I think you're onto something there."

"We gotta get out of Toronto," Jorge complained as they turned onto their street. "It is not the city I moved to a few years ago."

"It's not the city I grew up in," Paige muttered.

"Who is in our driveway?" Jorge asked. "Is that a police car?"

"Are you sure you didn't do anything to Mrs. Dundas?" Paige asked.

Jorge exchanged looks with her and didn't reply.

CHAPTER 26

"What the hell is this about?" Jorge asked as he got out of his SUV and walked toward the black man as he got out of his car. "Don't tell me Mrs. Dundas has you here to arrest me for being…abrupt with her?"

"Who?" Mark Hail appeared confused. Paige caught up to the two men, and he gave her a quick hello before returning his attention to Jorge. "Is this something we should be talking about out here?"

Jorge said nothing but pointed toward the house. The three of them headed inside before anyone spoke again.

"If that woman…."

"Is there a crime scene that I…"

"Is this about Maria?"

The last question came from Paige and caused the two men to stop speaking and turn to her.

"No," Mark replied immediately before glancing between them. "This is kind of a private matter."

"We can go to my office," Jorge ushered them in that direction. "Now, you have me curious."

"Look, I wouldn't normally come here for this," Mark started once the three were in the room and the door was closed. Jorge pointed toward a seat. "But it has to do with my niece and I…I'm limited as a cop."

"Really?" Jorge asked as he sat behind the desk, and Paige sat beside Mark. "Do you not still carry a gun and have the ability to arrest people?"

"There are limits," Mark reminded him. "Lawyers will scream conflict of interest if I'm not careful. It doesn't take much for people to get away with their crimes these days."

Jorge merely grinned at this last comment.

"So, what happened to your niece?" Paige asked. "How old is she?"

"Sixteen," Mark replied with some hesitation. "Look, she came to me recently and confessed something that happened to her over the Christmas holidays. I debated taking her to the department and filling out the paperwork, but deep down, I knew it would go down the gutter before she even finished telling her story."

"Oh no," Paige showed concern. "I don't think I like where this is going."

"Well, that would make two of us," Mark quietly replied, waiting a moment before he continued. "My niece, she's like a little girl to me. I know she's 16, but I look at her, and I see a kid. You know what I'm saying?"

"I know," Jorge nodded. "We do everything to protect our children, our family. You do not have to explain this one to me. What happened, and more importantly, what would you like me to do to resolve this issue?"

"I want you to kill the man who raped my niece," Mark spoke with some emotion. "Because I know the court system and what it'll take out of her if we go through it. It's not worth it. They'll drag her through the mud, and for what? So this motherfucker can get a slap on the hand?"

"I think you are being generous to suggest he would get that much," Jorge nodded in understanding. "And I respect your decision to come to me. You have helped me in the past, so of course, yes, I will take care of him. Give me a name, whatever information you have on him. You can find his corpse hanging from a tree or never find him again. It is totally up to you."

"I agree with everything Jorge is saying," Paige jumped in. "But murdering this man won't make your niece feel better. She's going to need counseling and probably a lot of it before she ever feels safe again."

"Teach her to shoot a gun," Jorge added. "My Maria, she is learning self-defense. She will feel better if she can protect herself."

"Maybe teaching her to use a gun is a bit hasty," Paige warned. "This isn't our kid, Jorge. Self-defense is fine, but having said that, I'm with Jorge regarding taking care of this...."

"Soon to be a dead man," Jorge cut in. "And I assure you, it will not be a simple, fast shot to the head. I will make sure he's tortured."

Mark sat up straight in his chair and nodded. His eyes grew small and dark.

"Yes, he is going to experience *his* private hell here on earth," Paige assured Mark. "How old is this man?"

"He's in his early twenties."

"We will need a name and other information," Jorge continued. "But as for your niece, we do not need her name. Let her continue to have her privacy."

"I appreciate that," Mark nodded. "I just....I don't know if I can get her to go to counseling. She barely talked to me about this and refuses to talk to her parents, so I'm in an awkward situation. I don't want to betray her trust and tell them what happened when she begged me not to tell anyone."

"When she came to you," Paige asked. "Didn't she realize the legal route would make that difficult?"

"She was hoping I could arrest him," Mark attempted to explain. "And that was that. She didn't understand the entire process. I guess she naively thought there was a way we could take care of this without her parents knowing. I told her that would be impossible."

Jorge leaned back in his chair and exchanged looks with Paige.

"You know," he thought for a moment. "What if she were to spend some time with Maria? I mean, they are about the same age, right? She could show her some self-defense moves she knows, maybe encourage her?"

"That's a good idea," Paige nodded. "I know she would, but maybe Mark isn't comfortable with his niece spending time with our family. In fairness, we probably aren't exactly the typical Canadian family."

"We are a mixed family," Jorge shrugged. "How much more Canadian can you be then that?"

"That's not what I mean," Paige muttered and gave him a look, which amused Jorge.

"I don't care," Mark admitted. "I know she's safe with you and your daughter. Look, my niece is naive for being a city girl. She could use a stronger friend, someone with some street smarts."

"Well, Maria, she is that," Jorge nodded. "Plus, she could use some friends."

"Yes," Paige agreed. "Maria doesn't have a lot of friends, especially in the school she's in."

"Well, she will not be there much longer," Jorge complained. "They want to kick her out because the girl has got a mouth."

"Can't imagine where that would come from, can you?" Paige turned her attention to Mark, who merely grinned.

"Hey, they want to put kids on pills or get rid of them," Jorge complained. "They say my Maria isn't a good fit for the school."

"I think that's happening a lot," Mark nodded. "I keep hearing about this program that appears to be more about Big Pharma making money than anything else."

"And everyone is ready to throw their kids to the wolves," Paige added with a sigh. "It's discouraging enough without parents being so compliant."

"They want sheep," Jorge said as he leaned back in his chair. "They do not want kids to think for themselves or to be smart, just moronic sheep because they are easy to control."

"Your boy Athas *still* not on this yet?" Mark asked.

"He is, but they are fighting him every step of the way," Jorge pointed toward his window. "But as usual, the power behind this is bigger than him."

"Then what can you do?"

"Hey, I said it was bigger than him," Jorge leaned forward in his chair. "I did not say bigger than me."

Mark smiled and nodded.

"Now, you must give me a name so I can torture this fucker who hurt your niece," Jorge leaned ahead on the desk. "I can get Marco to do some research too."

"His name is Jacob Leon," Mark Hail replied as he took a piece of paper from his leather jacket pocket. "His parents are rich, and from what I can see, he never had a job. He's a professional student who shows up for classes when it suits him."

"So, what does he do all day?" Jorge asked. "Sleep? Play video games? Watch porn? What?"

"Well, he seems to be involved in various causes through his university," Mark replied. "He can't be bothered to go to class, but he has time for this shit on the side."

"What causes?" Paige asked. "Please don't tell me he's a feminist because he's concerned about women, or I will kill him myself."

To this, Jorge grinned and winked at his wife.

"Yeah, well, not far off," Mark replied. "He has protested with women's groups before, so I think he will jump on any train that passes."

"But how did he meet your niece?" Jorge was curious. "Is she not only in high school?"

"They try to recruit kids in high school," Mark explained. "They go in and talk to the kids..."

"Wait, what?" Paige turned in her chair. "Like about the environment, that kind of thing?"

"Oh yes," Mark nodded vigorously. "That's one of their top causes right now, climate change, the environment..."

Paige and Jorge exchanged looks.

"Someone was at my daughter's school today," Jorge said. "The blue-haired fuck that was speaking, he slashed my tires once and said I was a climate criminal. I see him today talking at Maria's school and let the principal know what I think of this here."

"Blue-haired guy?" Mark asked as he took in everything Jorge was saying. "I think...that could be the man who raped my niece. I can find you a picture."

"See," Jorge shook his head and looked at Paige. "I should have killed him when I had the chance."

CHAPTER 27

"Why do I have to babysit her?" Maria complained, appearing disgruntled from the other side of the desk. "Why did you volunteer me to teach this kid not to be dumb?"

"Maria!" Jorge snapped at her. "I cannot believe you would say this. She is the same age as you and something terrible happened to her. I thought you'd be more compassionate."

"Well, you thought wrong," Maria corrected him as she sat up straighter and crossed her legs. "*Papá,* I'm stressed out enough with school always hassling me. I don't have time for this too."

"Maria, you are fortunate to be a strong young woman," Jorge pointed out, noting that his daughter was looking away. "This girl, she was a victim. Can you imagine how she must feel?"

"Since when have you worried about the feelings of 16-year-old girls?" Maria challenged. "And why is this *my* problem?"

"I never said it was *your* problem," Jorge explained. "I just say..."

"And why were you at my school today anyway?" Maria cut him off. "What did I do wrong *now?*"

"You are doing nothing wrong," Jorge insisted. "We think that maybe it is a good idea to look at other schools this fall...."

"She kicked me out, didn't she?" Maria grew agitated. "That old bitch, Dundas, she wants me out, doesn't she?"

"Maria, I…."

"She told you to find me another school," Maria continued to rant. "I know because I'm not the only one. They ask anyone who's not a good sheep to leave."

Jorge waited for her to finish but said nothing. He watched his daughter, full of vigor, suddenly deflate before his eyes.

"Maria," Jorge finally spoke. "It does not matter what she wants. The point is that this school is not good for you."

"Maybe no school is," Maria said.

"Then we will make our own fucking school," Jorge insisted. "Or we will hire you a home tutor, but you will not return to that school this fall."

"It's only February," Maria reminded him.

"That is fine," Jorge nodded. "It is only a few more months."

"I don't know if I can stand it," Maria replied. "All they do is try to control us. Even today, that freak talked to us about the environment, and the teacher wants us to write an essay explaining why he was right."

"What did he say?" Jorge was curious.

"That basically," Maria shrugged. "We're all terrible and use too much gas, shouldn't eat meat, and stuff. We weren't allowed to disagree even if we had valid reasons why we did. It was 'tell us why he was right or fail.'"

"They say this?"

"No, but it was implied," Maria said. "I said what I thought, but I assume I won't pass this test."

"Life, Maria, is a series of tests," Jorge reminded her. "But you have to look at who's giving the test before you decide if it's valid."

Her face grew pink, but she said nothing.

"Maria, I ask you to spend one afternoon with this girl," Jorge requested. "That is it. Remember, she had something terrible happen to her and is in a dark place. All I ask is you offer to show her some self-defense moves. That is all. This is for Mark Hail. As you know, he has helped this *familia* in the past."

Maria nodded and looked down.

"Now, regarding your school," Jorge continued. "We will find you somewhere better. It is too late in the year now to leave, but there are always other options. If the school does not want my money, I will find a school that does. Maybe other parents will do the same."

"So," Maria thought for a moment. "It was that guy from today at school, that raped this girl?"

"Yes, Maria," Jorge nodded. "We connected the dots. He's part of a group paid to protest for various causes."

"People are paid to protest?"

"To push their agenda," Jorge corrected her. "Then, they find people who are impressionable to join them. That is why they go to high schools. They find people like Mark Hail's niece to get involved because they are young, easy to manipulate."

"But they don't always rape them, I hope."

"Of course not," Jorge said. "But it's clear that this man, he saw an opportunity to do so and recognized that she was unlikely to say anything."

"So, he's probably done this before?"

"*Si.*"

Maria grew angry.

"You have to remember," Jorge said. "You were brought up differently than many kids these days. You come from a unique family. Most do not teach their kids about what is out there in the world. Probably because they don't want to face it themselves."

"So, what about the guy who did this?" Maria showed signs of concern. "Will he be arrested…or something."

Jorge grinned and hesitated before answering.

"…or something," He finally replied, and Maria nodded.

"Is that why this guy came to see you today?" Maria asked.

"Maria, it is better if you don't know too much," Jorge suggested. "You have your task, and we have ours."

"I understand."

A knock on the door interrupted their conversation.

"Come in," Jorge called out.

Paige stuck her head in the door.

"Tom Makerson is doing the story in a minute," Paige reminded him. "I know your phones are off…."

"Thank you, *mi amor,*" Jorge nodded as he reached for his laptop. "Now, Maria, this here, he is also the man that slashed my tires…"

"Oh! I remember that," Her eyes widened. "He talked about slashing tires today."

"Please do not tell me he suggested you all do this," Jorge asked as he opened his laptop.

"No, he talked like other people did it," Maria said. "But he claimed he never did, that it wasn't smart."

Jorge rolled his eyes, and Maria giggled.

"*...extensive criminal record,*" Makerson was speaking to the camera. "*But when we contacted the school in question to ask for a statement, they did not return our calls.*"

"No shit," Maria muttered.

"*A student from the school sent me this video of Mr. Leon speaking,*" Makerson continued, showing a short clip, followed by another one of the same man hunched over a tire, a knife in hand. "*And here he is slashing tires in the GTA, claiming that those who own larger vehicles like SUVs are climate criminals. Leon was also previously arrested...*"

"They sure know how to pick speakers for your school, Maria," Jorge complained. "I am glad my money is going toward bottom feeders like this one here."

"But the school didn't seriously pay this guy, did they?" Maria asked.

"They did," Jorge nodded. "A large speaking fee."

"He wasn't worth it."

"He must have some kind of connections to be allowed to do this," Jorge assumed. "Then again, in today's world, who would know?"

"Marco didn't find anything?"

"Just what we talk about in the news," Jorge replied. "We are still looking into him."

"*....protests continue in the downtown area,*" Makerson continued. "*Parents both for and against making it mandatory for children to take medication....*"

"Look, Maria, at the signs," Jorge pointed toward the laptop screen as he moved closer. "Look at the back."

He was pointing at a sign that said, *Take your vitamins, sheep,* featuring images of sheep lined up to take a pill before entering a school behind them.

"That is clever," Maria commented.

"It is the truth," Jorge reminded her. "Maria, I must ask you something. How would you feel if we left Toronto someday?"

"You keep bringing that up," She spoke skeptically. "I used to love it here, but things are getting weird."

"That is how I feel too."

"I'm tired of fighting with every school," she continued. "Like, why is it so bad to be myself?'

"It is not," Jorge shook his head. "But only they benefit from you thinking it is."

Maria appeared sad as the two made eye contact.

"Think about it," Jorge encouraged.

"But what about our friends, our family?" Maria asked. "Diego, Marco, and…"

"Maria, you and Chase are no longer close," Jorge reminded her. "Diego, we never see because he is busy with work. Marco, honestly, he is also thinking of getting his family out of the city too. And Jolene, don't we want to avoid her anyway?"

To this, Maria laughed.

"I am putting this idea out there, Maria," Jorge said. "It is for you to consider because you're old enough that it affects you. We can still be close enough to come to the city if needed, but maybe it is time for us to leave this insanity."

The two shared a look of understanding.

It was time.

CHAPTER 28

"Once upon a time," Jorge said as he brought his shoe down hard on Jacob Leon's hand, causing him to let out a loud, piercing scream blunted by the cement basement floor of the crematorium. "There was a *very* bad man. And this *very* bad man pretended to care about the world. He pretended to care about the environment. But he was a wolf in sheep's clothing because what he did, was slash people's tires and rape teenage girls."

As if suddenly realizing what was about to happen, the blue-haired man attempted to sit up, his eyes scanning for an escape, when Chase rushed over and pointed a gun at him.

"I wouldn't fucking move if I were you."

"You should take his advice," Jorge calmly added. "Because the more you struggle, the harder this will be for you."

Jacob Leon's body suddenly relaxed and fell back as if accepting his fate. He said nothing but watched Jorge in silence.

"Now, we thought about how to do this," Jorge continued. "At first, we thought an accident would be a good way for you to die, but then I thought, this here didn't send a message."

"Then," Jorge continued as he hovered over the terrified young man. "I thought I would have you 'commit suicide', but then I thought no one would believe you would have the courage. I mean, look at you."

Jacob seemed to stiffen with Jorge's insult, and tears formed in his eyes.

"And then I thought," Jorge hesitated for a moment. "I could make it look like a murder because, you see, a murder sends a message. It says that you cannot be a specific kind of person, or the world will turn on you."

"Do you know what it means for the world to turn on you, Mr. Leon?" Jorge continued as his voice grew louder. "It means the world is sick of you and your bullshit. It means time out. We're done here. We're done with you and everything you represent. This woke shit? We're done. People, they are done. They do not want to be lectured by a weasel fuck like you on how to live their life. Blue-haired Jesus does not exist in anyone's world but yours."

"So," Chase suddenly spoke up. "What are we doing to him?"

"I don't know," Jorge thought for a moment. "What would you suggest for a man who has raped a young woman?"

"If she was my daughter, I know what I would do," Chase replied, glaring at the man on the ground.

"It wasn't like that, she wanted to..." Jacob Leon attempted to explain, but his words halted when a huge boot suddenly come down hard on his neck. Chase stepped back while Jorge leaned down to check. He was dead.

"I think you decided for both of us," Jorge looked at Chase, who showed no remorse. He was no longer the young man Jorge hired many years ago, a man who would never consider killing someone in cold blood. "Now, what do we have for lunch? Can you make *that* decision?"

Glancing down at what he had just done, Chase shook his head at the sight of blood running down the side of Jacob Leon's head.

"I'm not hungry."

"I will go find Andrew so we can clean this up," Jorge stepped away, watching the blood quickly gathering on the plastic underneath their victim. "No one will be looking for this piece of shit."

"They'll think he went underground after the news yesterday," Chase suggested. "After all, that's what cowards do."

"I will get Andrew," Jorge repeated as he headed for the stairs.

"I'll be here," Chase calmly said. "To help him."

Jorge didn't reply but headed up the stairs.

"That was fast," Paige was waiting nearby as he arrived on the final step. "I thought this would've been a longer, more torturous process."

"I'm getting old, maybe getting a little soft," Jorge shrugged and glanced toward the basement. "Chase, on the other hand, did not waste much time."

Paige nodded.

"But *mi amor,"* he moved closer to her. "You know how these things can bring out my primal..."

"Are we good?" Andrew interrupted them as he entered the room. "I mean, I got a thing to do at HPC after this, so if you need me to turn up the fire, I gotta do it soon, you know?"

"He's all yours," Jorge pointed toward the basement. "Chase is waiting for you down there."

"Aye, aye, Captain!" Andrew saluted Jorge before heading toward the basement. "Please tell me you used plastic this time? It's so messy when you don't."

"Of course," Jorge replied, exchanging looks with Paige before watching Andrew head down the stairs. "*Mi amor,* let's get out of here."

"Sounds good to me," She muttered as they headed for the door, and Jorge slid his hand over her back. "Maybe we could...."

Before her words were out, her phone buzzed, indicating a message.

"Now what," She muttered after glancing at the number. "It's the daycare."

"Fucking wonderful," Jorge quipped as they headed outside toward the SUV. "If it's not the school, it is daycare."

"They want to speak to us at our earliest convenience," Paige said as she listened on her phone.

"Paige, are we surprised?" Jorge asked as they got into their vehicle. "This is not the first time we've received a call from his daycare or Maria's school. It is always something. They cannot just do their job and teach kids something. They must tell us why we are bad parents."

"I'm so tired of this," Paige confessed, showing rare signs of emotions. She was always so calm, but Jorge could see her exterior was starting to crack as he reached out to touch her hand. "Are we terrible parents?"

"Paige, are you serious?" Jorge squeezed her hand. "We are the best parents because we teach our kids to be themselves, think for themselves, to be smart."

"Then what is the problem?" Paige shook her head as her eyes grew sorrowful.

"*That* is the problem, *mi amor,*" Jorge insisted. "They do not want this for our kids. They want them to be dumb, obey, and conform. And Paige, our kids, they will never do this. And if they do, it will be over my fucking dead body… or someone else's."

"We can't kill every teacher and principal that pushes this crap," Paige reminded him. "As much as I'd love to put a bullet in Dundas, we have to be careful. There are other ways."

"I agree," Jorge took a deep breath. "We must learn where she gets her instructions."

"That's what I'm wondering."

The couple drove in silence the rest of the way. Paige appeared defeated and discouraged as she stared out the window. Jorge thought about his conversation the previous day with Maria.

"You know, yesterday, Maria and I talk about moving."

"You did?" Paige appeared skeptical.

"I want to move for many reasons," Jorge reasoned. "It is like you talk about staying under the radar. This is one way to do it. It will never be the case in Toronto."

"Yes…."

"And Maria, she was happy with the idea."

"She was?" Paige appeared surprised. "I thought…"

"She is growing up," Jorge reminded her. "And she sees why being here does not benefit her."

"But if we move, where will she go to school?" Paige asked. "You aren't thinking of sending her away to private school, are you?"

"Put her in regular public school," Jorge shrugged. "Maybe it is good if she is surrounded by real people and not rich, lazy kids like she is now."

"Really?"

"Paige, I pay a lot of money for her private school," Jorge cut her off. "And what is she learning?"

"Well, you have a point there."

"It is…something I am considering," Jorge continued. "I haven't figured out the details yet, but I am thinking about it."

Paige nodded as if slowly absorbing the information.

"Of course, Tala would come with us," Jorge insisted. "And Marco, he is thinking of doing the same. He is growing frustrated."

"Are his children having problems?"

"Different kinds of problems," Jorge replied. "He can work from anywhere, so it is fine for him. The others will still be here. We won't be far away."

Paige smiled, then fell silent for the rest of the drive.

Miguel's daycare was in a newer building. Flowers with smiley faces were painted near the door, indicating an uplifting, fun environment. However, this is not what Jorge and his wife found when they walked inside. Children were crying, and adults were comforting them while others attempted to clean up a mess of paint on the walls, floors, and the kids.

"Oh no," Paige muttered as she looked across the room.

It took Jorge a moment to realize what she saw, but once he did, all Jorge could do was laugh. He stopped after Paige shot him a look.

Across the room stood Miguel, holding hands with a staff member. He had green paint in his hair, red splattered on his face, and various colors on his clothes. While the other children appeared traumatized by whatever had happened, Jorge watched his son laugh hysterically.

CHAPTER 29

"I do not understand," Jorge shrugged and glanced briefly at his wife before looking back at the young, black woman behind the desk. "If you do not want things like this to happen, you don't give small children paints."

"Mr. Hernandez, this isn't about the paint," She attempted to reason. "It's about your son's behavior issues."

"He's *three!*" Jorge shot back. "He is just a little boy. Is this here daycare or military school?"

"I think it's reasonable to expect a certain amount of discipline from children," She continued. "We can't have Miguel bullying other children. It's completely unacceptable."

"Bullying?" Paige repeated and shook her head. "I understand that Miguel can't start putting paint on other kids, but in fairness, I don't think he was doing it to hurt anyone."

"He's *three!*" Jorge repeated with more anger this time. "He is a *child.* Children do stupid things and do not realize they are stupid things. I do not think he planned to terrorize this daycare as part of what? His evil plot?"

"Look, Miguel has done this at home, too," Paige continued. "His sister gave him paints for Christmas..."

"And I tell her then," Jorge cut her off. "If he makes a mess, *you* are cleaning it up."

"Which she did," Paige continued, "and…."

"Because he's *three!*" Jorge cut off his wife. "He is a *child.* Miguel was going to paint his sister. He thought it was great fun, again, because he is *three.* That is what children do. Why did you have children playing with paints in the first place? Are they toxic? You realize that kids at this age put everything in their mouth?"

The daycare worker stiffened in her chair.

"I have to agree," Paige shook her head. "I don't know how I feel about such young children having paints. Even if they're non-toxic, it seems like a recipe for disaster."

"Noted," The young woman nodded. "We will remove them from the daycare, but this isn't the first time we've had issues with Miguel. We've had other incidents before, as you know. We can't have him continue to do these things."

"So, you want to kick my son out because he got paint on other kids?" Jorge shot back. "Is this here what you are trying to tell me?"

"What I'm saying is that maybe Miguel is too excitable. I'm not kicking him out."

"He's *three!*" Jorge shot back. "He is supposed to be excitable."

"I'm just concerned that it…"

"Look, lady, I do not know how long you have worked at this daycare," Jorge cut her off. "But children, they act funny sometimes. It's normal. Can we move on from this and agree that you shouldn't have paints in a daycare?"

"We do agree on that point," She nodded. "But what I'm saying is we can't have Miguel constantly disturbing the other children. Now, what some parents with similar issues have done is try their children on a medication that helps to relax them, and I've been told about a new…"

"Ah, no, no, no," Jorge cut her off again. "You are not medicating my *three*-year-old child. This here is not happening."

"It would just be for a while," She explained. "Sometimes children go through a phase…."

"Lady, if you think you will be putting my son on medication just because you cannot look after the children while they are here," Jorge snapped as he stood up. "You got another thing coming to you."

"We don't need a daycare," Paige calmly added as she rose to stand beside her husband. “We thought it would be a good opportunity to help his social skills with other children.”

“And that, clearly, is not going well,” Jorge added. “Why can you not allow children just to play, to be themselves? Why must you try to drug them up?”

“We aren’t trying to…”

“Come on, Paige,” Jorge turned toward his wife. “Let’s get Miguel.”

It wasn’t until they were on the way home that Paige broke down, catching Jorge off guard.

“*Mi amor,”* Jorge reached over to touch her arm as he watched the traffic ahead. “This here is ok. Miguel is like every child at that age. She did not say he could not come back. We will find him another daycare eventually.”

“But we had issues finding this one,” Paige reminded him as she sniffed, grabbing a tissue from a nearby box. “But he won’t understand why he’s suddenly away from his friends. He’s a little boy.”

Glancing in the rearview mirror, Jorge watched his young son looking out the window without a care. He fidgeted, causing the car seat to make a noise, which caused him to squirm more and giggle.

“Paige, I do not think this here is upsetting him as much as it upsets you,” Jorge reminded her. “He is no different from Maria. We always had issues with her, even when she was young.”

“But Maria struggles,” Paige gently reminded him. “With making friends, with life, I don’t want this for Miguel.”

“Maria seen a lot in her young life too,” Jorge reminded her. “Miguel, he is a curious little boy. Everything will be fine. Paige, you worry too much. He is fine.”

“Maybe….”

“Miguel,” Jorge looked in his rearview mirror, catching his son’s eyes. “Who’s your girlfriend?”

“Tala!”

“See,” Jorge winked at his wife. “He’s already into older women.”

Paige smiled and shook her head.

“Everything is fine,” Jorge assured her. “And maybe moving, it would be good for him too. Out in the country, away from these morons, he can play in the mud and chase squirrels around the yard. Let him be curious and have fun."

With reluctance, Jorge turned on his phone as he sat in traffic. It quickly came to life, and he sighed loudly.

"It looks like I must meet with the others after I take you and Miguel home," Jorge sighed. "This here, it never ends."

This time, Paige touched his arm as a sign of comfort.

The phone rang, and Jorge glanced at a nearby screen before answering. "*Hola!*"

"Sir, can you come to the production house?" Marco's voice filled the SUV, causing Miguel to laugh in the backseat as he looked around in wonder. "There's a few things that we need to discuss."

"I will be there shortly," Jorge replied. "I will be there soon. Anything I should know?"

"It's in the news that there was a counter-protest against those protesting the medication in schools," Marco explained. "And one of the people at the protest pulled out a knife. Many say this person was a plant because they do not want violence."

"But it's a nice story on the news to make them look bad," Jorge nodded. "I know the game."

"Unfortunately, people believe it," Marco emotionally replied. "It was bad, sir. A fight broke out, and the police called. They showed up in riot gear. It was extreme."

"Riot gear?" Paige repeated. "How bad was this fight?"

"Not very bad," Marco replied. "We have footage at the production house.

"Also, Jolene is here and wishes to speak to you."

"Oh, fuck!" Jorge complained.

Miguel giggled in the backseat.

"Jorge, he's hearing everything," Paige muttered.

"So, I got to deal with Jolene too when I get there," Jorge cringed, "wonderful, just fucking wonderful."

"I think, sir, you will be happy with the information she has for you," Marco suggested. "We will talk about it more when you get here."

"Ok," Jorge spoke with some reluctance. "But why are you at the production house? I assume that has something to do with what you want to discuss with me?"

"I did some research, sir," Marco replied. "I will discuss what I have learned when you arrive."

"See you soon."

He ended the call and exchanged looks with his wife.

"If the protesters look crazy," Paige quietly said, "we know who is at an advantage."

"It is for the news," Jorge reminded her. "To make protesting parents look unstable and unreasonable. That is how they work. Then they will have a nice-looking, calm doctor come on the television and talk about how remarkable the medication is and how every kid needs it for their 'own good', and that is the plan. I tell you that now."

"Maybe I'm naive," Paige said. "But I always thought Canadians would see through this."

"You thought wrong," Jorge commented, automatically recognizing that he was perhaps too harsh. "*Mi amor,* as I have told you in the past. Canada is as corrupt as Mexico. They hide it a little bit better than other countries. But these things always come out. And you have seen it for yourself since Athas got into politics. And it's about to get even worse."

"I thought he could stop it."

"This here," Jorge assured her. "Is bigger than him."

CHAPTER 30

"….and I start next week," Jolene followed Jorge as he headed toward the boardroom at HPC. "They say I will answer phones and help out this man. I make travel arrangements…."

"And you think this here will help you get information?" Jorge asked as he entered the boardroom to find Marco and Makerson. Jolene trailed behind. "They are not going to let you get to anything secure."

"Sir," Marco spoke after glancing at Jolene and then Jorge. "There're some things I can't hack that she will have access to…"

"Before they fire me," Jolene finished his sentence, causing Marco to grin and look down. "Because I lie to get the job."

"What did you lie about?" Jorge asked with disinterest as he sat across from Marco.

"That she's a competent employee," Andrew's voice came from the doorway. "Because we know she ain't that."

"That is not why!" Jolene glared at him as he joined the others at the table while she continued to stand. "It is because I do not know all these computer programs that they ask me to do. I lie about that. Also, making travel arrangements for this man…"

"Make arrangements to send him back to hell where he belongs," Jorge suggested. "Whoever he is."

"I was gonna say send him to a fleabag hotel," Andrew shrugged. "But that sounds better."

"We'll make sure we have what we need in place before she leaves," Marco chose his words carefully as he focused on Jorge, ignoring Jolene, who continued to stand inside the door. "This will be easy for her to do. I have a way to gain access to everything in their company."

"Then do it," Jorge replied. "Preferably the first day since we do not know how long she will last."

"I am standing right here," Jolene reminded them. "Are you saying I cannot last more than a day?"

"I am saying, Jolene, that we must act fast," Jorge corrected her, turning his head around. "Now, can you close the door on your way out?"

Without saying anything, she nodded and followed his instructions.

"Sir, she will not last long," Marco assured him. "I wrote her resume to suit the job and created fake online profiles to back up the information, but this is Jolene. She will not be able to fake her way through this job."

"We do not need her there long," Jorge reminded them. "Even if it is just a week."

"You're hopeful she'll last a day," Andrew smirked. "I give her a morning *if* that."

"I think she can muddle through at least a few days," Makerson suggested. "They'll just think she's nervous and probably be too distracted by what she's wearing to notice that she can't do her job."

"Good point," Andrew nodded. "She better wear something low cut then because that woman is incompetent."

"Let us not worry," Jorge insisted. "As long as she does whatever she needs to do, I do not care how long she lasts."

"I think we should take bets," Andrew suggested with an evil grin.

"This here, we can leave," Jorge shook his head. "We must move on. What else is going on?"

"I'm assuming Marco filled you in?" Makerson asked. "We think they planted someone with the protesters to start shit with the counter-protesters."

"Probably with someone else *also* planted," Andrew suggested. "That's my guess."

"So the police show up?" Jorge shook his head. "With riot gear? Was this not only two people?"

"Well, others jumped in," Makerson nodded. "But it was still a relatively small group. I mean, it seemed extreme."

"But it sure looks good on the mainstream news," Andrew added. "Which is what they want."

"Yeah, the news cameras just happened to be there too," Makerson added. "The only day they covered the protests, I might add."

"Nothing suspicious about that," Jorge quipped. "I see, so this was planned to prove their case and try to stop the protests."

"They're trying to pass some kind of law to stop it," Makerson replied. "At least, that is what I heard. Meanwhile, it creates a dark image of people protesting over their kids taking pills to go to school. It makes them look like lunatics, which I assume was the motivation."

"Yeah, gotta get that propaganda in when you can," Andrew said. "Both sides are freaking out on Twitter…I mean, *X*. But once it's on the news tonight by the *trusted sources*, people will believe the lies."

"Plus, they'll have their doctors," Makerson added. "Their experts on the subject, talking about how safe the pills are, how they're only short-term, how kids are so distracted and have ADD because of technology they grew up on. They'll make a case to explain why it makes sense, and people will go with it. After all, who hasn't been at a restaurant or a grocery store, and someone's kid was out of control? That's what people will be thinking."

"They're out of control because they are lazy fucking parents," Jorge insisted. "People don't want to do their job, as I always say, and parenting is a job."

"At the coffee shop the other day, I heard a young woman say that she was so relieved that she had the internet and streaming services because it kept her child preoccupied all day," Marco added. "I thought, this woman, she is not a good mother."

"Why do people have kids if they don't want to look after them?" Andrew complained. "Just don't fucking do it."

"People are lazy in every other area of their lives," Jorge reminded him. "Why would parenting be different?"

Andrew nodded.

"Now," Jorge continued. "What are we going to do on our news tonight?"

"The opposite," Makerson replied. "Talk to doctors that say these pills aren't safe, talk about other options, talk to protesters on the scene for their view of the situation, show the other side of things. Fortunately, our people were also there today."

"Ok," Jorge nodded. "This here is good."

"We've already posted some teasers on social media," Andrew added. "Just so people will tune into us, not them."

"So, Marco, was there not something else you wanted to discuss with me?" Jorge turned his attention toward the Filipino. "Did you not say you found something?"

"Oh, sir, I did," Marco nodded vigorously. "The Toronto school board plans to have an emergency meeting tonight to discuss the matter, but the plan is already set behind the scenes to make the medication mandatory by pressuring the provincial government despite what Athas has put into place federally. I did find the proof."

"Can we release this here?" Jorge directed his question at Makerson.

"I think we can, but we have to be careful so it doesn't look hacked," Makerson replied. "We can say something like, 'a source has told us' and let the chips fall where they may."

"That will cause them to be paranoid of one another."

"But really," Jorge shook his head. "Where is this coming from? Yes, the school board and the opposition try to push it, but where does it come from? The drug companies? Is this about Big Pharma making money, or is this about something else? Like control?"

"My feeling it's about control," Makerson commented. "I mean, the drug companies will make money off this, but it's not easy to prove a kid needs the meds."

"I'd think it will take some time to get approved," Marco added. "And put rules in place. At least, that's my hope."

"These here rules," Jorge shook his head. "They will *not* get in place, I assure you of this. I will find out where it comes from, and I will take care of it."

"I gotta agree," Andrew jumped in. "This ain't about money. It's about power. They want to control kids. I was in school a few years ago, and that's how it was then. You had to go along with whatever they wanted and no questions asked."

"But who?" Makerson wondered. "Who is trying to control us?"

"Have you talked to Athas lately?" Andrew asked.

"No," Jorge shook his head. "But I will be after this meeting. He is against it, but whoever it is, they were working against him with his cabinet and the opposition. We must find out where this comes from."

"I wonder if this is happening in other countries," Makerson wondered. "I have some contacts in the US and some countries in Europe. I should reach out. Maybe it's not just Canada."

"And if it is," Andrew continued. "Why us? What the fuck is going on?"

Jorge said nothing.

"Maybe hacking into Big Pharma through Jolene will give us answers," Marco suggested. "They are working with someone."

"Or *for* someone," Andrew said.

On his way home, Jorge considered everything presented to him. Nothing he had learned was surprising, but was he missing an obvious clue? Was this something new, or had it been brewing for some time? Had Maria not had issues with schools for years? Perhaps it wasn't just her behavior that was the problem. Was she provoked? What if all the kids were? By the time he got home, Jorge was exhausted. It had been a long day.

"I just saw…" Paige started after he walked in the door, but Maria barged into the room before she could finish. She flew across the room to meet Jorge.

"I am *not* taking pills to go to that school!"

Paige and Jorge shared a look.

CHAPTER 31

"You are serious?" Jorge asked as he leaned back in his office chair and stared at the secure line on his desk. "You can do this?"

"You're the one who taught me that I'm the fucking prime minister, and I can do whatever I want," Athas shot back. "And I will."

"Hey, you got no complaint from me," Jorge smirked and nodded. "I am asking if you do not have to go through the Senate before passing a bill like this?"

"Technically, there are many things that politicians are supposed to do," Athas replied. "But it doesn't mean they do. It's all for show, so the public gets a sense of comfort."

"Again, you got no complaints from me," Jorge was slightly impressed but didn't show it. "I am thinking that you might get stonewalled."

"Since the various school boards and provinces seem to have their own agenda," Athas informed him. "I will say it's an emergency measure, and therefore, we can't take the time to go through the usual procedure. This is a serious matter. These pills are new, and I don't give a fuck about how safe and effective they are supposed to be. I know that kids are sensitive to medications. They can't pass this out like it's candy. Some schools won't allow the sale of soft drinks, but they have no issue forcing new pills. Give me a fucking break."

"So, Athas, we were trying to figure out today," Jorge leaned ahead to speak directly into the phone. "Who is behind this? Who's pushing this?"

"I assume, Big Pharma," Athas replied. "I mean, wasn't it them who tried to infiltrate my cabinet?"

"And the opposition's cabinet," Jorge reminded him. "I know, but to me, this is too easy. I feel like this is something more. I feel this here isn't just about making money off pills."

"They stand to make a lot," Athas reminded him.

"Yes, this is true," Jorge nodded. "But do you think this is about selling pills, or is this about control?"

There was a pause before Athas answered.

"That has crossed my mind," he finally replied. "I can't say that it's entirely about money. With some good marketing, they probably wouldn't have to make it mandatory. We know parents would voluntarily do this, so maybe it is more about control."

"But who?" Jorge asked. "Who would benefit from this?"

There was another pause and a loud sigh at the other end of the line.

"Do you think they are working with someone on this?"

"That is what I wonder," Jorge said. "I have my people looking into it, but do you have some thoughts? Is this about having compliant children or a compliant future? Is this a long game, or is there something else going on? I am curious."

"If I had kids in school," Athas admitted. "I may have more insight."

"Well, I have children in school," Jorge reminded him. "And I am constantly getting called over, what they call, *behavior* issues. Like my Maria misgendered a teacher recently, and this is word violence or some shit like that."

To this, Athas laughed.

"I know, I thought it was ridiculous myself," Jorge admitted.

"It is," Athas replied. "But that's not why I'm laughing. I find it ironic that of all families, yours gets accused of *word* violence. Your mean words should be the least of their concern."

Jorge grinned at his comment.

"I'm supposed to play along with this woke shit," Athas continued. "We have to get back to *actual* reality, not that strange, play land world where unicorns are the official mascot. People must stop being sensitive over words and worry about the real problems out there!"

"I am enjoying this new and improved Athas," Jorge commented. "And I do agree with everything you said. Unfortunately, in this *brave new world,* the unicorn is probably a person who *thinks* they are a unicorn."

"Don't even get me started," Athas retorted, causing Jorge to laugh. "We get letters where people want to be officially recognized, *legally,* as cats, dogs, you name it. One person identified as a cactus."

To this, Jorge laughed again.

"Anyway, the point is, we have to return to *some* sense of reality," Athas continued. "But I can't say that in my press conference later today. I have to remind them that medicating kids is *bad.* In the meantime, if you can find out if there is more than Big Pharma behind this, I would like to know what kind of monster I'm dealing with."

"If I find out," Jorge clarified. "You won't have to deal with that monster because I will."

They both knew what that meant.

"That sounds good to me," Athas replied after a brief silence. "Maybe this is a bigger problem than we originally thought."

"There is something more to it," Jorge admitted. "I think it goes much deeper than it appears at first glance."

"We'll be in touch," Athas said. "I have to deal with this bullshit."

"Good luck," Jorge replied before ending the call. "Keep an eye for stray bullets."

Turning his iPhone back on, he saw a message that Constable Hail was waiting to see him. Rising from his chair, Jorge headed for the door while turning his phone off again. Sticking his head out, he could hear Mark Hail talking with Paige in the living room.

"I am free now," Jorge called out, hearing their chat end. Seconds later, Mark was making his way toward the office.

"Paige said you were on a call…"

"Yes, with Athas," Jorge replied as the constable set his phone outside the office on a table. "We were discussing his news conference later today."

"I heard it's about the mandatory pills," Mark said as he walked into the room, turning around to see Jorge closing the door behind them.

"They warned us to prepare in case there is any kind of retaliation over the announcement."

"Let us hope not," Jorge replied as he walked to the desk. "We were trying to figure out where this bullshit was coming from."

"Pushing pills on kids?"

"Yes," Jorge sat behind his desk while Mark took his usual seat. "Is it just Big Pharma here, or is there something more?"

Mark didn't reply but watched him with interest.

"Sure, they'll make money," Jorge continued. "But is there something more?"

"Teacher's union wants more compliant kids," Mark suggested. "But this does seem much bigger than them. I mean, I suspect Ontario is the testing ground for this shit, and if it works, we'll see it in other places after."

"Have you heard anything?"

"If we hear anything," Mark said. "It's usually from the top of our food chain, but where those people get their instructions is a whole other story."

Jorge nodded but said nothing.

"I have noticed," Mark continued. "We're getting a lot of calls to go to schools now, something we didn't see when I first started."

"Is that so?"

"Well, it's usually something stupid," Mark said. "Where we have to escort an unruly student off the property."

"Unruly?"

"Their definition, not mine," Mark replied. "That's the problem because, by the time I show up, the school probably has pushed their buttons so much that they *are* unruly or aggressive. I get the feeling that it may not have started that way."

"Oh, are we back to this here word violence again?"

"Yeah, something like that," Mark replied. "I heard the schools will no longer have special, *paid* guests to talk climate change."

"Is this so?"

"Jacob Leon's family is looking for him," Mark continued. "He's missing."

"You don't say."

"Will he be found?"

"What do you think?" Jorge grinned.

"That's *exactly* what I thought."

"He will not be an issue again," Jorge insisted. "Although that is probably not of much help to your niece."

"I guess this is more for me than my niece," Mark admitted. "Because I would find him myself if no one else did."

"You should keep your hands clean," Jorge reminded him. "People like him are not worth anything. They are human garbage. So you put them exactly where most garbage goes."

"That seems like a good place."

"So, is there anything else I can help you with?"

"No, but I owe you," Hail said as he stood up. "For this and Maria's help with my niece. You tell me if you need anything."

"I will keep this in mind."

After Mark Hail left, Jorge turned his phone back on and watched the live news conference with Prime Minister Athas.

It was time to take out the big guns.

CHAPTER 32

"I don't care what the government says," The middle-aged woman spoke to the reporter outside an elementary school. *"It's up to all of us to ensure that our children are safe at school. Parents who know their children have issues should be medicating them. It's for the safety of all our children. It's the selfless thing to do."*

Jorge rolled his eyes and sat back in his chair. Glancing at his wife, who sat across the desk, his heart sank when he saw her expression.

"What if the parents feel that medication isn't the answer?" The mainstream reporter pushed. *"What about the parents who don't feel their children need to be on medication?"*

"Well, they have a right to say no," The woman stood up straighter, her eyes grew colder. *"But maybe their kids don't have a right to be in school either, endangering other students."*

"Is this woman here, for fucking real?" Jorge snapped as he leaned ahead and closed the laptop, sensing his wife's concern. "*She* is the one who needs medication."

"Jorge, I'm worried," Paige admitted as her face grew pink. "We can't put our kids on medication."

"We don't gotta."

"Well, no," Paige shrunk in her chair. "But it sounds like they will be ostracized if they don't."

"Paige, it's none of anyone's business what, if any, pills they are taking," Jorge reminded her, attempting to calm her. "That is the reality here."

"I don't get that feeling," Paige shook her head. "Every interview I see lately indicates that kids who won't take this medication won't be allowed to participate in extracurricular activities or go on day trips for school. They're suggesting that due to behavioral issues, those who don't demonstrate either that they behave or are on medication won't be allowed to go."

"I would like to see them try to tell me this," Jorge growled.

"They will," Paige reminded him. "They've already told us both our kids fall in that category. They're sending a message. Do what we want, or you can't be a part of society."

"Paige I don't think it is..."

"Trust me," She cut him off, shaking her head. "It starts here. And it's not going to stop. Parents are compliant. They'll fall in line and expect their kids to do the same."

"Pathetic," Jorge shook his head. "Why do people have no backbone?"

"It was a slow progression," Paige gently reminded him. "It's been building up for years. They trained us. Staring at a device all day hasn't helped."

Jorge didn't respond. He felt a heaviness in his chest.

"Paige, is this here about some psychopath at Big Pharma, or it is about a crooked politician," he hesitated momentarily before continuing. "You know, you kill someone, and that is that. But this time, who do we kill? What do we do? Our children are held hostage in this insanity, and parents like this one we just watched cannot see. It is concerning. Does she think putting her kids on pills will solve these problems?"

"She's scared," Paige attempted to understand. "The media has been all over this lately, saying there's an increase in violent incidents with kids. They don't mention the person stabbed on the subway unless a kid was somehow at fault."

"HPC news will go against this here, Paige," Jorge reminded her.

"But is it enough?" Paige countered. "Most people turn on the television and believe whatever they see because they think it is a trusted source. Even though we keep proving it isn't."

"You know," Jorge thought for a moment. "I wonder what Holly Anne Ryerson knows about all this. She is the media liaison for Big Pharma."

"After the controversy, I didn't see or hear anything more about her," Paige said then, thought for a moment. "I wonder if they fired her."

"This is a good question," Jorge considered. "I should try to talk to her. It might be easy to get her on our side if they did fire her. Maybe she has a bone to pick with them. Maybe she has some secrets to tell."

"It might be an option," Paige paused for a moment. "But I'm starting to think this problem is even more than we originally thought."

Jorge didn't reply, but the two shared a look.

Feeling defeated, he headed to the bar later that day to meet with Marco. Unlocking the door, he found Chase standing behind the bar, staring at his phone. He looked up and sat the phone down.

"My ex-wife is messaging me," he said with no expression. "Telling me she thinks my kids should be on meds because they're too energetic and aggressive lately. Somehow that's my fault."

"Is that so?" Jorge asked as he walked across the room and sat at the bar. "Tell me, how does this happen when you barely see them?"

"It's what she calls their 'Indian side' coming out as if we're all aggressive and crazy," Chase complained. "Even though she was batshit crazy when I met her."

The latter comment caused Jorge to laugh.

"Women, they are often crazy," Jorge insisted. "But they say it is men that make them this way."

"Well, she can think whatever the fuck she wants," Chase shook his head. "My kids aren't taking pills."

"I hate to tell you this, Chase," Jorge reminded him. "But you may not have a choice. It does not sound like she was asking your permission."

"I don't got many rights left with my kids," Chase spoke quietly. "I signed them away against my better judgment. But it wouldn't matter anyway. She never listened to me. She ain't about to start now."

"Your kids," Jorge guessed. "Are just energetic little boys."

"They call that a behavior issue now," Chase reminded him.

"Oh, I know about this here," Jorge nodded. "I have two behavior issues at home."

The door opened, and Marco walked in, awkwardly pushing a bicycle beside him. Leaning it against a nearby wall, and headed toward the bar.

"I am sorry to be late," he spoke to Jorge. "We had an issue at the *House of Pot*. They were trying to hack our system. I managed to get things under control, but it was a very stressful morning."

"Do you know who it was?" Jorge asked as he pointed toward a bottle of tequila on the shelf. Chase nodded and reached for it, pouring them each a shot.

"No, sir, I was hoping you would have some thoughts on this,' Marco said as he reached for his share of tequila. Without hesitation, he knocked it back and made a face.

"I got a lot of enemies," Jorge reminded him as he reached for his own. "Pick one."

"Sometimes it's the one you don't suspect," Chase reminded him as he picked up his shot of tequila. "And there are a lot of uncertainties these days."

"If I have an enemy and know who it is," Jorge said as he glanced down at the tequila before picking it up and knocking it back. The liquid burned down his throat. "I do not worry. It is when I don't know who's coming around the corner that I am concerned."

"It is hard to find, sir," Marco replied. "I was trying to do some research today, but then this happened, and it took hours to get under control. I worry now that they will be successful next time. It was close today."

"This here, it stresses me," Jorge confessed. "I am tired, Marco. I am tired because this never ends. Maybe this time, we cannot do anything. How can we fight an enemy when we do not know who that enemy is?"

Marco and Chase said nothing but shared a knowing look.

"Maybe Jolene will help," Marco suggested. "I gave her a task today."

Do you think they caught her doing this task, and that's why someone tried to hack us?" Jorge asked.

"No, sir, I feel this is more than Big Pharma," Marco confessed. "I cannot explain. I guess it is because we've gone against them before but never had this issue. I feel like this could be government, a country, someone powerful."

"Whoever's behind this shit," Chase guessed. "This is such a head fuck."

"We will figure it out," Marco assured them both. "Everything leads somewhere."

"And everything leads to money," Chase added.

"That reminds me," Jorge turned to Marco. "Have you seen anything on Holly Anne Ryerson lately? Since that scandal, she seems to be off the radar."

"Normally, sir, I'd think that's a good thing," Marco commented. "But you're right. She has disappeared from the media landscape."

"Probably waiting for the exposed photo thing to blow over," Chase suggested.

"But it has," Marco reminded them. "Now the media is attacking Athas because he does not want to put our children on pills. Have you seen the news today? They are tearing him apart."

"I saw that before I left home," Jorge replied. "They're making him look like he is the bad one because he won't force pills down our kid's throats."

"What is wrong with this country, sir?" Marco complained. "Why do people now think it's normal for their kids to take medication to behave? I do not understand. It's troubling. My wife, last night, even talked about moving back to the Philippines because she has a lot of fears about where this is going. She worries a lot. Our kids are good, but who knows what they will see as being behavior issues."

"Do not worry," Jorge assured him. "It will not get to that point. We must find out where this is coming from and take them down. There is no other way around it."

"What if we can't?" Marco asked skeptically. "What if this is bigger than all of us?"

"It's not going to be bigger than me," Jorge spoke confidently. "That, I can assure you."

CHAPTER 33

"Paige, like the song says, I'm not for everyone," Jorge commented with a sober expression, which caused her to laugh.

"That's an understatement," She finally replied as she reached for her cup of coffee, watching her husband across the breakfast table. He winked at her, then smiled before his expression grew serious again.

"But *mi amor,* I do worry," he continued while glancing at the nearby stairs as if he were about to share something he didn't want the children to hear. "What if I am losing my touch? Remember when that boy with the blue hair? He slashed my tires, and I let him live? Only to catch him later and kill him. He hurt that one girl, what if he..."

"Jorge, you can't put that on yourself," Paige cut him off, knowing where he was going with this thought. "Some might even say that it's *good* not to murder him based on something so minor."

"But the signs were there," Jorge reminded her as he leaned closer. "At one time, he never would've made it out alive."

"In the end, he didn't," Paige spoke thoughtfully.

"But sooner," Jorge shook his head. "I cannot let things slide so casually. Again, maybe I'm getting soft with old age."

"You're in your 40s, not 100," Paige shook her head. "Besides, if you're old, *I'm* old too. Let's say you gave him some rope, and in the end, he chose to hang himself."

"That is fair," Jorge seemed to accept her answer. "But look at *House of Pot.* They try to hack it the other day. What does this mean? Who feels so comfortable doing so and why?"

"They try to hack every company," Paige spoke calmly. "To some people, it's just a challenge. It's not personal necessarily."

"Let us hope not."

"Marco will figure it out."

"He hasn't been able to yet."

"Give him time."

"He says Jolene did something to the computers at this Big Pharma company," Jorge continued as he reached for his coffee. "But so far, there is nothing. Maybe Marco is losing his touch."

"I somehow doubt it," Paige said. "I think he's just met his match. And there haven't been any other attempts against you since then. He will figure it out. You'll see."

Jorge didn't appear convinced, and the two shared a look.

"You also have to remember," Paige continued. "This may *not* be Big Pharma this time. We can't look in one dark corner when the monster could be on the other side of the room."

"That is the problem," Jorge said as he rose from his chair. "*I* used to be the monster."

"In many circles," Paige replied as he approached her, kissing her on the head. "You still are."

Jorge winked at her, smiled, then headed for the door.

"To be continued," he said before rushing out of the house, leaving Paige alone with her thoughts.

After the kids had gone to school and daycare, she started her usual morning routine. Yoga, meditation, and finally, she had her adult children to check in on. In most cases, they were as vulnerable as Miguel and Maria. She started with a call to Diego.

"What's going on today?" She attempted to sound cheerful despite the anxiety she sensed from the other end of the line. "How are things at the office?"

"Back to normal," Diego replied with an exaggerated sigh. "As normal as this place ever is."

"Hacking issue resolved?"

"You know Marco, he's on top of it," Diego replied. "He got some new security measures he told me about. I dunno Paige, I didn't understand half of what he was talking about, but it sounded good."

"Yes, most of that stuff is way over my head," Paige admitted. "You aren't working too much?"

"I'm fine," Diego replied with some hesitation. "If you're worried that I'm back to the coke…"

"I didn't say that," Paige spoke calmly, thinking about the issues her friend dealt with the previous year. "But you know what happens when you burn the candle at both ends."

"It's ok," Diego promised her, but a drop in his voice concerned her.

"What are you not telling me?" She calmly asked, showing no judgment. "Is something wrong?"

"Nah, just, you know," Diego sounded fidgety, distracted. "Things with Sonny, I don't know…"

"You say that about every guy," Paige reminded him.

"Maybe I'm not great at this relationship thing," Diego admitted.

"There's a bit of an age gap," Paige reminded him and attempted to joke. "as in, a *lot* of an age gap."

Diego laughed.

"Please take care of yourself, ok?" She said as the call began to wind down. "That's all I ask."

"I will, Paige, I promise," Diego spoke solemnly. For the first time in the conversation, she felt reassured.

"We will get together soon."

"*Si,*" Diego agreed. "I gotta go. I have a meeting."

The conversation ended on a high note, but she was still worried. She worried a lot.

Glancing at the news highlights, she wondered how Alec was managing. Where her husband was losing confidence in his abilities, the Canadian prime minister was picking up steam. Constantly being attacked by the media for his insistence that medication wasn't the answer to behavior issues with children, Alec was fighting back and showing no signs of backing down. Paige wasn't sure what was worse, the force that started this evil or the parents that went along with it.

Chances were good that she'd end up homeschooling both her

children. In many ways, that might be better, but it was with a heavy heart that she even had to consider it. Then again, if they got out of the city as Jorge was proposing, maybe it would be different in a rural setting. People thought differently in the country. They had their values and own concepts of justice.

Her phone beeped, and Paige picked it up.

Mi amor, I think Marco might have some information. I am going to see him now.

Keep me posted.

I will.

She sighed a breath of relief, but the concern was still there. Paige spent many years of her life as an assassin and was aware of the darkness beneath the surface. It wasn't the local thugs she worried about but those carefully hidden behind the scenes that concerned her. There were some evil forces in the world. She and Jorge had gone head to head with many already. These were the people who would blow up a plane to kill one person. They were ruthless. She had to think about her family.

Her phone beeped again. She glanced at it and frowned.

It was Maria's school.

Please be informed that your child has had behavioral problems, and you are required to meet with Principal Dundas as soon as possible. Please call if there will be a delay.

They couldn't even call half the time anymore. When Paige was a kid, teachers picked up the phone and called parents regarding any issues with their children. Of course, there were *real* issues, not the current alarmist view. When people didn't have real problems, they tended to make them up.

She decided not to contact Jorge. This time, she would deal with the principal on her own.

Heading to the garage, she jumped in her car and centered herself before heading to the school. She needed to stay calm. The mistake people made was allowing their emotions to take over.

Before long, she was sitting in traffic and resenting it. She used to love Toronto. The city had been vibrant and alive. Now, it was defeated and dreary. The memories she had of her youth faded away. Many of the landmark businesses were gone as if they never existed at all. There was a sense that the city no longer had a soul. Looking out her window, she viewed unhappy people walking on the sidewalks. No one was talking. Most stared at a phone as if the world around them didn't exist outside their bubble.

That was the problem. Everyone was in a bubble these days.

Arriving at the school, Paige resented the confrontation with Mrs. Dundas. It was time to put an end to this bullshit.

Jumping out of her car, she approached the school. It wasn't even necessary to check in with the security guard outside. He recognized her and moved aside.

"Good morning, Mrs. Hernandez," he gave her an apologetic smile, probably because he knew the nonsense taking place.

"Good morning," She replied. "Lovely day, isn't it?"

"Spring is in the air today."

"Let us hope."

Once inside, Paige made her way to the principal's office. She noted the silent hallways, barely a murmur from students behind the doors, but it didn't feel like a building filled with young, energetic people. She wondered how many of them were already on medication.

Taking a deep breath, Paige entered the room she saw as enemy territory. It was ironic considering the amount of money expected to do the simple job of teaching children. Of course, it was no longer so simple.

"Hello," Paige grabbed the secretary's attention. She looked up from her phone. "I'm here to see Mrs. Dundas."

"Do you have an appointment?"

"I *have* a text message to come here as soon as possible," Paige clarified. "And I'm here."

"And you are?"

"Paige Hernandez," she replied. "I'm here regarding Maria…"

"Oh, yes, I just sent the message out," She spoke excitedly. "You got here fast!"

"May I see her?" Paige pushed.

"Yes, of course," the young woman obediently tapped on her phone. She finally looked up. "Mrs. Dundas will see you now. Go right in."

Paige nodded and followed instructions. Inside the room, the older woman sat behind the desk and looked relaxed, unlike when Jorge was a part of the meetings.

"Hello, Mrs. Hernandez," She pointed at the chair across from her. "Please come in and sit down."

Closing the door behind her, Paige said nothing but crossed the room, sitting on the chair. She noted the almost gleeful expression on Mrs. Dundas's face and waited for her to speak.

"Thank you for coming today," She finally said in a relaxed tone. "I also appreciate you doing so alone. We can have a more productive discussion without your husband here."

"Is that so?" Paige asked as she sat her purse down and moved ahead on her chair. "Because when we're finished here, you might *wish* it was Mr. Hernandez that you're dealing with."

The principal's expression fell.

CHAPTER 34

"She said she'd never come near me again if I didn't shave," Chase commented as he ran his hand over his long goatee. "So I grew a beard."

To this, Jorge threw his head back in laughter while Marco giggled at the end of the bar.

"*Amigo,* you gotta do what you gotta do," Jorge finally composed himself. "We are talking about Jolene."

"I couldn't get her out of my life any other way," Chase shook his head, his tone lowering. "I mean, she's relentless."

"I think the accurate term is needy," Marco volunteered from the end of the bar.

"I think the accurate term is *crazy,*" Jorge corrected him, causing Marco to giggle again while Chase nodded vigorously. "You are being much too generous to this woman."

"This is true."

"Now, Marco," Jorge said as he looked across the bar at Chase, who leaned against the adjacent cabinet, then back at his IT specialist. "Do you have some news for me? Maybe some good news this time? Did Jolene find us some information at Big Pharma, or is she too busy chasing down her next boyfriend?"

A glance at Chase indicated that he agreed, a simple smile on his face.

"Sir, I have still not found anything from that location," Marco said. "Although, in fairness, she did follow my instructions."

"Maybe it's not them," Chase suggested as he crossed his arms over his chest. "I mean, I'm sure they're on for the ride, but I don't think they're driving the vehicle."

"The problem is," Jorge added. "Who is? Have we learned that, Marco?"

"Not quite, sir," Marco spoke with regret. "The information I have found *is* limited, but something stood out to me. Do you remember last year, before the election, when we dealt with that woman Susanne Nestor?"

Jorge nodded. He remembered almost being killed by one of this woman's henchmen. If Paige hadn't shown up on time, he would no longer be on this earth. Only his wife knew how close he had come to meeting his maker, but the experience had left him shaken, far less confident than he had been before that night.

"I know that she is," Marco hesitated as if to pick his words carefully. "No longer in the picture, but I wonder if that movement died with her."

Jorge said nothing. At the time, they were pretty sure if they killed off the head viper, that the others would die. Until now, there have been no signs of life in the group.

"Weren't they the people that kind of controlled everything?" Chase asked. "The ones that rule the show from behind the scenes?"

"Everything from politics to propaganda," Jorge nodded. "They get together and talk about how we got too many people in the world, how people are not compliant enough, how we are useless. They think the rich elites are the only relevant people and, the rest are merely slaves and bottom feeders."

"Nice," Chase spoke sarcastically, running his hand through the beard. "So, in other words, we're taking up space and air?"

"And resources," Marco threw in. "In their minds, we use up all the freshwater, cause all the pollution…"

"Yeah, cause their private jets and 15 vehicles aren't doing that?" Chase countered, causing Marco to grin.

"I did not say they are not hypocrites," Marco reminded him, causing Chase to nod.

"So, these people," Jorge picked things up. "You are saying there is more, that they didn't die off once we murdered their queen?"

"At first, sir," Marco agreed. "It did seem this way. I carefully watched them, and that is what I saw. No one was picking things up. I thought they were scared and saw that as a warning to let it go. But now, I feel that it's them behind all this with schools. It does follow their thinking and how they want to create a new society."

"But are you sure?" Chase asked. "You don't just think it? You got some proof?"

"Not so much proof," Marco replied. "As a hunch after I found this video."

Marco turned his laptop around for both men to see. An older woman with faded red hair was standing at a podium. Although it was difficult to tell her age, the wrinkles on her neck gave away more than her smoothed-out face. After he hit a button, the video came alive, and her voice echoed through the empty bar.

"We owe it to the future generations to make this world a better place to live," She spoke coldly despite the topic of children. "Our world is no longer a place I recognize from my childhood...."

"Things have changed since the 30s, sir," Marco muttered, causing the other two men to laugh.

"....children are overly stimulated by computer games, are alarmed by everything they see in the news, and are often unsure how to socialize properly. That is why we at the World for Children Society must help make these kids feel safe again. We want them to feel confident about their future and to ease through childhood in a way that promotes positive mental health. We feel that once children have reached this point, they've grown more mature, their brains fully developed, and better able to cope with the problems in the world without having to spend years in agony."

"Currently, children have the highest rate of suicide that we've ever seen," She made a dramatic pause as if to make sure that her words fully sunk in. "This is a travesty. It's heartbreaking. And we have to find a way to stop it."

"That lady don't look heartbroken to me," Jorge abruptly commented as he pointed toward the laptop. "She looks cold as fucking ice from here."

"That's because she is, sir," Marco stopped the video and turned his laptop back toward him. "Her name is Heidi Pierce."

"Heidi?" Jorge repeated her name while scrunching up his nose.

"Do you know her, sir?"

"No, but isn't that a name for a doll or something?" Jorge continued to make a face. "You know, for kids?"

"I think it's a book," Chase replied. "I was thinking more of a stripper name."

"Either could work," Jorge nodded. "That woman there does not look like a Heidi. I thought since she was German, you would say something like Ingrid or some old lady name."

"I know, sir," Marco laughed. "I do see your point."

"It doesn't make any of this less disturbing," Chase said. "I mean, she's trying to work on people's fears and sympathy, but that woman is one crazy bitch. I can see it from here."

"You got that right," Jorge nodded. "She does not care about children, I will tell you that. She is creating a narrative."

"One that television and the internet have picked up on," Marco threw in. "The things she says in these speeches are the same words we hear from world leaders, not to mention in the media. It's not a coincidence that this is the case, sir. They're fed this information."

"Is she connected to Big Pharma?" Chase asked. "I mean, there's gotta be something in this for her. She ain't doing this out of the goodness of her heart."

"Especially when she looks like someone who eats children," Jorge commented, causing Marco to laugh. "Now *that* is a children's book, am I right?"

"Yup," Chase nodded. "You got that one right."

"This book sounds more scary than anything this woman is talking about," Jorge commented. "And yet, that book did not cause kids to have these mental disorders like she has suggested."

"I think part of the problem is that parents plunk their kid in front of a computer all day so they don't gotta look after them," Chase complained. "My ex does that to shut the boys up. Like, her new man, why can't he take them outside? Teach them to do something productive. Get them into sports?"

"Because people are lazy," Jorge repeated the same lecture he gave all the time. "Too lazy to go to work, too lazy to read a book, too lazy to raise their kids. We are a world of gluttons with no motivation. Sit in front of the computer and watch crap all day or play games. That is all the people want to do."

"And sir," Marco shook his head. "Her numbers are exaggerated. This was clearly to scare people. Parents will do anything to be sure their children are safe and happy, so they will listen to whatever she says."

"But is she saying that the kids should take pills?" Jorge wondered.

"Not here," Marco shook his head. "But I suspect that is soon. This foundation has become the so-called expert on children of the world. They're supposed to be doing all this work in third-world countries but try to find any information about their funding vs. what they're spending it on. It's sketchy at best. It is relatively new, so I don't know how they can proclaim themselves experts or leaders of anything."

"People do not do their research," Jorge reminded him. "And if they own the media, the equally lazy reporters will report whatever they are told, especially for the right price."

"So, do they make money plus gain control?" Chase asked. "I don't understand."

"That's what I'm trying to find out," Marco admitted. "I found this lady and her organization, but I plan to hack their systems, her phone, whatever I can do to learn the truth."

"You're a good man," Jorge nodded as he turned his phone back on. "You must keep me posted."

"Will do, sir."

Jorge saw his phone light up and immediately noticed a message from Paige. Shaking his head, he let out a sigh.

"Paige, she tells me that Maria's school has called again," he complained. "I cannot wait to see what kind of *behavior* problem she has this time."

Both Chase and Marco looked concerned.

CHAPTER 35

"So, is there a mess for me to clean up at the school?" Jorge teased his wife shortly after arriving home. "Some blood? A body? What are we dealing with here?"

"There is no blood, no body," She laughed and sipped her coffee. "All I left her with was some words to contemplate."

Jorge raised an eyebrow, waiting for more information, but the couple was interrupted when Maria came stalking into the room.

"Did Paige tell you?" She asked as her face filled with rage. "I hate that fucking school!"

"Maria, calm down," Jorge raised his hand as he turned toward his daughter. "And do not use that language when your brother could be nearby."

"He's upstairs taking a nap," Maria shot back. "And it doesn't matter anyway. He's a baby. He doesn't understand what we are talking about."

"He's learning new words," Paige reminded her. "We don't want that word to be one of them."

"But he swears all the time," She pointed toward Jorge. "Like *all*...

"Ok, Maria, that is enough," Jorge cut her off. "What is it you did this time?"

"Why do you assume I did something wrong?" Maria countered, crossing her arms over her chest. "Maybe I did the right thing this time."

"She did, actually," Paige agreed. "But they didn't see it that way."

"What is it you did?" Jorge was curious. "Dare I even ask."

"I helped a teacher that a student was attacking."

"Helped?" Jorge raised an eyebrow.

"Yes, *Papá,* I took a gun out in class and told him to fuck off!" Maria spoke dramatically, her voice heavy in sarcasm.

"Ok, Maria, enough of this," Jorge spoke sharply this time. "There is no need for this here attitude. I just asked you a question."

She seemed to relent and step back before taking a deep breath and answering.

"One of the guys was being a prick to her," Maria attempted to explain. "And when she nicely asked him to calm down, he called her a cunt and got in her face. She looked terrified and defenseless because, you know, teachers aren't allowed to do anything, so I did."

"As in?" Jorge tilted his head with interest.

"First, I told him to leave her alone," Maria stood up a bit taller. "And when he ignored me and grabbed her arm, to the point that she started to cry, I moved in and told him to back off, and he put his hand out to shove me, so I twisted his arm and dropped him to the floor."

"Wow!" Jorge clapped his hands together in approval.

"But I'm apparently the bad one for defending a teacher from this guy, who's like a big, nasty football player, but he walks away with a prescription and probably some cookies to comfort *him.*"

"Wait, what am I hearing?" Jorge turned toward his wife. "Am I understanding this correctly? My daughter defends a teacher and herself from an aggressive student, and *she* is in trouble. What was everyone supposed to do? Nothing? Let him attack the teacher?"

"So," Paige calmly nodded. "Teachers aren't allowed to defend themselves, even if they feel threatened, which she did."

"And he's allowed to attack a teacher and walk away?" Jorge asked. "Is my English bad, or am I not understanding?"

"Your English is fine. You completely understand," Paige nodded.

"Isn't that messed up?" Maria chimed in. "I mean, really? *I'm* the bad one? What is wrong with these people?"

"The student who attacked the teacher has a little drug problem," Paige continued. "Which isn't his fault, apparently, but we all have to stand back and allow him to express his emotions, then put him on medication because, again, it's not his fault."

"Are you fucking kidding me right now?" Jorge shot back.

"*He* swore!" Maria pointed out to Paige.

"It's fine," Paige ignored her step-daughter and turned her attention to Jorge. "They wanted to suspend Maria, but Mrs. Dundas and I came to an understanding."

Neither Maria nor Jorge responded to this comment but watched Paige with interest. However, she turned and walked into the kitchen.

"Come on," Jorge pushed. "You mean to tell me that you're not going to tell us what happened to change her mind."

"She's a reasonable woman," Paige replied over her shoulder as they followed her into the room. "I think sometimes words are more powerful than actions."

"These here must have been some kind of words," Jorge quipped, causing Maria to giggle.

"The words were probably 'I'm gonna kill you'," Maria offered and giggled some more while Jorge joined in.

"Don't worry about it," Paige assured him. "It's taken care of, and that's all you have to know."

Jorge assumed she'd tell him more later, so let it go. Maria appeared intrigued.

"Maria," Jorge turned to his daughter. "I do not care what the school said. I think you did the right thing today, helping that teacher. Maybe the school and the teacher don't appreciate you, but I am very proud."

With that, Jorge swooped in and gave Maria a tight hug. He affectionately kissed her on the top of her head. A ringing phone suddenly diverted his attention.

"I think that's your secure line," Paige said as Jorge slowly let go of his beaming daughter.

"It is," Jorge took a deep breath. "I must see what Athas wants this time."

Rushing to his office, he closed the door and headed across the room. Reaching for the phone, he abruptly answered.

"Yeah, you got something for me?"

"I got a rumor for you today," Athas replied. "There's a rumor going around that it's not Big Pharma but somewhere else…."

"I got that already," Jorge cut him off. "It's much higher."

"That's what I'm hearing," Athas confirmed. "This might be out of our hands, especially if it's from another country."

"I see your pushback on the medication for children isn't going so well," Jorge commented as he glanced toward his bulletproof window. "The media, they are not your friend."

"Were they ever?" Athas asked.

"That's a fair question," Jorge nodded. "I think they know who is and isn't buttering their bread. And they know it won't be you. This here is to make sure you throw money their way."

"And since I've taken it away," Athas agreed. "There's no reason to help me but go after me instead."

"The media is a whore that only gets wet when someone pulls opens his wallet," Jorge reminded him. "And son, you put yours away."

"I've had enough of fucking journalists," Athas bitterly complained. "And now Holly Anne Ryerson has made an appearance again."

"I was wondering where she went," Jorge replied. "Where did she turn up this time?"

"At my door," Athas replied.

"Oh, really?" Jorge grinned. "So, did you fuck her this time, *amigo?*"

"She came to my office door."

"Your point?" Jorge asked. "Do not tell me you're particular about where you get it now?"

"She made an appointment, which I approved," Athas admitted. "Because I wanted to see what she had to say."

"And?"

"They quietly fired her from her fancy position because of the pictures," Athas replied. "Now she has signed something to keep quiet about what she knows regarding Big Pharma."

"Oh," Jorge's eyes widened. "Do tell!"

"That's the problem," Athas said. "She can't. She wanted to see if there was a way to override this stipulation, to get around it on the sly, but it looks pretty legally binding."

"Well, she may not be able to show us the way to Grandma's house," Jorge said. "But she can drop a few crumbs."

"That's what I was thinking."

"Did you want me to meet with her?" Jorge asked.

"I was thinking that might be a good idea."

"Tell her to call me," Jorge said with a sinister smile. "She might come in handy."

"She did hint that things could get pretty bad," Athas said. "And we might not be able to do much about it. I suppose Big Pharma has its propaganda."

"They also have help," Jorge assured him. "Tell me, have you ever heard of the World for Children Society or Heidi Pierce?"

There was a pause.

"No, I don't think so," Athas said. "Is that here in Canada?"

"No, it's German," Jorge replied. "At least, the woman is, so I assume this here is taking place in Europe."

"But it affects here?"

"That is what we are looking into now," Jorge replied. "There may be a connection."

"I will look into it."

CHAPTER 36

"When he is quiet, the media eats him alive," Jorge nodded toward his laptop as he closed it and pushed it to the side of his desk. "And now that he pushes back, the media says that Athas is too aggressive and is using *word violence,* whatever the fuck that is?"

Across from him, Holly Anne Ryerson didn't respond at first, as if choosing her words carefully. Pushing a piece of dark hair behind her ear, she almost appeared uncertain whether or not to speak.

"They're trying to create a narrative to tear him down," she finally replied as Jorge leaned back in his chair, studying her. "To discredit him in any way they can."

"Oh, is that so?" Jorge spoke in a mocking tone. "I hadn't noticed."

"Is that why you asked me to come here today?" Holly Anne asked in a nervous voice. "To discuss how the media purposely tears people down?"

"Well, if anyone would know what that was about," Jorge shrugged. "I would say that would be you."

"I will remind you I gave Alec some positive coverage during the last election."

"I will remind you," Jorge countered as he sat forward in his chair and gave her a cold stare. "That you gave him *more than* positive coverage during the last election. I think he also gave *you* something."

Her face turned red, and she looked away.

"But that's not why you are here," Jorge reminded her. "We must talk about Big Pharma and the little secrets you learned before they fired you."

"I signed a contract that…"

"I'm well aware of your contract," Jorge cut her off. "Yes, you cannot give away the company secrets, but I think you can at least lead me in the right direction."

"But the problem with that," She attempted to explain. "Is if I get caught…"

"You won't be."

"I know information that isn't accessible."

"Ms. Ryerson," Jorge shook his head. "I assure you, there is no such thing as information that isn't accessible."

"These are dangerous people," She spoke in a lower tone this time. "Anyone who doesn't play ball has a way of turning up dead. It never looks like a murder, but there are other ways…"

"People who haven't played ball with me have a way of….well, we won't get into that today," Jorge smirked as he watched her nervously shrink back. "Let's just say that you're fucked either way. Who do you want to cooperate with, lady? Who do you think is most dangerous?"

She didn't reply, but her eyes said it all.

"I am not asking you to spill everything," Jorge reminded her. "I am asking you to let me know if I am getting hot or cold. Does this have anything to do with this World For Children Society bullshit group and the old lady that runs it?"

"You're getting hot," Holly Anne replied. "It sounds like you might not even need my help."

"I assume she's why schools around the world are encouraging children to take pills to get them through the *stressful* period of childhood?"

"So far, I think it's only in Western countries," Holly Anne nodded. "The belief is what starts here will spread elsewhere."

"But why?" Jorge asked. "This is not just about money."

Holly Anne clasped her mouth shut.

"Oh, come on," Jorge encouraged her, and with a smooth grin, he leaned across his desk. "Do not tell me this is where you decide not to talk? Do you not care about the children affected by this matter? I would think this here would be a concern."

Flustered, she looked away. Her eyes showed emotion as she attempted to avoid Jorge's dark stare.

"I can't….if I say anything…"

"As I tell you," Jorge reminded her. "You do not have to tell me a thing. You help point me in the right direction. I have people who can learn the truth."

"They will be in danger."

"Why is that?"

"This is bigger than Big Pharma. It's bigger than this World For Children Society," Holly Anne finally looked up. "If they even thought I was talking to you about this…"

"They'd what?" Jorge asked. "Kill you?"

"I didn't only leave my job with a large cheque promising to keep quiet," Holly Anne replied as tears formed in her eyes. "I left with a gun to my head. Reminding me what happens to people who know too much and talk. I thought….I thought they were going to kill me that day. They said….they'd make it look like a suicide and considering everything that happened, especially after the humiliating pictures were released…."

"So, this was never about the pictures," Jorge asked. "You knew too much?"

"I stumbled on something…."

"And they found out?"

"Yes," Holly Anne nodded as tears rolled down her face. This did not affect Jorge. "They watched me all the time, monitored me through my phone. I had no idea."

"So, the pictures were?"

"A cover-up," She reached for a tissue and quickly wiped away tears. "They put them out there to humiliate me. It was to take away my power. I knew too much."

"What did you know?" Jorge pushed. "I need to know. I can protect you."

"You can't protect me," She shook her head. "This is bigger than you."

Jorge stiffened at the comment.

"Lady, no one is bigger than me."

"I can't, they said if I ever told," She shook her head. "They'd find out and kill me."

"Then why are you here today?"

"I was hoping you'd offer me a job," she admitted. Shrinking in her chair, she continued, "In case they were still monitoring me, that's what I told friends."

"Ok, so first of all," Jorge thought for a minute. "I have someone who can find out if someone is tracking you. That same person can also find out whatever it is you feel you cannot tell me. You have to put me in the right direction. Is there a person? A company? Is it this Heidi lady that we need to dig more into?"

"She can hide things well," Holly Anne told him. "She has a lot of people protecting her."

Jorge nodded but didn't say anything.

"This is much bigger than her."

"So, someone bigger than her wants kids to be drugged?" Jorge pushed. "So this is about compliance?"

"Short term," she nodded. "Yes, they want kids to be compliant, but that's something that happens regardless. It happened when we were in school. Sit down, open your book, close your book, and go to the principal's office if you don't behave. We were made compliant for years. Now, it's more. It's disturbing."

"So, what else do these pills do?" Jorge pushed. Her lips automatically tightened, and she started to cry again. Taking a deep breath, he relented. There was an unmistakable and intense fear that he had seen in the eyes of those about to die at his hands. She had it. His compassionate side would get him further than his usual, dominant personality. "This here, it is very bad? What do the pills do? It is worse than making kids behave?"

She nodded as more tears rolled down her face.

"I…I can't sleep," Holly Anne continued to sob. "I have nightmares. I worked in journalism for a long time, and I thought I saw the darkest side of the world, but that was nothing like what they wanted to do to the children. What they've threatened to do to me if I told anyone? These people are sick. They are monsters. They are psychopaths. They are evil."

Jorge felt his defenses drop as he listened, carefully watching Holly Anne as she fell apart.

"I found studies," she continued as Jorge picked up the box of tissues and passed them to her. Holly Anne grabbed two and wiped her eyes.

"Disturbing studies about what happens both short and long term. They don't care. They don't care that these are children. Fuck, it's not even about money. It's sick."

"They fix studies so they look safe," Holly Anne continued. "But the real studies, they tell a different story."

Jorge took a deep breath and thought for a moment.

"I can't tell you anything else," Holly Anne took a deep breath and cleared her throat. "I can't. They will know. I know they will know."

Jorge nodded, seeing the fear in her eyes. He doubted her but said nothing.

"Ok," he calmly replied. "I think you have given me enough information for now."

"It's dangerous," Holly Anne insisted. "They must never know that I..."

"I called you here to offer you a job," Jorge cut her off. "You're excited, and you will tell your friends and family that we had a great meeting. You are relieved to be working for independent media, and this is a new chapter in your life. Maybe you will do a light, fluffy show that will not be as serious? They will not look at you if they think you're stepping back."

Hope filled her eyes, but she said nothing.

"I will have someone check to see if they're spying on you," Jorge continued. "If they are, we will give them information that makes you safe. Meanwhile, I will take what you have told me, and my people will dig deeper. They won't even know. I will inform Tom Makerson that you are working for him next week. You two can work out the details."

"Oh, ok," Holly Anne shook her head as if she were in a deep fog and finally finding her way out. "I...ok, yes, thank you."

"Now, go home and tell everyone I offered you a job," Jorge reminded her. "And when you leave this office and pick up your phone outside, show no signs of being upset but excited about this new opportunity. Just assume someone is watching you until we tell you otherwise."

CHAPTER 37

"They're coming for our children?" Jorge asked as he looked across the conference room table at Makerson at Marco. "Is that what you are telling me?"

"It's not just here," Makerson reaffirmed as he gestured toward his closed laptop. "It seems the more developed countries are pushing for this same agenda. Keep the kids compliant, but where it used to be more focused on behavioral issues, now it's as if they won't even allow it to get to that stage. Rather than punishing kids for acting out, they don't even want to get to the point where they *are* acting out. They've quietly normalized medicating children in some parts of Europe, almost like it was their testing ground."

"So, what you are saying?" Jorge attempted to grasp what they were telling him. "Is this here isn't new?"

"Not like we thought," Makerson replied with concern in his eyes. "I originally thought maybe we were the testing ground, but now I'm seeing pockets of Europe where children were experimented on. They told parents the medication is safe and effective, but then…."

"But then?" Jorge raised an eyebrow.

"Kids started having issues," Makerson went on. "But they insist it's related to something else. It's never the medication."

"And people believe this?" Jorge asked.

"People believe officials, sir," Marco reminded him. "If you have a nice title and a platform, they make you their God."

"There's a lot of psychology that goes into this," Makerson continued. "It's essentially an elitist form of marketing. 'We know better than you, so you should listen'. They know how to manipulate people, and unfortunately, most don't question authority because they've been told not to. The police know better. Politicians know better. Doctors know better. Scientists know better. The average person who questions anyone at this level is mocked."

"Yes, this is also part of the plan," Marco eagerly jumped in. "'So you think you know better than a doctor? Better than a lawyer? Better than this highly educated person?'"

"Exactly," Makerson nodded. "It belittles you, so you shut up and don't express your doubts. And if everyone feels the same way, no one talks."

Jorge nodded and said nothing.

"It's very…concerning," Marco added. "It depresses me."

"So," Jorge felt his anger build. "What you're telling me is that this may not be for money or to make children compliant, but to make them sick?"

"We are not sure," Marco said. "That is what we are trying to figure out now."

"It's like walking in quicksand," Makerson admitted. "You just keep sinking and sinking. There doesn't seem to be an answer that makes these people less psychopathic, and it's hard to see where this starts and ends. Who's at the top of this? It's such a tangled web, and the information we're getting is scattered, so it's hard to connect it."

"Did you verify if this is true?" Jorge asked.

"Yes," Makerson nodded. "Unfortunately, it is. I hoped it was a conspiracy theory, but it's not looking that way. The people talking about this come with a lot of credentials. I've researched them all. There's no bullshitting here."

The three men silently exchanged looks.

"The good part about Holly Anne coming here," Makerson finally spoke. "Is that she might be able to point us in the right direction? It sounds like she knows more than she's saying."

"This here is true," Jorge agreed. "But we must keep her under the radar. We cannot allow them to think she is looking into this but make it look like she is doing fluff pieces about local events and silly stuff."

"That won't be a problem," Makerson confirmed. "Put her with Sonny."

"But do not allow him to know anything," Jorge insisted.

"We keep him on a need-to-know basis," Makerson said. "We keep everyone here on a need-to-know basis. It's better that way."

"You never know, sir," Marco remarked. "There always could be a spy."

"Speaking of spies," Jorge changed the topic. "Is Jolene coming up with anything?"

"Sir, maybe we need to get her out," Marco suggested. "I do not think she is finding anything new. I am worried the longer she is there, the more likely Jolene will screw up something. So far, the information she helped me obtain was of little use, and in fact, it is information I can get without her help."

"Tell her to quit," Jorge said as he leaned back in his chair.

"Then she's gonna want a job here," Makerson reminded him.

"No," Jorge said. "This here it will not work. I will think about it, but I do not want her here."

"No one does, sir," Marco spoke honestly, causing Makerson to laugh.

"We will find her another job," Jorge thought. "I will send her to the *House of Pot* office to help Diego. I will talk to him tonight."

"Very good, sir," Marco nodded with some relief. "That seems like the place for her."

"There's a better place for her," Jorge grumbled. "But she is Diego's sister. So, you will both continue to look into these pills?"

"Yes," Makerson said and cleared his throat. "I have a retired medical expert going over the studies from Europe to see what he can find. What stands out to him, and what he thinks is concerning. I started to read it all, but I'm no scientist, so I would rather he let me know what it comes down to."

"There is a slight chance there's nothing wrong with these pills," Marco said. "But, sir, it is very slight."

"That's the impression I'm getting," Jorge replied. "Why people trust Big Pharma, I will never know."

A knock at the door interrupted their conversation. Jorge turned to see Sonny standing outside. He gestured for him to come in.

"Yeah?"

"Paige is on the phone for you," he said. "She said she knew you'd have your phone turned off…"

"Where's the phone?" Jorge jumped up, glancing around the room, quickly spotting a landline in the corner. "I see it."

"We will give you privacy, sir," Marco stood up at the same time as Makerson, but Jorge was already on the other side of the room and picking up the receiver.

"Line one," Sonny called out before leaving, along with the others.

"Paige, what is wrong?" Jorge immediately asked.

"Calm down," she automatically replied. "There's no emergency."

"Is it Maria? At school?" Jorge guessed.

"No, nothing like that," Paige assured him. "One of the kids at Daycare bit Miguel and…"

"What?" Jorge cut her off. "Is he ok? Why did he bite him?"

"Because they're kids, Jorge," Paige calmly reminded him. "The little boy said he was a lion and bit Miguel, and he needs a tetanus shot…"

"Oh great!" Jorge complained. "So, what? He identifies as a lion. So now, we must humor him and pretend he's a real animal? Is that why Miguel must get a shot?"

"Actually, no," Paige laughed. "Although, if that were the case, I wouldn't be surprised. They recommend a tetanus shot if you're bit by a human too. Who knew?"

"Are you sure about this here, Paige?"

"I promise you," Paige insisted. "We'll have lots of time waiting at the hospital for me to do some research."

"Ok, well…he is ok?" Jorge asked again. "Are you sure?"

"He is," Paige assured him. "But better safe than sorry."

"Is there something wrong with this kid that he acts this way?"

"Other than being a kid?" Paige asked. "Probably not, but I'm sure they'll try to say that he needs medication to behave. What he probably needs is to be taught how to behave and eat less sugar and processed food. I see what these parents feed their kids."

"Ok, well, if you want me to go there with you?"

"No, it's fine," Paige insisted. "I will see you home later."

"Ok, *mi amor,*" Jorge said before ending the call.

Looking around the empty conference room, he took a deep breath and closed his eyes. He couldn't admit to the others that he felt as if everything was spinning out of control. They looked to him to be powerful, strong, to fight against anything that came along, but could he this time?

There was a vulnerability that came with children. He understood why parents were quick to do whatever the so-called experts said because part of him wanted to do the same. It sprang from a fear deep inside him, one that people played on and used to their advantage. And this fact alone made him furious. It made him want to find whoever was attempting to manipulate this situation and for what reason so he could make them pay.

But that was the problem. Who was at the top of this mountain? What were their motives? He would need much more information before making a move. He would feel powerless until that time.

Thinking ahead, he sent a message to Diego.

Can I meet with you at your place this evening?

Is everything ok?

We aren't sure yet.

CHAPTER 38

"Hell is empty because the devils are all here," Jorge repeated his earlier comment to Diego as the two men enjoyed a drink in the Colombian's lavish living room. "Is that not what they say?"

"Isn't that Shakespeare or something?" Diego twisted his lips, squinted his eyes, and looked into his drink. "I gotta tell you, this sounds like a plot for a movie, not real life."

"Do you not think that all these books, movies, television," Jorge gestured around the room. "That this here is not a warning of some kind? Maybe the artists, they see what the rest of us ignore, and that is why they're artists?"

"No," Diego shrugged. "I don't know anything about being an artist."

"Well, you should," Jorge pointed out. "Don't you gays do a lot of artsy stuff?"

"Some," Diego shrugged. "But don't ask me to write no book or anything."

"Diego," Jorge started to laugh. "You have far too many other things for you to do. Just keep running my company, and I will be happy."

"Hey, you want to send Jolene into the mix," Diego inquired. "And I will be too busy putting out fires to run anything."

"Just stick her in an office somewhere and have her watch cat videos," Jorge suggested. "I don't give a fuck, as long as she's out of my hair."

"If we have her on standby," Diego considered. "She'll be around if we need her at the last minute. You never know what might come up."

"This is true," Jorge glanced around the room, noticing the lime trees in the adjoining sunroom. They were his friend's pride and joy, along with the annoying little dog that slept in a fluffy bed nearby. "So, you got Sonny living here now, or what?"

"Do you see him anywhere?" Diego countered as a wall grew between them, something unusual for a twenty-plus-year friendship. "I don't got anyone living here."

"I thought you had him back?" Jorge wasn't offended by the sharpness of his question. "I just ask..."

"No," Diego looked down as his body shrank in stature. "I don't need that in my life."

"I thought you two had something going on, you know?" Jorge wasn't exactly sure how to word it. Although he had never been uncomfortable with his homosexual friend, having emotional conversations wasn't for him. "I thought things were better since you...."

"Recovered?" Diego attempted to finish the sentence and held up his drink. "Not completely recovered, or I wouldn't have this in the house?"

Jorge looked at his drink and mused.

"Then, maybe you shouldn't?" He finally asked. "I mean, you have a whole bar over there."

"I know," Diego nodded. "But I gotta have something. If it ain't that, it's gonna be what? Food? Sex? Drugs again?"

"Is it not the point to stop being addicted to everything?" Jorge asked. "I mean, this here is what I thought was the whole idea?"

"I guess I'm not great with rules," Diego countered with a shrug, apathetic, if not depressed, in his reaction.

"Well, Diego, if you need more help," Jorge spoke in the most gentle voice he could muster. "You know that..."

"I can't do that again," Diego shook his head. "I was trapped in that house with someone who wanted to talk about my feelings all day. I can't do it."

"You weren't exactly trapped in prison," Jorge reminded him before finishing his drink and setting the glass on a nearby table. "I had you in my brand new safe house, which is as big as my house here in Toronto.

Out in the country, quiet. If anything, I think I envy you. I would love to be *trapped* in a house, away from all this here insanity."

"Talking about your feelings *all* day?" Diego countered. "Really? Come on!"

"Well, maybe, I don't know," Jorge spoke frankly. "To be honest, some days, yes. I would rather that than deal with the constant bullshit I have to deal with."

"Like, what is going on now?"

"*Si,*" Jorge nodded. "You know, at one time, I would have loved this and jumped in with both feet. But not now because there is too much on the line. My family, I worry about them. I feel as if the whole world is going to fuck, and I can't do a thing."

"Yeah," Diego seemed to drop his earlier defenses. "I see what you mean there."

"Maybe I am getting too old," Jorge continued. "I do not have it in me anymore to always slay dragons, you know?"

"We agree on that one."

"So, I have thought about leaving Toronto."

"And what?" Diego appeared stunned by the news. "Go back to Mexico?"

"I have thought of this too," Jorge admitted. "My son, he could see his culture. My daughter could remember where she comes from, and in Mexico, I know where I stand."

"You stand in danger," Diego reminded him, with concern in his eyes. "You can't go back to Mexico. Remember why you left?"

"Well, I left because Maria wanted to go to a Canadian school," Jorge laughed as he remembered. "Because my wife, she was a Canadian lady. I guess that was the main reason. Had it not been for that, maybe I would have stayed."

"I don't think it's a good place for you," Diego insisted. "You're not gonna sleep better there at night."

"No, this is probably true," Jorge considered that he was romanticizing the concept. "But actually, I was thinking of moving to the country, somewhere more rural. Somewhere that I can hide under the radar."

"Wearing suits that cost more than some people's entire wardrobe?"

Diego sniffed as he pointed toward Jorge's designer outfit. "You gotta be kidding me?"

"Maybe I dress differently?" Jorge shrugged. "Go shopping at *Walmart* or something?"

"Oh, Jesus Christ," Diego made a face, causing Jorge to laugh. "There has to be some more reasonable middle ground."

"Hey, I am just saying that it might be better to have a smaller world for my children to grow up in," Jorge reminded him. "So they can grow up normally and not with all these fucking freaks in Toronto."

"You don't think there are freaks in the country?"

"Different kind," Jorge reminded him.

"But they might lose their edge if they're away from the city too long," Diego suggested. "I thought I would."

"Is that why you insisted on getting out of that *prison* early?" Jorge referred to his safe house, watching Diego deflate in front of him. "Tell me, my friend, are you truly ok?"

"Yes, I am," Diego looked him in the eyes to answer. "I just....I don't know. I like to keep to myself more. I guess it's part of the healing process."

"But, Diego, you know a disease," Jorge reminded him. "It wants to isolate you."

Diego appeared emotional but didn't say anything, so Jorge continued.

"If it gets you alone," Jorge continued. "It can kill you. It is no different from the devils around us that will do the same. It is no different from the psychopath that breaks into your house and puts a gun to your head. It is an enemy much worse because if you shoot it, you're dead on the floor. Do you understand, *amigo?*"

He knew his words were harsh. Jorge could see it in Diego's eyes, but they were words that had to be said.

"Now," Jorge continued. "I do not say this to be cruel. I do not say it to be a terrible person. I say it to you because you are my *hermano,* my oldest friend, and I do not want to see you go down the wrong path. I can stop anyone who tries to open that door and shoot you," Jorge pointed at the nearby entrance. "But I cannot stop that person that is inside your head. The only way I knew how was the way that Paige suggested, but you did not like that way. That is why you must do everything to keep that voice away."

"I will," Diego barely muttered, his eyes filling with tears.

"Now, as much as your sister is fucking *loco,*" Jorge continued. "She does want to help you, and she will. I know this because when you went missing last year, Jolene thought I had killed you. She was ready to kill me too, but then I tell her the truth. She loves you very much, and I have asked her to watch over you, support you at work, or help with whatever you need. That will be her new responsibility. This will be her new job."

Diego perked up, and his eyes widened.

"Do we understand each other?" Jorge asked after a long pause. "Do you understand what I am saying?"

"Yes," Diego finally answered as he sat up straighter and carried more strength than he had been in months. "But is that necessary? I don't need no babysitter."

"Not a babysitter," Jorge assured him. "Now, if there is a problem you need help with or you're just having a bad day, you go to Jolene. No matter what. She is there to help you. Within reason, of course. I have already talked to her about this here. She knows my expectations, and I assure you, she will follow them."

"Is this….are you doing this because…" Diego hesitated, "You're leaving, aren't you?"

"Diego, at this time, I cannot say," Jorge admitted. "It is only winter, but the spring, it is coming. I must wait until Maria has finished school for the year, and then I will see. We may experiment for the summer, or we may stay. We will see what the next few months bring. In the end, I must do whatever is best for my children. If that means getting them out of this psycho circus, I will do it."

Diego nodded in understanding.

"But for now, I am trying to protect those I love," Jorge said. "Because I think we are preparing for a war. Unfortunately for the other side, I was trained in the Mexican cartel, and we are the most dangerous army in the world."

CHAPTER 39

"Jolene, I do not have time for your nonsense today," Jorge waved his hand in the air and glanced toward the bulletproof window in his office. "The point is that you are lucky that I give you a job. It is simple. You look after your brother, which you should be doing anyway, and keep out of everyone else's way."

"I know, but I can do more," Jolene insisted as she sat forward on her chair, her hand gently touching the expensive handbag beside her. "I promise you this. I have done good work for you before."

"And you will again," Jorge assured her. "If I need you, I will let you know. Until then, you will be at the office as Diego's assistant, and you are to help him with whatever he needs, but mostly, you are there to watch him. To make sure he is ok. No drugs, nothing. He has not been himself, and I cannot be watching him all the time. Do you understand?"

"I do," Jolene assured him. "But he already has an assistant to do everything for him, and she will not let me do anything..."

"Then let her," Jorge cut her off. "Why is this a problem, Jolene? You have a job doing nothing all day. Most people would love this. Fuck, I would love that job right now. Just go to the office, shop online, or watch videos. Jolene, I do not care. Keep a close eye on Diego. That is all."

"He won't like this," Jolene stumbled through her English. "He does not want to be babysitted."

"Jolene," Jorge took a deep breath and chose his words carefully. "Diego and I, we have already discussed this issue. He knows that you are there to help him if there are any problems, that I am assigning you to watch over him."

"So, he knows?" Jolene appeared confused. "And this is no problem?"

"I didn't exactly give him a choice," Jorge replied, and they both fell silent for a moment. "Jolene, this here may seem like not a big deal to you, but it is an important job. I need you to understand the seriousness. Diego does not seem to be himself, and you have nothing to do. That is why I will pay you to look after him. Check on him. Monitor his behavior. Make sure he's not using drugs again. Make sure the pressure is not getting to him. If the pressure is getting to him, or if anyone is betraying him in any way, you are to let me know."

Jolene nodded, sitting back in her chair as if suddenly understanding the depth of what he was asking.

"This is not a job for just anyone," Jorge reminded her. "This is your brother. You know what is best, and you have his interest at heart. But it is important to me. Will you do this?"

"Of course!" Jolene nodded. "Of course. I would look after my brother regardless of this…"

"But this is your *main* job, Jolene," Jorge reminded her. "This means you cannot get distracted by the latest fuckboy you meet. You must be focused."

"I will be focused."

"Now, I have an important call from Athas coming in," Jorge informed her as he stood up, and she did the same. "So, you must leave, but I want regular updates."

"Regular updates," She repeated as she reached for her purse.

"And I want you to take this seriously," Jorge added as the two walked toward the door. "This isn't a game."

"I know."

"One last thing, Jolene," Jorge said as he reached to open the door. "If anything happens to Diego on your watch, you're next!"

He said it so smoothly that it seemed to take a moment for Jolene to understand what he was saying, but the moment she did, her eyes widened, and her mouth fell open.

"But I…"

"I don't want to hear it," Jorge abruptly cut her off. "These here are my terms."

"But, I cannot…"

"Have a nice day, Jolene," Jorge spoke in a snappy tone as he all but pushed her out the door. His secure line rang as he returned to his desk.

"Athas," Jorge put him on speakerphone. "Tell me what kind of nonsense is happening in Ottawa today."

"Well, I just met with an advisor who suggested I use the terms 'racist' and 'misogynist' to shame the public if they don't fall in line," Athas spoke sardonically, his voice echoing through Jorge's office. "They've done research which suggests that being called these names causes the public to feel shame and fear that others will see them the same way. Welcome to the world of politics in Canada."

"Name calling?" Jorge started to laugh. "Is this here, high school?"

"You would wonder," Athas agreed. "Our society is being reduced to a juvenile mentality, and it's getting worse all the time. This is not the government I joined a few years ago. I used to deal with oil lobbyists who wanted pipelines or environmentalists who wanted to hug trees. Now, I have people wanting kids to take pills and conform."

"I want to know why this here is," Jorge spoke bluntly. "I feel as if there are a lot of layers, and I'm wondering what will be under the last one."

"I'm scared of what this means for our country," Athas admitted. "I don't know where this takes us."

"Well, you know," Jorge replied. "You are the fucking prime minister. Nothing happens unless you let it."

"I'm not so sure about that," Athas reminded him. "People are being gaslit about a problem that doesn't even exist. I never in my wildest dreams thought people would fall for this kind of shit. But I got parents complaining to my office and my MPs that we aren't taking this seriously enough. And the fucking news isn't helping. That's all they ever talk about."

"We must see who is buttering their bread, and it's not you," Jorge reminded him. "That is where the money comes from. Someone is telling them to push this stupidity. My people are looking into it."

"I know, but there's a force behind it," Athas reminded him. "And they're coming for our kids."

"My people, they think this here pill might make kids sick," Jorge informed him. "But we are not sure yet. They are still looking. It has been an experiment in Europe, and they claim success."

"I did hear that," Athas confirmed. "That has been their justification when they come to my people, but no one seems to have the information I'm looking for, like long-term results or most prominent side effects. They try to talk their way around things and downplay it while pushing it on parents. They know they're vulnerable when it comes to their kids. There's a lot of propaganda out there, and like I said, it starts with the media."

"Of course!" Jorge nodded. "That reminds me, Holly Anne is now working for me. She's doing a casual show. It has nothing to do with news."

"Does she know anything?"

"We gotta make her talk," Jorge confirmed. "They have her too scared to do so."

"That in itself should say something."

"All I know," Jorge replied. "Is that there is a powerful force pushing this, and I must find out who this is because it's not just here, in Canada. They are infiltrating all countries, convincing them they do not care about children if they are not on board."

"And they're potentially racists and misogynists if they don't play the game," Athas quipped. "Yeah, it's all coming together."

"Were you told to say that in this situation?"

"No," Athas paused for a moment. "They gave me no specifics. It was more of a general thing. They talked about the studies they did that suggest these words are the most offensive thing you can say about people, so their automatic reaction is to disprove it for fear of being viewed the wrong way. Interestingly, society is so insecure that we even care what people think."

"Ah, yes!" Jorge laughed. "We all have a public image now because of social media. Except we don't all got media training."

"I'm noticing celebrities also talking about this shit," Athas continued. "I heard one big Hollywood type talking about putting his kids on these pills and how it changed their lives. They hadn't realized how unhappy they were before that time. You get the idea."

"Until the big cheques rolled in," Jorge mocked. "They are famous, so that must mean they're also smart, well-educated people. Am I right?"

"Yes," Athas continued to rant. "People who spend their lives playing a role, pretending they're someone else, are, for some reason, the same people we're supposed to take life advice from. I'm not sure what about their profession makes them experts on everything, but for some reason, they are...."

"Ah, yes!" Jorge quipped. "If a celebrity tells me to put my kids on medication, I must do it."

"They're getting paid to sell these pills," Athas observed. "But people don't see that."

"And yet, cartels are the baddies because they push drugs," Jorge quipped. "Some things never change."

"Cartels don't push the right ones."

"*Si,* this is what I've been saying all along," Jorge glanced toward his bulletproof window. "But the truth is it has a way of slowly coming out. And this here, it will not be any different, my friend. I will find out who is at the top of this here bullshit and hang them out to dry."

"Since I'm talking to Jorge Hernandez," Athas laughed. "I assume you mean that *literally.*"

They both laughed.

CHAPTER 40

"Last night, I did an *Instagram* story about how I had entered a phase in my life where I preferred to talk about the wonderful people in this country and what they're doing to make a positive impact on society," Holly Anne said the words as if she was reading from a script, while across from her, Jorge nodded in approval. "I built it up and asked for topics my fans would like covered. I had them really involved in the process."

"So, what is your first fluff piece?" Jorge showed mild interest as he glanced at the clock behind her. "Is Sonny helping you?"

"We're interviewing a woman who has a series about her dog on YouTube," Holly Anne shrugged. "It's as light and fluffy as you can get."

"That is what you want," Jorge nodded as he started to get up.

"I wanted to talk to you about that," Holly Anne stopped him, and Jorge sat back down. "I'm worried that they might not buy it. If they see what we're really doing here …"

"You'll be dead?" Jorge finished her sentence. "That is what you worry about?"

"Yes," Holly Anne's face turned pink. "I know you have no reason to be loyal to me…"

"Holly Anne," Jorge cut her off. "Loyalty is important to me. We protect those who help us. This here, I assure you. They're monitoring your old phone, so you use the new one to talk to us. Marco has extra security on that. We have checked your home, your computers, everything."

"It's not that part I'm worried about," Holly Anne confessed. "I can't sleep at night, I…."

"I can get you security," Jorge suggested. "I can have protection at your home. What is it you want?"

"I want a gun."

"I will get you one."

"I don't have a firearms license."

To this, Jorge's head fell back in laughter.

"Lady, do you think I do?" He countered. "Do you think anyone in my family does? Trust me. You don't need one. You're with us now."

She seemed to relax and nodded.

"Do you know how to shoot?"

"Yes, my grandfather used to take me to the range when I was a kid."

"My associate, Jolene, she will be in contact with you," Jorge replied. "Anything else? Lady, you tell us, we will make it happen."

Relief filled her face.

"I'm not sure."

"Think about it," Jorge stood up. "Then let me know. Jolene will be in contact with you soon. She will also help. She will be your main contact. And if you ever have a problem, we will take care of it."

She nodded and appeared calmer as Jorge left and headed for the conference room. He could see Marco, Makerson, and Tony were waiting for him.

"You got our new employee sorted out?" Makerson didn't look up from his laptop when Jorge walked in, the door closing behind him. "She seems very nervous."

"She might have a reason to be," Jorge replied as he sat in his usual seat. "She's not fucking around with some bullies from down the block."

"We all could be in danger," Tony reminded Jorge. "If we get too close to the fire."

"Yeah, well fuck them," Jorge grumbled. "I plan to expose every one of their secrets."

"So far, sir, it looks like they have many," Marco responded as he closed his laptop. "These pills, they are not good. They are worse than we originally thought."

"They hid a lot," Makerson nodded as he closed his laptop and pushed it aside. "Of course, the studies aren't long-term enough because the pills are still pretty new, but already, we're seeing where addiction might be an issue."

"They cause dependency," Marco nodded, concern on his face. "So it may not be easy to stop using them later."

"Which is what they want," Makerson continued. "Either that or to put them on another addictive medication, or let them fall off the wagon and into street drugs."

"People are easier to control if they're not in their right mind," Jorge nodded. "Get them while they are young, and you have a lifetime customer."

"Sir, that is the thing," Marco replied. "It may not be a long lifetime."

"We're also seeing infertility might be an issue," Makerson calmly continued. "They're trying to downplay it, suggesting it's a minimal risk, but still…"

"With no long-term studies," Tony jumped in. "I'm not sure how they can assure us of this or anything else, for that matter."

"Put someone in a white coat on television saying it's ok," Makerson replied as he sat back in his chair. "And everyone believes him. Why would a doctor lie?"

"Certainly not for money," Jorge spoke sarcastically. "This here has *never* happened."

"That's another thing," Tony added. "We want to see if there's financial ties to these companies. If we can link that with dangerous side effects, people will have no choice but to listen."

"Unfortunately," Jorge shook his head. "I am not sure they will."

"The media is hyping it up to seem like kids are about to go off the deep end if they don't have this medication," Makerson complained. "Big Pharma is paying them well to keep the propaganda going."

"They are shaming people if they don't listen to the scientist," Tony reminded them. "That's the key phrase on these news shows. If you don't *listen to the science,* you must be stupid or ignorant."

"This is what we're up against," Makerson said, shaking his head. "The problem is that we can have all the proof in the world. People hear what they want and trust certain voices more than ours. Unfortunately, it's more dicey because it's about their kids."

"Sir, you would think this would make them much more careful," Marco spoke gently. "But even at my kid's school, I see parents trying to force *other people's* kids to take these pills because they think they will somehow influence or hurt *their* children. It is strange."

"Did the whole world just get stupider?" Jorge raised an eyebrow. "Sometimes I wonder."

"All we can do is explore the truth and see where it takes us," Tony suggested. "I just don't know if the world is interested in listening."

"Athas, he said celebrities are speaking out," Jorge glanced around the table. "We need one of these YouTube stars to come out and speak for our side."

"Sabrina Supergirl again?" Makerson referred to the young woman who had helped them previously when Athas was running in the election. "She was against hurting children. Maybe this would be something she'd be interested in."

"*Make* her interested in this," Jorge suggested. "Anything new with the World For Children Society? We find out where this shit starts from or what?"

"Still hitting a wall," Marco admitted. "I am finding some information, but I feel like I'm circling the drain more than I am finding where this begins."

"Maybe it's not in just one place," Tony suggested. "Could it be this children's society has links with other organizations that *also* benefit from kids taking these pills?"

"Other than Big Pharma?" Jorge asked.

"Well, it seems like lots of people working together," Tony replied. "Big Pharma makes money, this children's society, what do they get?"

"A compliant generation?" Makerson shrugged. "But why?"

"Isn't it obvious?" Jorge asked. "I mean, a compliant society is easy to control. It's what dictators do, is it not?"

"Maybe that's why they've tried so hard to get Athas out," Makerson suggested. "Maybe he's not going to fall in line with their way of thinking."

"It would make sense," Tony added. "I mean, the assassination attempts before the last election, all this underhanded shit with his cabinet and behind his back, pretty much since the day he started. Maybe it's all connected."

"They know he won't play ball," Makerson said as he reached for his coffee. "It seems more first-world countries are pushing these pills."

"Too much freedom," Marco suggested. "These countries allow their people to do whatever makes them happy."

"Harder to control," Makerson nodded.

"Much harder to control," Marco agreed. "Unless medicated to do so."

Everyone fell silent until Jorge spoke again.

"I am intrigued to see who is at the top of this mountain," he watched the others nodding. "The fact that we have not been able to find out who yet, this here tells me that someone is going to great lengths to hide their identity. They are very protected. I am curious why."

"Maybe it's more than one person," Marco suggested.

"Who benefits from a more compliant society?" Makerson repeated an earlier question that floated through the room.

"Rich people," Jorge replied. "People who think the world is out of control."

"It may be, sir," Marco agreed. "But is this the answer?"

"It is if you are a psychopath," Jorge replied. "And psychopaths, they rule the world."

"So how much does Holly Anne know?" Makerson asked as he glanced around the table. "I know she's scared to talk, but she needs to put us in the right direction because we're hitting mostly dead ends."

Jorge thought for a moment before speaking.

"It has been my experience that if you can't find the rats," he hesitated. "You set the place on fire until they all run out."

CHAPTER 41

"Isn't that the girl," Paige pointed at the laptop that sat in the middle of their kitchen table as she leaned in closer, "that helped you during the election? She has a large social media following?"

"Yup," Jorge nodded as he relaxed in his chair and drank his coffee. "That would be the one."

"Is it safe for her to talk about the consequences of these pills," Paige appeared concerned as she sat beside Jorge. "If Holly Anne is scared, then…"

"Paige, this is her opinion," Jorge cut her off, pointing toward the screen. "She is just going to say there are rumors that these pills have serious side effects. We need to create doubt and make people start to think. Sometimes they eat more if you throw them crumbs rather than the whole slice of bread."

"I hope you're right," Paige seemed to relax, if even slightly. "I just worry because Holly Anne hardly seems like a lightweight. If they're making her scared to talk, then I don't think we should take any chances."

"Paige, I fear no one."

"Jorge," She hesitated until he made eye contact with her, and she pointed toward the screen. "This isn't about you. We don't want her walking on a landmine. Trust me, some people control our world in ways no one understands or suspects. They keep off the radar, but they aren't people you want to mess with."

"Maybe you have some thoughts about where this comes from?" Jorge raised an eyebrow. "Point me in the right direction, *mi amor.*"

"I don't necessarily know who is running the show this time," Paige gently answered. "I just know that in my previous life, powerful people were above politicians and big executives. They controlled everyone like puppets. They aren't public people at all. They sometimes hired me to resolve problems, but I never met them. Their identities are secret, and that's how they want it."

"So, logically, these people could be walking down the street," Jorge pointed toward the door. "And we would not know."

"Probably not," Paige shook her head. "And that's the scary part. They can get to you, but you can't get to them."

"That is because, Paige, if we knew who they were and could get to them," Jorge turned toward his wife. "They know they would have no chance. It is like the man who hides behind the curtain in *The Wizard of Oz.* You're only powerful in dark corners, but once the world sees you, you're fucked."

"I suspect that's what is happening here," Paige confirmed. "But we have to find out who's behind the curtain. The problem is, it mightn't be as easy as it has been in the past."

"*Mi amor,* we have found these people before, and we can do it again," Jorge reached out and touched a strand of his wife's blonde hair. "You and me, we can do anything."

"I'm not sure about this time," Paige lowered her voice. "We have to think about our family. We don't want them in the line of fire. That's what worries me. It's not just us. These people, they'd think nothing of hurting our children to keep us in line."

"Paige that is no different than…"

"That's the problem," She firmly cut him off. "I don't think you realize that this time *is* different. We are talking about a whole new level of power that we've never dealt with before, and I'm concerned. This isn't a chance I'm willing to take, and neither should you."

He didn't respond but attempted to comfort her while considering her words. Was he in over his head this time?

Sitting in his office later, Jorge felt defeated in the face of his new opponent. Did his family make him weak? He never used to think so, but it certainly was a vulnerability. As much as he wanted to find out who was attempting to hurt the children, he had to think about Maria and Miguel. He would rather rip out his heart and set it on fire than allow anything to happen to his *familia*. Then again, he'd prefer to find out who was behind all this bullshit and rip out their heart instead.

Literally.

Jorge heard his phone beep and reached for it. Makerson sent him a video from question period at the House of Commons. He tapped the button and sat back.

Loud applause took over Jorge's phone as he watched the opposition gleefully react to something asked.

"The right, honorable prime minister…"

Athas abruptly stood up from his seat, an annoyed expression on his face.

"Mr. Speaker, the opposition seems intent on allowing our children to be nothing more than test subjects in an experiment that only benefits Big Pharma and their shareholders. And from the information I recently obtained, my understanding is that the leader of the opposition's wife is one of these shareholders. Is this how the government works now? Is it about who can fill their wallets the most and the fuck with the Canadians who voted them in?"

Jorge felt his jaw drop as cheers and jeers filled the House of Commons as the Speaker of the House stood up and chastised Athas for his words.

"As the prime minister, you should know better…."

The background noise continued as some yelled comments back and forth while Athas stood rigidly and spoke.

"I withdraw my remarks," Athas spoke with strength in his voice while his body appeared to inflate slightly in size. *"But I do not apologize for standing up for Canadians."*

The uproar continued, and the video ended.

Jorge grinned. This was what Athas should be doing.

A text from Makerson interrupted his thoughts.

I'm looking into how many others have money invested in Big Pharma on both sides of the aisle. It might explain why Athas' party seems to go up against him.

Jorge grinned.

Like I said the other day, set the fire and see how many rats run out.

I suspect there are lots more, but Athas shook the can today. Legacy media is trying to justify why the leader of the opposition's wife has shares in the company, trying to downplay it. I plan to do the opposite.

Jorge wondered how many others were making money off the world's children. And even more so, why no one seemed to care.

His phone beeped again.

Jolene is here to see you. I wasn't sure if you were on a call.

No, let her in. Also, mi amor, I have a video for you to watch.

He forwarded what Makerson sent him.

A knock at his door pulled him from his joyful place. He grew serious.

"Come in, Jolene."

The door opened, and the Colombian walked across the floor. She was wearing a heavy coat.

"Jolene, you can take your coat off," Jorge pointed toward the door. "It is not that cold in this house."

"Paige, she asked me, but I cannot stay long," She spoke breathlessly. "I want to go next door before Diego gets home."

"Why, is something wrong?"

"I check his office," Jolene replied. "Carefully, when he is not there. I could not find anything."

"So, you want to, what?" Jorge was confused. "Search his house?"

"Before he gets home today, *si,*" Jolene nodded. "I feel he is acting weirdly, so I want to see if there is anything to be concerned about."

"Do you think he's taking something?" Jorge felt his original elation fall flat. "The cocaine again?"

"I do not know," Jolene shook her head. "Maybe you know, it is just me, but I find him different. I am not sure if it is good or bad. He seems peaceful, not himself."

"Jolene, cocaine, it does not make you peaceful. Maybe it is something else?"

"I know," She said. "But I do not know this for a fact, so I look. I will see."

"If he has drugs, he might have them on him."

"I know this," Jolene nodded. "But at work, it is tricky. You cannot be too careful."

"Ok," Jorge sighed. "I guess we will have to find out for sure, but let us hope he is ok."

"I do not know for sure," Jolene admitted. "I just...I do worry. I know you think I do not care for anyone but myself, but I love my brother and don't wish this for him to take something that can hurt him. He is not a young man anymore. This is not good."

"None of us are young anymore, Jolene," Jorge reminded her. "But I cannot have someone who is taking drugs looking after my company, and I cannot have my best friend addicted. Neither of these things work."

She seemed to process the information and began to stand.

"Oh yes, Jolene, also," Jorge said. "Did you speak with Holly Anne?"

"Yes, we have this settled," Jolene nodded as she adjusted her coat. "I give her a gun to use."

"Did she know how to use it?"

"She think she knew how to use it," Jolene corrected him. "I show her the right way."

"Interesting," Jorge nodded.

"This woman, she has to know that it is not like the television," Jolene reminded him. "She does not see that it must be close because the people who break into your house will not wait for you to unlock it from a safe place. This stupid government rules. They do not understand this."

Jorge grinned.

"Maybe Athas can change this law," Jolene continued as she walked toward the door.

"I suspect it is not a good time," Jorge remarked, amused at her comment. "Making everything goosey loosey with guns, it may not help."

"Goosey? What?" Jolene hesitated and looked back.

"Never mind, Jolene," Jorge was humored by her expression. "Go check Diego's place and try not to get caught. And let me know what you find."

"Will do."

After she left, he let out a sigh.

"Please, God, may it be nothing that she finds."

CHAPTER 42

"You know, when I first met Paige, Valentine's Day was this magical time," Jorge informed Chase as he sat at the empty bar at *Princesa Maria,* which sat closed for a few more hours. "I would try to do all these beautiful things for her, but now, I hand her some flowers, and that is it. I guess this is marriage?"

"You're talking to a guy that didn't do well with marriage," Chase reminded him, and they laughed.

"But you were a child," Jorge shook his head. "You knew nothing of the world, let alone marriage, at that time."

"Not to mention that I didn't want to be married in the first place," Chase reminded him. "Maybe that will change someday, but it soured me of the experience so far."

"Well, that makes sense when that is all you know," Jorge reminded him. "But with Paige, I find the longer we are married, the more everything becomes routine. There is always so much going on, so many things to deal with, that we never get time together. I guess that's one of the reasons I am thinking of going to the country, at least for this summer."

"So, you're going to do it?" Chase asked. "After making fun of me for growing up in a hick town, now you're thinking of moving to one yourself?"

Jorge laughed and glanced down at his beer.

"Well, you know things, they do change," Jorge reminded him. "And Toronto is not the same city it used to be."

"Yeah, I heard lots of people disappear now," Chase teased, causing Jorge's head to fall back in laughter. "Or are found dead."

"It is becoming a more dangerous city, do you suppose?" Jorge continued to smile as he took a drink of his beer. "Maybe it is a good time to leave then, *si?*"

"It won't be the same without you here."

"I got a big safe house with lots of room for visitors," Jorge reminded him. "And we will not be that far away. Although sometimes I think about going even further."

"So, this thing you're working on now," Chase leaned forward. "With the pills, they want to give kids?"

"Yes, it is not looking good," Jorge nodded. "The more they look, the worse it gets."

"Marco was telling me," Chase nodded. "Do they want to make our kids zombies or what?"

"That and maybe unable to have children in the future," Jorge added "I do not understand."

"Yeah, what's that about?" Chase wondered. "I did watch a video the other night where some guy was saying these assholes at the top think the world has too many people. That might be part of the reason."

"The world might have too many people," Jorge agreed. "But unfortunately, the people we need to get rid of are the same ones trying to get rid of the rest of us."

"So, it's this World for Children's Society group?"

"Yes, but there are more at the top," Jorge said. "We cannot find who those people are yet. They are well hidden."

"There must be an arm you can twist to find out who," Chase suggested as he crossed his arms over his chest. "People got a way of talking if you turn up the heat."

"Oh, I have lots of heat to turn up," Jorge reminded him. "A whole crematorium of heat."

"That would make most people talk."

"You find me the people, and I'm there," Jorge raised an eyebrow. "Let us hope Marco can learn something new. Until then, we have a few things in the works to shake their cages. See what falls out."

"I gotta tell you," Chase shook his head. "I kinda give up on the world at this point."

"I gave up on the world long ago," Jorge insisted. "But, I do everything for my *familia,* including sorting out this here."

"Speaking of which," Chase tilted his head toward the door. "Did you find out what was going on with Diego? Is he back on..."

"No," Jorge said, letting out a sigh. "I know, this is what I was thinking too, but I had Jolene check it out, and he was fine. Turns out, he's into all this stuff like Paige, like mediation. I guess it makes him seem different, so we assume the worst. He's clean. He caught Jolene searching his house, and they had a big argument."

"So, the usual," Chase offered. "Did you ask her to search his house?"

"No, I ask her to keep an eye on him," Jorge said as he reached for his drink. "You know, monitor his behavior, that kind of thing. She took it to an extra level and searched his house. He has cameras and saw her doing it from the office and came home to confront her. Maria said she could hear them yelling when she got home from school."

"Jolene takes everything to the extreme."

"And if anyone would know..."

"Yeah, yeah, I know," Chase replied, his expression falling. "You warned me."

"Everyone gets caught in Jolene's trap."

"She never got you caught in it."

"Yes, well, I have known Jolene for a long time," Jorge reminded him. "I have seen and heard a lot. I know her games. The point is that you now see who she is, and you can move on."

"At the expense of losing a friendship," Chase reminded him, to which Jorge shrugged.

"Maria, she had a crush on you way too long," Jorge offered. "It was cute when she was young, but it started to be a little too much as she got older. As much as I did not like her seeing you with Jolene that day, I am kind of glad if that is what it took for her to move on. Sometimes, my Maria worries me. She can be very emotional like her mother was, but I must admit, this here is changing. I see her growing up a lot."

"That's good," Chase replied. "I guess everything is ok in the end."

"If we go to the safe house this summer," Jorge continued. "I think it will be good for her to get out. I do not like Toronto's influence on her. I would rather not have her in private school anymore because they are getting a little crazy, but I also worry about putting her in public school. I do not know the answer. She has issues no matter where she goes."

"Schools now aren't what they used to be," Chase reminded him. "Doesn't your friend Athas have any control over schools?"

"It is provincial," Jorge reminded him. "And he don't have control of anything else, so why would this be different anyway?"

Chase laughed.

"I don't think they want him to have control," he suggested. "They want to be in control of him. He is getting stronger. He threw out that f-bomb during question period the other day."

"Yes, now the media says people feel he is too harsh, too mean," Jorge rolled his eyes. "They like him soft, fluffy, like a stuffed animal. People now do not like strong men. They want us weak and pathetic. Powerful men are automatically too aggressive. They want to drain us of our testosterone."

"Yeah, I get that in the dating world too," Chase reported "I talked to a woman the other day that seemed turned off that I was into boxing. She said it was too violent, too alpha male. I'm too scary."

"Then tell her to date women," Jorge quipped.

"That's the funny part," Chase laughed. "Some of them are more aggressive than me."

"The world lacks courage," Jorge reminded Chase. "But that's what they want. They want us scared because scared people are easier to control. That is why they have us fearing our children will be depressed and crazy if they're not on these pills that they want to push. They work on our fears. They've always worked on our fears, but people never question it."

Jorge heard his phone make a noise to alert him. Pulling it out of his pocket, he saw a message from Makerson. He read it and laughed.

"What's that about?" Chase asked.

"Well, in this here continuing drama with Athas," Jorge set his phone on the bar. "There was another argument between him and the leader of the opposition. Things escalated, and he suggested they 'get in the ring' to resolve it."

"Oh my God," Chase shook his head. "As if these prissy boys could fight to save their lives."

"It would be entertaining."

"Would it?" Chase asked and began to laugh. "This is getting ridiculous."

"A million things they can talk about in a day," Jorge reminded him. "A million important things and no one pays attention until it's dramatic and entertaining."

"That's discouraging," Chase pointed out.

"Yes, but did you ever consider that's why they do it?" Chase leaned against the bar. "If politicians weren't controversial, the people would forget they are there. Do you think anyone gets into politics to get lost in the shuffle?"

"It would work to their advantage if they did," Chase considered. "I mean, look at how much they could get away with."

"They already do."

Chase nodded.

"I must check something," Jorge grabbed his phone. "That lady, Sabrina Supergirl, is supposed to bring up something for us today."

"Oh, I got it," Chase pointed toward the television over the bar. "We can play it on here."

"You are much more techie than me, my friend," Jorge grinned as Chase turned on the television and found the *YouTube* channel. Sabrina Supergirl was speaking to the camera.

"Don't know about that."

"Is this live?" Jorge squinted at the screen.

"Yes," Chase said, and they both paused to listen. "She's talking something about her fans sending her gifts."

"How long does she talk on this here?" Jorge asked.

"I think her shows run at least an hour."

"Please do not tell me I must listen to this all day."

"As usual, I want to open them live with all of you so you can see the wonderful treasures people send me from all over the world."

"How do some people have the ability..."

Jorge didn't hear the rest of Chase's question. He stared at the screen and felt his heart race and his throat got dry. Something was wrong. He was about to reach for his phone to text Makerson when a loud noise came from the screen, and the video went black.

CHAPTER 43

"Are you kidding me right now?" Jorge swung around with such abruptness he almost ran into Makerson in the conference room doorway. "So the terrorists, they focus on twenty-year-old YouTubers now? Is this what you are telling me?"

"They're trying to say it's an attack on free speech," Makerson explained with a shrug. "You know the media, they gotta explain it someway."

"That's not untrue," Tony said from the conference room table as Jorge and Makerson joined him. "It is an attack on free speech, just not in the way they're trying to spin it."

"Why?" Jorge asked as he sat in his usual seat. "What way are they trying to spin it?"

"They're trying to say that it's because she was going to speak about how kids need these medications to stay calm," Makerson attempted to explain, but Jorge was already furious.

"What? You mean to tell me," he began to rant. "That they are trying to say the *opposite* of what is happening? Are you shitting me right now?"

"Yeah, they're essentially trying to say that people who are against kids taking pills," Makerson tried to sort it out as he explained it. "Are extremists who will go to great lengths to stop it. You know, similar to the pro-life people blowing up a doctor's office, that kind of thing."

"That makes me wonder if *that* was even true," Tony raised an eyebrow.

"Once you've worked in the media or politics for some time," Makerson said as he sat down. "You begin to question a lot of things you once believed."

"So," Jorge cut them off. "Let me get this here straight. The mainstream media is saying that people who *don't* want kids drugged are *extremists* who blow up YouTubers on the air to keep them from speaking about certain topics. And in this case, they are saying that it was not her speaking against the pills, but the other way around?"

"Basically," Makerson nodded while Jorge closed his eyes and shook his head. "Things are becoming very twisted."

"We live in a clown world," Jorge announced as he opened his eyes again and looked around the table. "We must speak against this, but do so in a way that doesn't link us to her."

"We could say a source told us she was supposed to be speaking against the pills?" Tony suggested.

"I was thinking about Sonny since he knows her," Makerson nodded. "But then, I considered that they know he works here…."

"No, this here won't work," Jorge shook his head. "Maybe we could say a source we cannot identify."

"That might work," Tony agreed. "We have to break away from this narrative."

"I still can't believe it even happened at all," Makerson glanced at his phone before pushing it back into his pocket. "That poor girl, she was just a kid."

Jorge felt a heaviness in his chest. What would've once sent fire through his heart, this time, it sent a sadness. She was not much older than his daughter.

"The neighborhood was evacuated and checked," Tony informed them. "But it looks like she was the only person targeted…at least, directly. But I guess we already knew that."

"She lived alone?" Jorge asked.

"She lived with her family, but they were at work," Makerson spoke gently. "Police expect to be there for hours."

"Is CSIS involved?" Tony referred to the Canadian Security Intelligence Service. "Since it's a *terrorist* attack?"

"Nah, that's only the media's assumption," Makerson replied as he sat back in his chair, showing exhaustion. "The police aren't saying anything yet. They're more likely to play the same hand as the media."

"Regardless," Jorge spoke with authority as he took charge of the situation. "We must do two things. The first is to go against this mainstream media's suggestion that it was a terrorist attack because she was speaking up *for* the pills, and those attacking her were extremist lunatics against pills. We know this is wrong. And the second thing is we must find out who did this. How did they know she would be talking about this at all?"

"Maybe they didn't know?" Tony asked.

"No, she made some hints on social media," Makerson reminded him. "It may have been Instagram or one of them, but it showed she had a slant."

"Then how can they say that she was for the pills?" Jorge was confused.

"It was removed," Makerson said as he took out his phone to show them. "Someone went to a lot of trouble."

"She has a huge following," Tony reminded him. "A lot of influence."

"Where's Marco?" Jorge glanced around the room. "I thought he would be here by now? Maybe he can find us some answers."

"On his way," Tony confirmed. "He had to deal with an issue on the *House of Pot* website first."

"Do we not have other IT specialists that could do that?" Jorge muttered.

"I think it was a fairly big problem," Makerson calmly suggested. "Maybe a hack attempt again or something."

"Looks like Sabrina Supergirl wasn't the only person under attack for *wrong think* today," Jorge spoke wryly. "I would love to find out who is behind this because they may soon have an explosive package waiting for them."

"Athas is reacting," Makerson gestured toward his phone and hit the volume on a video.

"I would like to give my heartfelt sympathy to the family of Sabrina..."

"He is talking about this?" Jorge was confused. "A *YouTube* star, does that not seem odd?"

"She is considered....*was* considered one of the biggest YouTubers in Canada," Tony reminded him. "She was more powerful and had more of a following than some mainstream news programs."

"Try *all,*" Makerson corrected him. "But so do we at this point. No one follows mainstream anymore, except seniors, boomers…"

"I can't imagine why," Jorge muttered as his eyes left the screen of Athas speaking. "What next? Will they say Athas sent the explosive to her house?"

"Don't worry. If they could find a way to make it stick," Makerson replied as he continued to scan through social media. "They would."

"That would take care of two of their problems at once."

"Sorry I'm late, sir," Marco rushed into the room, his face flushed as he headed to the boardroom table. "I had a mess back at the other place, but I am here now."

"Chances are good their tracks are hidden pretty well by now," Makerson suggested. "But anything you can find would be a help."

"I am anxious to see what the police documents say," Marco said as he opened his laptop before sitting down. "But I also will try to see if any cameras in the area are working and if they caught anything. I assume the package was dropped off directly by the person behind this because it would be too risky to have a regular delivery service deal with it."

"I'm not sure what else you could do?" Tony looked around the table. "Maybe the dark web?"

"It has been quiet as of late," Marco replied as he began to type, not looking up from the screen. "I suspect these people are careful about leaving any proof behind."

"Someone has to know something, somewhere," Tony reminded them.

"No one is talking," Makerson reminded him. "There are a lot of unanswered questions, and we aren't the only ones wondering where this shit is coming from. There are indie journalists in Europe that I've been in touch with. We're comparing notes. We aren't the only ones hitting walls."

"Anything new on the pills, Marco?" Jorge asked. "Research? Anything like this?"

"There was a new study that they're trying to keep buried," Marco nodded as he continued to type. "More of the same, if anything, it is stronger indications that the pills have serious side effects that aren't as rare as they wanted everyone to believe. They'll do studies until they find one slanted to their side, then release it to the public. But so far, everything is saying the opposite. The pills are linked to infertility if used for long periods."

"Which is what they want, by the way," Makerson reminded them. "Kids are stuck on them forever."

"Nah, just the 12 years or so they're in school," Tony spoke mockingly.

"Yes," Marco nodded. "And they can cause heart problems. Kids have passed out because their blood pressure is much too low."

"And people want to give their kids this?" Jorge raised an eyebrow. "Over my dead fucking body that my kids take these pills."

"Me too, sir," Marco looked up from his screen. "I cannot believe people are so fast to do so. Parents at my kid's schools, my wife says they are more than happy to go along with this suggestion. They insist that the provincial government wouldn't tell them it was safe if it wasn't."

"The fly in the ointment is Athas going against their narrative," Makerson reminded them. "Can you imagine if he didn't?"

"The parents say that he is against it because Big Pharma won't contribute to his party."

"Because he won't promote them," Makerson laughed. "This is what I mean. They twist everything around. They'd donate money to his party if he said what they wanted, but since he won't, they turn it around."

"This here," Jorge reminded them. "Is why I want to get out of this city."

"The aliens," Marco gestured toward the ceiling. "They can take me anytime, sir."

Laughter followed Marco's announcement.

Jorge's phone rang.

CHAPTER 44

"Let me get this straight," Jorge didn't hold back his hostility as he glared across the boardroom table at Holly Anne Ryerson. They were alone in the room, the others gone to work on their various projects in light of the death of Sabrina Supergirl. "You feel *safer not* working with me? You feel *safer* sitting home, alone in your pathetic little apartment with no protection from me and my people?"

"No, I just think..." Holly Anne appeared flustered as she attempted to explain.

"No, lady, you're not thinking at all," Jorge abruptly corrected her as he leaned ahead on the table, staring into her frightened eyes. "This is not the time to put down your weapon. If anything, you are *less* safe if you do not have me in your corner. I am not here protecting you out of the goodness of my heart. Lady, it is because we need your help. If anything, I could throw you under the fucking bus now because, so far, you gave me nothing. Now, a girl is dead. What do you think about that?"

Holly Anne burst into tears.

"Don't even bother, lady. These tears aren't working on me," Jorge grumbled as he glared at her. "Shit just got fucking real. You walk out of here today, and you will be dead by the end of the week because they got every reason to kill you. You know more, and that's what they got their panties in a knot about now. What will you say?"

"That's why I thought I should leave," Holly Anne attempted to explain. "I could say I decided to get out of the news completely and leave...."

"Don't be a fucking coward," Jorge shot back. "I am so *tired* of all you cowards that claim to be journalists but would rather play the game than tell the fucking truth. We got lots of them on television, and you know what? If we had journalists that weren't a bunch of fucking sheep, these pharmaceutical companies wouldn't get any of this shit out there in the first place."

Holly Anne couldn't even look him in the eye as her sobbing stopped; she stared at her hands.

"Now, if you want to be safe," Jorge continued to show no compassion. "Get your fat ass into Makerson's office and tell him everything you know about Big Pharma and these pills, *or* you get the fuck out of here. But if you do, lady, I hope you know how to dodge bullets better than you know how to report the news."

With that, Jorge jumped up and headed for the door.

He was done dancing with the devil. Time was up.

Jorge exited the conference room and glanced down the hallway before heading toward the main door. However, he hadn't quite reached it when he heard a familiar whimper from behind. He turned, expecting to see Holly Anne, but instead found his daughter.

"Maria?" Jorge was shocked to see tears running down her face. He forgot she was working that day. "What is wrong, *niñita?*"

"*Papá,* that girl was killed and..." She rushed toward him, and Jorge pulled her into a hug.

"Maria, I did not know you followed her."

"I don't, really," Maria sniffed. "But she was a big deal to a lot of kids. That's all anyone talked about in school today. Just about what a good person she was and stuff. But I didn't know she was for these weird pills."

"She wasn't, Maria," Jorge let go of his daughter and attempted to explain. "That is just the media. They must explain her death away, so they say...."

"But that's what her social media posts say," Maria spoke matter-of-factly. "I was surprised you'd work with someone like that, but..."

"What do you mean?" Jorge cut her off as he stood up straighter. "I thought her posts hinted that she was against the pills."

"Maybe they did before," Maria appeared confused. "But not now because the teachers talked about this in school today."

"I am confused why they would talk about it at all," Jorge asked. "Do teachers not *teach* anymore?"

"Well, some kids were upset, so they canceled classes to discuss our feelings," Maria explained. "I know. I thought that was a lot too."

"They took the whole day off to talk about your feelings?" Jorge rolled his eyes. "So, what did they say about this Sabrina girl? Someone on the internet that you don't even know? What the hell did you talk about?"

"That she was for the new pills and killed for that reason," Maria replied. "Something about a terrorist attack? I didn't know terrorists killed people for something like this, *Papá.*"

"No, Maria, they are trying to suggest that a terrorist attacked her for promoting the pills," Jorge attempted to explain.

"So, everyone is lying?" Maria's eyes suddenly turned cold. "She wasn't advocating for these pills? I thought the terrorist attack story sounded weird."

"Maria, the propaganda is strong," Jorge reminded her. "I do not appreciate your teacher skipping a class to talk about this rather than what I fucking pay the school to teach you."

"Yes, not just a class, almost all day," Maria spoke bashfully, watching her father closely. "Now, I feel stupid for believing what they said. It doesn't even make sense!"

"Maria, this is not you," Jorge reminded her. "I want you to go to Makerson. Tell him what they say to you in school today."

"But he's in a meeting..."

"Interrupt," Jorge pulled his phone out of his pocket. "I will send him a text. Tell him what they try to tell you in school, how much of the day they wasted, everything. Tell Marco to hack your school. I want to know if the teachers were *told* what they say to you. I am curious."

"Ok," Maria's eyes widened. "I can tell them everything the teachers said, everything."

"This is good, Maria," Jorge nodded. "I am proud of you. Go talk to them."

Jorge tapped a message to Makerson as his daughter walked away.

He decided to call his wife.

"*Mi amor,*" he started as soon as she answered the phone. "Can you check at the bar with Chase? I need him to be more vigilant after today's incident."

"I was thinking the same," Paige calmly replied. "I've also discussed this with Tala, and I'm watching the house."

"We cannot be too careful."

"What about Diego?"

"There is always a lot of security at head office and the stores," Jorge answered and stopped to think. "But maybe call him as well. I'm at the production house, and we got things looked after here because the shit is about to hit the fan. We cannot wait anymore."

"Do you have something?"

"I got them working on it now with Maria," Jorge replied. "I will tell you more later. I'm heading to the crematorium. Andrew is working there today."

"Do you think we're in danger?"

"*Mi amor,* we both know that today was a message to us all," Jorge muttered as he glanced over his shoulder. "They want everyone to run scared, but we will not. We must have courage."

After ending the call, Jorge headed to the door. Glancing around as he left the building, he considered that he might be the next target. The last thing Jorge wanted was for his family to worry. His main concern was protecting them. He didn't care about his own life.

Once in his SUV, he left the parking lot and headed toward the crematorium. A flutter of snow swirled around his window, and he turned on the wipers. The skies were grey, indicating something more sinister was around the corner. Nature had a way of letting us know these things.

Arriving at the crematorium, Jorge noted that only Andrew's car was in the parking lot. All the others had gone home.

Approaching the building, he was cautious, looking around for anything suspicious, but nothing caught his eye.

He went inside, locking the door behind him.

It was quiet. No one was around the reception area. All the offices were empty, indicating Andrew was probably in the basement.

"Hey, where the fuck are you?" Jorge called out, reaching for his gun. Just in case. "I gotta talk to you."

"I'm down here," Andrew called out. "I got a bit of a problem."

Jorge rushed ahead, gun in hand, taking the steps two at a time.

What he found was unexpected.

A fat, white man was on the ground.

"What the fuck is this?" Jorge asked, pointing at the middle-aged man. He was dressed professionally in a shirt and tie, his eyes closed. "This one dead or what?"

"Or what," Andrew answered. "I was just about to call you. I found him roaming around in the office, so I hit him over the head."

"Are you sure he isn't legit?"

"Nah, he was snooping through files and shit."

"How did he get in?"

"Good question because I locked all the doors."

Jorge carefully inspected him.

"Did he say anything?"

"Didn't get a chance," Andrew shook his head. "I don't fuck around with this shit."

Jorge grinned and nodded.

"This here is fair," he replied and nudged the guy with his foot. "We got to find some answers. Decide what to do with him."

The man moved slightly but didn't wake up.

"How hard did you hit him?"

"Whatever, man," Andrew shrugged. "I wasn't gauging this shit at the time, you know?"

"Check for ID."

"Already did," Andrew shook his head. "There's nothing."

"Why come here?" Jorge wondered.

"You got me there," Andrew replied. "Less security than the other places."

"Yeah, and that's going to get tougher," Jorge reminded him. "After the incident today."

"I figured as much," Andrew nodded. "The psychopaths are out full force."

"Do not think they're ever far away," Jorge reminded him as he nudged the man again, noting that he almost opened his eyes but stopped. He exchanged looks with Andrew. "That's ok. You know he might not come back from this. Just throw him in the oven."

The man suddenly sat upright, eyes wide open.

CHAPTER 45

"Who the fuck are you?" Jorge asked the older man as he regained consciousness. Jorge looked down at his balding head, noticing he appeared smaller than only moments earlier. "And why are you in my crematorium?"

"Oh, this is a crematorium?" He responded as if in a daze. "I'm sorry, someone hit my head, so I don't..."

"Cut out the bullshit," Jorge lifted his gun as if to remind the man that it was still there. "I don't got all day, asshole."

"And don't bother sayin' you're here to preplan your funeral either," Andrew snapped at him. "Although considering the current circumstances, it might be a good idea."

Jorge continued to stare down the pathetic man as a look of panic crossed his face.

"Look, I can't remember..."

"*NOW! MOTHERFUCKER! NOW!*" Jorge impatiently screamed.

"Like he said," Andrew jumped in. "We don't got all day."

"Someone hired me to come here," his words were sudden, erratic.

"Why?" Jorge shot back. "And by who? I want to know everything, and I want to know it now."

"I will tell you everything you want to know," he responded. "If you stop pointing that gun at me."

Andrew and Jorge exchanged looks.

It was growing dark when Jorge finally got away and drove through the streets of Toronto. He was fuming. No one deceived him and thought they could get away with it. Sometimes Jorge was surprised who was disloyal, but most times he wasn't. The key was to make everyone know that it was unacceptable and that there would be consequences.

Arriving at his destination, he called Paige.

"Is something wrong?"

"You might say that."

"You sound upset."

"I was," Jorge mused for a moment. "But it is good to know what cards you've dealt and which ones to get rid of."

There was a slight pause.

"Oh."

"We will talk soon, *mi amor.*"

"Let me know if you need help."

"I got this covered."

Ending the call, he stared at the building and thought for a few minutes before exiting his SUV and going inside. The truth had a way of always getting back to him. Those who didn't see this were fools.

Entering the *Hernandez Production Company*, Jorge nodded to the security guard who stood outside. The black man was there for appearances more than anything. He had no idea what was going on the other side of the door. And that was a good thing.

Walking through, Jorge noted that the daytime staff were gone. Even the parking lot had shown signs that only a few were left inside. The person he needed to see was still there. That's all that mattered. It was time to deal with this problem.

Makerson walked out of the boardroom and appeared surprised to see Jorge.

"Hey! Did you see my report?" He walked toward him. "I just..."

"No, did you learn anything?"

"Well, Marco found some information..."

"Is he still here?"

"Yes, in the boardroom."

"Who else is in there?"

"Ah....Tony, Holly Anne..."

"Maria?"

"No, Tala picked her up about twenty minutes ago."

Jorge said nothing but nodded.

"Is everything ok?" Makerson asked.

"It will be," Jorge nodded. "Come with me."

Without responding, Makerson followed him to the boardroom. Once inside, Jorge closed the door as everyone looked up from the table. Marco was sitting at the end, laptop opened. He was showing something to Tony, who was simultaneously eating a sandwich. A box of donuts sat on the table between them, and cups of coffee and napkins were scattered around. The men looked energized by whatever they were looking at, stopping briefly to glance up at Jorge; both nodded at him but continued to talk.

Holly Anne was at the other end of the table with a laptop open in front of her. She appeared calm and relaxed, if not surprised by his arrival. Not a basket case as she had been earlier in the day, this was the final piece of the puzzle that made the picture clear. Without skipping a beat, Jorge pulled out his gun and shot her in the head.

"What the……" Makerson stood beside him in disbelief, "Oh my God! I….I….what the hell…"

"She was playing us," Jorge replied as he sat his gun on the table and reached for his phone. "That's why she wanted to leave today. Not because she was scared. Trust me, I found out the truth. I *always* do."

The group appeared to be in disbelief.

"I should I…." Makerson appeared stunned.

"I got it," Jorge said as he held the phone to his ear. "I got people who can take care of this…but maybe we should go to another room. Is there anyone else in the building?"

"Just us," Makerson replied, clearly rattled by what had just happened. "I…."

"Come," Marco was already standing with his laptop in hand. "We will go to your office."

The three men were quick to rush out of the room. Jorge reached for his gun before glancing briefly at Holly Anne's lifeless body as it slid to the floor. After ending his cryptic phone call, Jorge glanced at the reporter's body and stared. Blood was all around her and creeping across the floor.

"You fucked with the wrong person, lady."

Exiting the room, Jorge found the others in Makerson's office. All the laptops were now closed.

"So, what happened here?" Makerson stuttered as he nervously sat behind his desk. "Our phones are off…everything is off…"

"Cameras," Marco added. "There will be no footage of this day. I have erased it."

"*Perfecto,*" Jorge nodded as he sat down.

"So, Holly Anne, she was…"

"Spying on us," Jorge replied with a brief nod, glancing at each to see their reaction as he continued to stand. "She was never here to help. Her story was a lie."

"But, sir, when I checked," Marco started to speak but quickly stopped. "Oh, now I see."

"Holly Anne did not have as much as she said," Jorge replied. "She probably didn't have anything, but it was a great way to win my trust. She wanted on the inside to learn about us, not the other way around. It was a game. When I put pressure on her to talk today, she cried to me out of fear, supposedly because she was terrified they'd kill her, and she wanted to leave. It was a lie."

"She told us some things," Tony nodded and took a deep breath. "But not much when I think about it."

"Just more of the same, really," Makerson replied. "About how she was in the room when her bosses were talking about these pills, but this wasn't earth-shattering, just other potential side effects, but who knows what is true. From what you're saying, she was playing a confidence game with us."

"This is why you must always be careful who you trust," Jorge reminded them. "Many, they are only out to protect their interests. They do not care about yours. This was a game all along. She just forgot who she was playing with."

"So, who was Holly Anne working for?" Makerson appeared to calm down. "And how did you find out?"

"We got someone snooping at the crematorium," Jorge replied. "Found out he was working for her. People have a way of spilling their guts when you got a gun to their head."

"What was he looking for?" Tony asked, appeared unfazed. "Like, of all places, wouldn't it be here that they'd look?"

"This man we found, he was at the crematorium trying to find proof that we burned more bodies than our official records show. Ryerson was working on a story in hopes of taking me down."

"Shit!" Marco's eyes widened. "What did she have? I searched her emails and..."

"Maybe get her phone," Makerson suggested.

"It was on the table," Tony reminded Marco as he stood up. "So, that was the plan all along? She was trying to find dirt on you?"

"It kind of makes sense, actually," Makerson said. "She was asking a lot of questions lately, but I wasn't talking."

"Who was she working for?" Tony repeated Makerson's earlier question.

"No one yet, but she was trying to get a job with a major news channel in the US," Jorge replied. "They were in negotiations, but first, she had to bring them something big. Guess what she decided would make a great news story?"

"Sir," Marco was returning to the office with her phone in hand. "I got in already. She did not have a passcode. This is strange."

"We could've been looking at it every time she went to the bathroom," Tony muttered as his eyes met with Jorge's, who said nothing.

"Not really," Makerson shook his head. "She took that thing everywhere. Even the bathroom. Never left it with us."

"Now we know why," Marco said as he tapped onto the screen.

Jorge's phone beeped.

"The cleanup crew is here," he announced. "Marco, you keep looking. I will go let them in."

It was going to be a long night.

CHAPTER 46

"Back in Mexico, we got a saying. Take the gold, or you get the silver," Jorge remarked as he looked across the desk at Makerson. Beside him, Marco checked Holly Anne's phone before returning to his laptop. "I guess Ryerson decided to take the silver."

"She judged that one wrong," Makerson observed with a dismal expression on his face. "If she thought you were dangerous enough to make a good story, then she oughta known better."

"You would think," Jorge muttered as he turned toward the door to see Chase Jacobs entering the room.

"It's taken care of," he tilted his head toward the hallway. "They're on their way to meet Andrew at the crematorium."

"Where she'll join her friend," Jorge replied as he exchanged looks with Makerson and Marco. "The real question is how much damage did she do?"

"Sir, from what I see on her phone," Marco looked up from his screen. "It doesn't look like she was communicating with anyone about this story. Holly Anne had notes in a file, but when she messaged her contact, she just talked about investigating you. But there's no reference to any angles."

"Unless she spoke to that person directly on the phone about it," Makerson added. "We gotta hack her contacts, see what we can find out."

"Already working on it," Marco insisted, and Jorge turned his attention back to Chase.

"Everything's clean?" He gestured toward the boardroom.

"You could eat off the floor," Chase nodded.

"I think eating is the last thing I wanna do about now," Makerson made a face, causing Jorge to laugh.

"Give it a day," Jorge insisted. "You'll forget about it and be eating your donuts and talking about stories in there again, trust me."

"You need anything else?" Chase asked as he moved further into the room. "Did she have an office? Anything you need me to go through?"

"No, she just worked with us in the boardroom," Makerson replied. "Nothing official since she just started."

"At least the fact that she recently started might mean she got nothing," Jorge commented.

"Nothing about you," Marco replied. "She had a few general notes of what happened each day but no deep, dark secrets."

"Well, we have a secret now," Tony returned to the room with a sandwich. "What are we going to say if the police come around?"

"The police won't be coming near here," Jorge abruptly assured him. "Besides, how the fuck should we know where she goes at the end of the day."

"Cameras weren't working all week," Marco looked up from the laptop with a shrug.

"You can seriously eat right now?" Makerson glanced at the sandwich as Tony unwrapped it and shoved it in his mouth.

"I'm hungry," Tony shrugged as he crossed the room and sat in his usual spot. He took a moment to pat his bulging stomach. "It's been a long day."

"That's putting it mildly," Makerson turned his attention to Jorge. "Forget the police. What about her family? Friends? What if people in the media start wondering where she is? She was a prominent personality in the news for years."

"Until she wasn't," Chase shook his head. "Just say she left work in a rush, and we don't know why."

"She probably was sick," Tony shrugged, going along with the game. "Had some kind of women issues."

"Let's not get too much into the weeds," Jorge insisted. "Keep it simple. She left, period. We don't know why."

"Still we don't want no one snooping around," Makerson insisted.

"Don't matter," Jorge shook his head. "They got no body, no footage on camera, and her car won't be at work. They can make all the assumptions they want, but fuck them because they got nothing."

"We've been down this road before," Chase reminded them. "You'd be surprised how fast things blow over when there are no cookie crumbs to find Little Miss Riding Hood."

"Just a fucking wolf that's got a full belly," Jorge added. "But if you got no proof, you got nothing."

"As long as we don't get the cops in our hair," Makerson replied. "We don't need that shit."

"I'm heading out then," Chase pointed toward the exit. "I gotta get to the gym. Let me know if you need anything else."

"We should be good for tonight," Jorge replied. "Thanks, Chase."

After he was gone, Jorge turned to the others.

"I'm not sure how much more we can find tonight," he commented. "My main concern is Holly Anne wasn't talking to anyone, shared any information, or raised suspicion that she was in danger."

"Well, we got her on her channel talking about how she loved being here," Makerson reminded him. "How she was doing stories on flower arrangement and some kid flying a balloon in the park, bullshit like that."

Jorge grinned.

"Sir, I am not seeing anything on her phone," Marco insisted. "I checked all her message sites, text messages, emails, but I do see where she's mostly communicated with her sister."

"Is that so?" Jorge asked.

"Nothing there about her job," Marco shook his head. "But she has attempted to check in with Holly Anne today. Should I respond?"

"Hey, as long as they can't track the text being from here," Makerson said as he looked toward Jorge. "That might solve one of our problems."

"Then we should get rid of the phone," Marco replied. "I uploaded the information from it, but we should get rid of it."

"What should we say?" Tony shrugged.

"Be normal," Jorge said. "Don't say anything that raises any suspicions. Just say, whatever…"

"Even if it gets them on the wrong track?" Makerson asked.

"We don't want them on any track," Jorge reminded them. "Good or bad. Nothing. We give them nothing."

"That makes sense," Tony said as he finished his sandwich. "It leaves a dead end. Maybe something like, 'Busy, message later.' Maybe check her previous messages to make it sound the same."

"If anyone asks, she left around 2," Makerson said. "Didn't say where she was going, but she missed our meeting."

"Be vague," Jorge reminded them. "We don't want no rehearsed story. She left around 1:30, 2, something like that, but didn't say where. We don't ask because it's none of our business, end of story."

"We're way too busy," Tony shook his head.

"I didn't even see her leave," Marco spoke earnestly. "Do you mean she's not here now?"

Jorge threw his head back in laughter.

"You mean, she didn't just walk by my door," Makerson jumped in, causing Jorge to laugh harder, and Marco giggled. "That might be pushing it."

"Hey, we don't know where she went," Jorge shrugged dramatically. "We don't got no daycare here. This is adults. Figured she was working on a story, headed out, and didn't return. We didn't think of it one way or another. Probably working from home because it's quieter than here. I dunno."

"That's our story, and we're sticking to it," Makerson added as the others nodded. "So, she didn't tell anyone anything. We got our cover sorted out. Now we're back to square one."

"We still don't know who's at the top of this shit pile with the kids taking pills," Tony jumped in. "But it's big. It's international, and if what I suspect is true, it's pretty scary stuff."

"Depopulation due to sterilization," Makerson added. "It may not have a consequence now, but it will in the future."

"But if this is the case," Jorge wondered. "Would they not start in countries where people have more children? Canada, many choose not to have children anyway. Why not a more populated country like India? China?"

"Are we sure they aren't doing it there?" Tony asked as he sat back in his chair. "I mean, you know, in a different way."

"If they are, it's not working," Makerson shook his head.

"Even in the Philippines," Marco offered. "I mean, I can check with family, but I do not think these pills are there."

"It would cause too much suspicion if it started in a third-world country," Jorge reminded them. "Maybe a poorer country would cause alarm. Start in a rich country, then share it with the others. That way, they think it's safe if a rich country like Canada does it."

"I dunno," Makerson wondered. "Maybe there's something else going on here. I mean, these are all theories. I was reading over the side effects, and the list is a mile long, so the more serious side effects are probably hidden in that twenty-mile list, ensuring we won't see."

"They list everything to cover their asses," Tony reminded him. "We got to have some reports from independent studies."

"I don't think there are any," Makerson said.

"Ain't that illegal?" Jorge asked. "But I suppose it's Big Pharma. They do what they want."

"I'm pretty sure any studies that aren't in their favor go missing," Makerson said. "We're going in circles here. What about Athas? He's government. He must know something."

"I do have to get in touch with him," Jorge nodded. "I will do so tonight. I will break the news about his former lover, Miss Ryerson."

"If anyone can find information about this shit," Tony wondered. "You'd think it would be him."

"More likely some of the people who're trying to influence him," Makerson suggested. "Lobbyists who are pushing the bill, for example?"

"I will look that up, sir," Marco started to type vigorously.

"We are getting closer, *amigos,*" Jorge nodded. "I can feel it."

CHAPTER 47

"Tonight, it has come to my attention that your friend, Holly Anne, she was not being honest with me," Jorge informed Athas while talking on their secure line from his office, glancing at his bulletproof window and then back at the closed door in front of him. "The work she claimed to want to do with *Hernandez Productions* was simply a way to win my trust while she researched me from behind the scenes."

"Oh, shit," Athas replied. "Do I even want to know..."

"All you gotta know is," Jorge cut him off. "It is never a good idea to fuck with me, *amigo.* I *always* find out, and I do not give second chances."

There was a long pause before Athas spoke again.

"So, you're certain..."

"*Si,* I had a long conversation with a man found in my crematorium earlier today," Jorge continued as he closed his eyes and relaxed back in his chair. "Let us say that people tend to tell me the truth when I ask. I am very persuasive when I want to be."

"And he was working with Holly Anne?" Athas asked. "Who was trying to win your confidence to learn something at the production house?"

"She was a snake, Athas," Jorge reminded him. "And no longer a problem, but I do not have all night to talk. My associates are looking into it. What I need from you is some information."

"About Holly Anne?"

"Holly Anne is no longer a problem," Jorge confirmed. "I am talking about the lobbyists trying to force these pills down kids' throats. I need to know who they are and who they work for."

"Well, they work for Big Pharma," Athas replied, then paused. "I can get you the names, but they're a small part of the problem."

"I must start somewhere."

"I understand," Athas sighed and paused again. "But this is getting out of control. You know, it's not about Canada or our government. This is international. If it started and ended here, it would be easy."

"Yes, I know," Jorge opened his eyes and looked at the phone. "We have already talked..."

"No, I know for a fact," Athas cut him off. "I had a... powerful person in my office today and was told, in no uncertain terms, that I'm to go along with this or..."

"Or what?" Jorge countered. "They unfriend you on Facebook? What?"

"Someone will kill me," Athas replied.

"They bluntly say this here to you?" Jorge laughed. "Tell me, why did you let this psychopath in your office in the first place?"

"I didn't let her in," Athas continued. "She was already here. My Chief Health Officer, Margo Weber, represents this international group that...."

"Wait, what the fuck?" Jorge sat up straight. "You mean to tell me that you have your Chief Health Officer walk in your office and threaten your life unless you go along with this bullshit and you let the bitch walk out again? Athas, have I taught you nothing?"

"Yeah, well, there are some things that you can do in your own home or say, one of *your* businesses that you can't necessarily get away with in a government building."

"But you *can* get away with *threatening* the Canadian Prime Minister in his office?" Jorge asked as he rolled his eyes. "This here, it is interesting."

"She didn't say it quite like that..."

"Then you must tell me how she said it."

"She said that this was how the rest of the world was going or had already gone, and we were obligated to comply."

"Get to the death threat," Jorge pushed. "Tell me where I can find this bitch because you don't fuck with my people."

"Ok, let's step back for a minute," Athas spoke calmly. "Let's not start shooting people right away. She was only delivering the message for someone else."

"Then give me their names, and I will take care of them all," Jorge spoke abruptly. "These people, they must remember, you work for *me.* You do not take instructions from them or anyone else. You take them from me, and I say these pills are not to be mandatory here in Canada. If parents are stupid and want to give them to their kids, this is their choice, but they will not become mandatory."

"But people are being brainwashed…."

"Then buy the media," Jorge cut him off. "They are always crying for money, so give them money, but tell them not to bite the hand that feeds them, or you bite back. That is how you play this game."

"I suspect we're too late in the game for that," Athas reminded him. "They're already bought by the other side. And I know your HPC news is countering the narrative, but they're making your people sound like crackpots and conspiracy theorists. The game is too big. We can't fight back."

"So, what you say," Jorge snapped. "That you're going to let them run you? Think about that, *amigo,* and think fucking hard. I made you, and I can destroy you too. But unlike them, I come from the cartel. We are not in the business of making our enemies comfortable."

"No, I don't, I mean," Athas stumbled through his words. "I don't mean I will go along with it. I'm not saying that. I *did* tell my chief health officer that you were my advisor and would have to discuss it with you."

"Give me her address."

"I don't know if you should…."

"Give me her fucking address," Jorge snapped. "Because when I finish with her, she will not threaten you again."

There was some hesitation on the line.

"Look, Athas, these people," Jorge reminded him. "They aren't fucking around, but neither am I. I have no qualms about shoving a gun in her fucking mouth and telling her to say her prayers. And if she's giving the instructions, she can also tell me who's giving hers, and I will work my way right to the fucking top and leave a blood trail behind. Now, give me the bitch's fucking address because this shit ends now."

"I….I think…"

"And tomorrow," Jorge cut him off. "You're doing a press conference where you say that this drug won't be mandatory and that we Canadians do not force anyone to take a medication. If they choose to take it, we cannot control that, but we will not enforce anything against their will because it is a free country, and free countries, they don't work that way."

"I would also suggest," Jorge continued. "That you speak openly about the pressure you've had on you to enforce this medication on children. Talk about not knowing how they might react to it, long-term effects, all of this stuff here. I can have Makerson send you the facts he's learned in his research. Let people know you are looking after them."

"And if they attack?"

"Attack back," Jorge instructed. "Like you did the other day when you told someone to fuck off during question period."

"They've raked over the coals for that one," Athas reminded him.

"What are they going to do?"

"Kill me," Athas reminded him.

"Athas, you have been down this road before," Jorge reminded him. "I can get you some extra security, my people, if this here makes you feel better."

"Well, I…"

"Or I can remind your security if anything happens to you," Jorge continued. "It happens to them too."

"These are RCMP officers."

"So?" Jorge countered. "I do not fucking care."

"Ok, maybe we should…"

"Athas, just make the speech tomorrow," Jorge cut him off. "Say what I tell you to say, and give me that bitch's address. I will take care of the rest."

"I might have a better idea."

After ending the call, Jorge sat back in his chair with his thoughts. He reached for his laptop just as there was a knock on his door.

"Yeah?"

The door opened, and Paige stuck her head in.

"You tore through here like a bull earlier," she quietly remarked. "Is there anything I should know about?"

"*Mi amor,* come in," Jorge nodded his head. "And you might want to close the door behind you."

"So it was that kind of day," Paige observed as she followed his instructions and started to cross the room. "Did you find out something more?"

"I found out Holly Anne was a lying bitch, that is what," Jorge replied. "She thought it would be fun to investigate me."

"Hmmm, I take it she's no longer in the cast of characters at the production house?" Paige asked as she eased into the chair.

"She's no longer in *any* cast of characters," Jorge corrected her, and Paige nodded, taking the news with ease. "And our chief health officer is about to be next."

"Margo Weber?" Paige raised an eyebrow. "So, is she connected with these pills?"

"You bet," Jorge replied. "Big mistake on her behalf. She thought she could go into Athas' office and threaten him. Only I control this man. They need a strong warning."

"So what's the plan?" Paige asked.

"I am so glad you asked, *mi amor,"* Jorge grinned as he leaned back in his chair.

CHAPTER 48

"Mind if we join your meeting?" Jorge barged into the room with Paige behind him. He noted that Athas appeared as alarmed as Margo Weber, even though he knew the two planned to crash their meeting. Jorge shot him a dirty look before continuing. "My wife and I have some things to discuss with your chief health officer."

"I didn't agree to this," Margot Weber jumped up and shot Jorge a dirty look. "I didn't come here to be ambushed."

"No one is ambushing anyone," Paige gently spoke as she closed the door behind them. "We're here as concerned parents to discuss this medication you wish to make mandatory. Surely, you'd like to meet with some actual Canadian parents to hear their input."

"We've already done that," Margo attempted to sound strong even though her body was frail, and her eyes carried unmistakable fear when she glanced at Jorge before quickly looking toward Paige as if he weren't there. "The majority of parents believe that..."

"Bullshit!" Jorge cut her off as he moved closer, noting she pulled back when he did. "Now, lady, I don't got all day to hear the speech you prepared for the media. We want the truth. You can start by telling me who's controlling your puppet strings, and if you're lucky, I will let you walk out of here today."

"You can't threaten me," Margo spoke with tears forming in her eyes, glancing again at an unsympathetic Paige as if grasping at straws. "Mr. Hernandez, we are not in Mexico, and threatening someone's life isn't accepted here in Canada just because you..."

"You mean, like you did with Athas yesterday?" Jorge sharply cut her off, watching the color drain from her face. "Look, lady, I get it. You live in a mansion while you suck off the taxpayer's tit. I get it. That's what you all do, so you got to answer to someone to keep that lavish lifestyle. You thought you'd come in here and tell Athas to do what your puppet masters told you, walk out, and everything would fall into place. But I got news for your lady. Athas does not take instructions from *you*."

"But we are interested in who told you to do this," Paige moved closer to the chief health officer, who appeared scared and glanced toward the door. "We need names."

"I can't give you the information..."

"Ah, but lady, you got to tell us," Jorge shook his head. "This here, it is not a polite request."

The chief health officer didn't answer, but her dark eyes grew in size while her breathing increased so intensely that you could see her physically strain. It was a clear sign of fear taking over while she weighed her options. Jorge made a point of moving his jacket aside to display the gun he was carrying. That was all it took for the lady who bravely threatened Athas a day earlier to surprise them by suddenly darting toward the door. Unfortunately for her, Paige was much faster.

Grabbing Margo Weber by the arm, the older woman gasped as Paige swiftly pushed her to the floor, causing her to hit it with a loud thump. This was when Jorge pulled out his gun and pointed it at her head. Paige put her foot on the woman's neck, and with a calm voice, she quietly informed the woman, "My heel can go through your neck and leave an ugly scar, or I can move it a little to the left and kill you."

"Trust me," Jorge said as he watched Athas jump up from behind the desk and rush over. "It is not a fast death either. You will struggle and die slowly. Unlike the bullet I have in this gun, you will know you are dying."

"This might be a good time to tell us the information we're looking for," Paige smoothly added. "Give us some names. Tell us everything. This is where this game ends."

Margo Weber glanced toward an unsympathetic Alec Athas, who crossed his arms over his chest.

"You might want to listen to them."

"I think…I think I hurt something…." She attempted to move but cried out in pain. "Please….I will tell you, but you must call an ambulance and…"

"Enough!" Jorge shouted while Paige pushed her foot harder against the woman's throat. "Lady, we don't got all day, and we aren't playing games here. Give us some fucking names and some fucking information, or you're dead. Period. You will not have to worry about calling an ambulance because there won't be anything to take away."

"I have all the information in my phone if you let me…"

"We can also take your phone off your corpse and have our IT people examine it," Paige replied without skipping a beat. "You're gonna have to do better than that."

"You know what? Never mind," Jorge shook his head. "That there is the easier way. This woman, she don't want to talk."

"I'll talk!" She cried out as tears filled her eyes and ran down her cheeks. "I will tell you whatever you want to know. Please! Please don't kill me. I have a cat that needs…."

"Lady, are you seriously begging for your life because you're worried about your cat?" Jorge shook his head and looked toward his wife. "Unbelievable!"

"Her cat has its own Instagram page," Athas muttered as he returned to his desk.

"Oh, is that so?" Jorge asked with mock interest. "Tell me, lady, does your cat have nine lives?"

"Or more importantly," Paige jumped in. "Do you?"

"It's not what you think," Margo Weber sputtered out.

"We already know these pills aren't really to calm kids," Jorge informed her, shaking his head.

"No, I know that show that comes from your production house," she replied. "Suggested that it was to cause kids to be infertile down the line. That's not what this is all about. This was never what it was about."

"Then what is it about?" Paige asked as she eased her shoe from the chief health officer's neck. "Compliance?"

"In part," she admitted as she slowly sat up, with unexpected spryness for a woman who had just claimed to be in pain. "But they plan to continue adjusting the medication over weeks and months, making it stronger."

"I don't understand," Athas said as he returned. "What's this going to do?"

There was a hesitation before she answered.

"What we said was true," she cried. "It will calm them but to a much stronger degree than we led people to believe. The medication will affect their serotonin. It will make them feel apathetic. In some cases, suicidal."

"You're trying to make our kids suicidal?" Paige gasped. "What is *wrong* with you?"

"That's just in some cases," Margo Weber attempted to explain. "It's not in every case, but we feel that it's a risk we're willing to take to maintain civility."

"Are you fucking kidding me, lady?" Jorge snapped. "You want to make kids miserable and want to kill themselves? But it's a risk you are willing to take to keep things civil? Is there something fucking wrong with you?"

"No, I know what this is about," Athas jumped in. "They were talking about this at one of my meetings. Haven't you noticed that the music and all the television shows winning awards now or getting attention are passionless? That's on purpose. It discourages people from having any strong emotions about anything. That's why movies and books that are at the top are usually about mindless topics and have no socially contentious issues involved. They don't want a generation of rebellious kids who question anything. They want kids to be compliant and apathetic about life. It all makes sense now. They were talking about it."

"Who?" Paige asked.

"Lobbyist," Athas shrugged. "People in my party, powerful people who probably don't want anyone questioning their motives. That's why everything now is about *toxic masculinity* and how saying mean things makes you a terrible person and canceled. They want to send a message that you must toe the line, keep your mouth shut, and not offend anyone. All that woke bullshit."

"Ah, yes!" Jorge nodded. "This here, it does make sense."

"So, this drug was just another layer of that?" Paige asked as she glanced at Jorge, causing him to nod in understanding. "Weak people are easier to control."

"They don't want you to have courage," Jorge said more toward Paige than the woman on the floor, who appeared to be relaxing as if she were off the hook. "It's like a cult. They beat you down until you do not have any fight left. No strength and, as I said, no courage. That's why so many kids Maria's age, are so spineless."

"Because they want them to be," Paige muttered as she looked toward Athas, who was pacing the floor. "Don't fight back, don't ask questions, just keep your mouth shut and go along with whatever they want. You can sure do a lot of damage when no one protests."

"So this is why," Athas was asking as he returned. "This is why you were threatening my life yesterday? Because you wanted me to go along with this shit?"

"I had no choice," Margo explained as Jorge glanced toward Athas, his eyes returning to Paige, who moved away and nodded as she stepped back. "I have an important meeting tomorrow with the man overseeing this project worldwide. Of course, Mr. Hernandez, your children are exempt from this rule, as are all the children of high-ranking individuals, such as yourself. This is just for the average, everyday, non-relevant kids that probably are taking up more breathing space than anything..."

Alec Athas appeared furious as he approached the chief health officer. She didn't notice the gun at first, but it was the moment that she did that it was too late. He shot her in the head.

"Thank God this here office is soundproof," Jorge spoke as if nothing unusual had occurred. "But we sure got one hell of a mess to clean up."

CHAPTER 49

"A kitty?" Maria gushed, reminding Jorge of the little girl she once had been. However, this illusion quickly disappeared when she returned to being a saucy teenager. "I'm not going to have to clean up after this thing, am I?"

Jorge looked down at the black cat, who appeared curious about the strangers as he sniffed his surroundings. He then looked back at his wife and shook his head.

"*Mi amor,* I can't win," he said as he turned to walk away.

"I…where did this cat come from?" Maria sounded suspicious, if not slightly nervous. "I thought *Papá* didn't want us to have a cat. I don't understand."

"He is a rescue, Maria," Jorge called over his shoulder as he headed into the kitchen. "His owner recently passed away, and they needed a new home for him."

"Oh," Maria's voice dropped down a notch in tone, indicating that she clued in. "Now, I think…"

"*Kitty!*" Miguel's voice boomed through the room, and Jorge turned in time to see the little boy running toward the cat, who appeared nervous but stood his ground. Collapsing on his bum, Miguel gently petted the cat and giggled. "George!"

"Miguel, that's our *Papà's* name," Maria attempted to correct him. "We can't name a cat..."

"George!"

Paige began to laugh.

"He wants to name the cat after you," Maria made a funny face before bursting out in laughter. "Seriously? That's so weird."

"George!" Miguel repeated as he continued to pet the black cat, who was now purring and rubbing up against the little boy. In turn, he giggled. "Soft!"

"I'm not sure this house is big enough for two of us," Jorge muttered as he shook his head. "Anyway, I got a meeting here shortly. Maria, can you help Paige get the cat supplies out of the SUV?"

"Yup," She agreed as Jorge pointed toward the office.

"Paige, I will be..."

"I will send everyone in when they arrive."

Once in his office with the door closed, Jorge opened his laptop and clicked on a link.

"....saddened by this news of her sudden resignation," Athas spoke to the camera in the same office where her body had recently lie dead. It took time, but his people had got it done without being conspicuous to those who worked in the building. As it turned out, the prime minister had a secret passage to get out of his office in case of a sudden emergency like a terrorist attack. It was handy when they were getting rid of Margo Weber's body.

"... private matter, and we must respect her privacy at this time...."

"It's a private matter, all right," Jorge turned off the video and sat back in his chair, glancing at the bulletproof window. A knock at the door interrupted his thoughts.

"Come in," Jorge said as he swiveled his chair around and waited. Paige walked into the room.

"They here?"

"Not yet," She replied as she walked toward the desk. "Jorge, I was thinking...these people are very dangerous."

"We are very dangerous too, *mi amor,"* Jorge replied without missing a beat.

"But if they're powerful enough to effect something like this worldwide," Paige started.

"You worry too much."

"I worry that our kids will get caught in the crossfire," Paige admitted as she stood across the desk from him. "That's what I'm concerned about."

"You mean, they aren't already?" Jorge asked. "Paige, I know you are concerned, but trust me, I got this. The problem with these people is that no one ever stands up to them. This time is different."

"But what if..."

"Paige, this is ok," Jorge spoke to her in a gentle voice. "I will have Marco look into it, and when this man arrives tomorrow to meet with our chief health officer and Athas, I will be waiting for him instead. I will be ready."

She didn't appear convinced.

"Paige, I have dealt with these people before," he reminded her. "This is not my first day on the job."

"I've dealt with them before, too," she reminded him. "They used to hire me to kill people like you that got in their way."

Jorge took in her words and shrugged.

"Then it's a good thing I have you on my side this time, *mi amor,*" Jorge winked at her.

"Just think about what I said."

"Paige, you know I will look at everything. I know what I'm doing. Do not worry."

The sound of the doorbell interrupted their conversation. Paige rushed to answer it while Jorge considered what she said. He needed a rock-solid plan. He needed to send a message.

Marco was the first to arrive, soon followed by the rest. Jorge sat in the office with Chase, Makerson, Diego, and Jolene. As much as he didn't want to bother with Diego's sister, he recognized that sometimes she was a necessary evil. She might come in handy in this situation.

After going over what had recently taken place, he observed the expressions of everyone in his *familia.* Shock and anger filled the room.

"So, let me get this straight," Diego was the first to speak. "These fucks want to make our kids depressed and miserable. Is that what you're saying?"

"Compliant sounds more like it," Makerson replied. "By the way, did Margo Weber *really* resign? What's with that?"

Jorge gave him a look, and he nodded.

"Gotcha."

"It don't matter," Jorge pointed out. "We don't got to deal with her anymore, and that's the point."

"Sir, there are people sending messages to her phone," Marco said as he scrolled through the screen. "People asking what is going on and why she resigned."

"Who?" Jorge asked.

"Most of the messages are from this man….ah….Roger Broaddrick?" Marco looked up. "I'm researching him right now, but he's the man who is coming here tomorrow to meet with her. He's asking if she's still available to talk and wonders why she stepped down. What would you like me to say?"

"Say you have something else in mind, and you will talk to him about it more tomorrow," Jorge said as he relaxed in his chair. "Except, of course, it won't be Margo Weber waiting for him when he arrives. It will be me. And we are going to have a nice talk."

"Are you seeing anything else?" Diego asked as he turned toward Marco. "Anyone else going to the meeting or what?"

"I just see him, sir," Marco shook his head. "She only has it listed that the meeting is with him and Athas. Does Alec know this?"

"He knows," Jorge replied. "He will be there."

"So, what?" Diego asked. "We gonna shoot and ask questions later or what?"

"Sounds like a good idea to me," Chase muttered.

"Who is this?" Jolene asked as she squinted her eyes and zeroed in on Jorge.

"Jolene, pay attention," Diego chastised his sister.

"I am!" She snapped back. "I just do not understand who he is."

"He is a powerful man in Europe, apparently," Makerson looked up from his laptop. "But that's a good question. Why is he so powerful? Who the fuck is he?"

"See, this here was not a bad question," Jolene pointed out to her brother. "He also wonders."

"He has declared himself head of this group that supposedly is concerned for the world and where it's headed," Makerson continued to read something on his screen. "But still, why him? Why does he stand on the top of this mountain? I can't understand why everyone does what he wants?"

"People are weak," Jorge reminded Makerson. "Sometimes people want a leader, and this would be that man. Why? This here I'm not sure about. I am about to find out tomorrow."

"Sir, I have turned off all the cameras and erased everything in Athas's office and nearby," Marco said. "No one will see where Margo Weber was last. No one will see when she left or if she did. I cleaned everything."

"*Perfecto,*" Jorge replied.

"I know Paige has some…concerns," Diego spoke cautiously, his head down and his eyes turned up. "I told her I would make sure everyone was ok."

"Paige, she worries…"

"She might have a reason," Chase reminded him. "If this man is so powerful, who's to say he won't threaten you too? I think it's legit to be concerned."

"If anything happens to me," Jorge looked at Diego and Jolene but didn't finish his sentence.

Concern filled Jolene's face while Diego looked away.

"Hey, this here is always possible," Jorge reminded them. "Let us hope not, but we cannot know the future. You must remember one thing. F*amilia* comes first, and it is loyalty above all. There are no exceptions. If I've said it once, I've said it a million times. This is what matters the most. You must never forget that."

The room was sullen.

"Come on, people," Jorge laughed. "Have some faith in me. Remember, I have dealt with the big dogs before, and I've won. If anyone should be worried, it should be this man meeting me. Because it may be the last fucking meeting he has."

CHAPTER 50

Courage. It's not always about running into a burning building to save someone or playing the superhero. Sometimes it's about being yourself and speaking your truth. It's easy to cave to the pressures, but it takes courage to stand up and say no or ask questions when it matters the most.

Even if it means you stand alone.

Even if it means you step on some toes.

Even if it means you push back; *hard*.

Jorge Hernandez was the king of pushing back.

As he sat across from the man who appeared powerful and invincible in public photos, spoke elegantly in speeches before thousands in the audience, and had a reputation for getting what he wanted, Jorge realized that none of it mattered. It was an image created much like a product sold in stores. This man appeared to be the most powerful person in the world in his expensive suits and polished photos, but looking into his eyes, Jorge realized he was as vulnerable as a child in person.

"This certainly is a surprise," Roger Broaddrick shuffled uncomfortably in his chair but attempted a smile as he sat with Jorge in Alec Athas's office. The Canadian prime minister sat in silence aside from both men. The combination of his thick accent and deep voice is why he appeared so authoritarian in the videos online, the hours of footage Jorge had viewed before the meeting. "Margo did not mention that you would also be in the meeting, but you know what I say? What a wonderful surprise, Jorge Hernandez! Your reputation, it proceeds you."

"It should," Jorge gruffly replied. He took a deep breath and moved his arms out on each side of the chair, making himself seem larger while not breaking eye contact for a moment. "I have a strong track record, but my record is not like yours."

"Yes, well," Broaddrick grinned bashfully as if given a compliment. "It has been my journey, my goal, to change this world. I look around and see all the people who contribute nothing, who have no goals, no ambitions, simply taking up space, and I think, what are we doing here? People are weak, Mr. Hernandez, as you probably already know. A man as powerful as you has something extra to make you come this far. You are in the 1% of the world. You are not one of them."

"You think I grew up rich?" Jorge pushed back. "I did not. I made myself who I am today."

"As did I," Roger Broaddrick attempted to explain. "Yes, my father had money but did not hand anything to me. He made me work hard. He put obstacles before me to test and prepare me for this world. It was not easy, but eventually, I made it to where I am today. That is why I have no respect for people who don't have motivation, who live in their parent's basements and play video games all day. It is pathetic."

Jorge considered what he said and nodded.

"Mr. Hernandez," Broaddrick leaned forward in his chair. "My father, he was not an easy man."

There was a moment of understanding between the men as Jorge didn't reply but nodded.

"Of course, these methods," Broaddrick sat back in his chair and glanced around the room while Jorge's eyes watched him. "They would not be acceptable today. Beating your children, you cannot do in this world. But as much as I hated every minute of it, hated *him,* I cannot deny that it made me the man I am today. If he had been soft with me, then I would be soft. If he had given me luxuries without consequences, I would also be one of these useless, spoiled people who expect to have everything handed to them. And now, look at the children of today. They do not work for anything. They cry if they don't get their way or have the latest gadget. They do not know what real struggles are."

"I cannot deny," Jorge finally spoke. "That children are spoiled today. Yes, you are right. It is a different time."

"But look at our world," Broaddrick spread his arms out while shaking his head. "It is, as they say, going to hell in a hand basket. Each generation is lazier, weaker, and has a sense of entitlement. Where does that take our world? Where does that put us? What will happen if this continues? They will burn down our planet and then wait for someone to save them."

Jorge nodded in understanding.

"That is why," Broaddrick seemed to grow more confident as he spoke. "I started an organization with others who share my vision. These are people who have worked hard and risen to the ranks. They have become powerful, rich, the leaders of the world. These are people who should be leading us in a better direction. That is my goal here. That is why I do everything I do."

"Is that why you want all the kids in the world on this pill?" Athas jumped in with anger in his voice. "Why do you want to control them?"

"It is not about controlling them," Broaddrick corrected him, glancing briefly at Jorge, who continued to watch him. "It is about saving them from themselves. When left to their own devices, you see what happens. Our environment is going to shit. Our population is growing too rapidly. We will run out of food to feed all these people, depleting our world of resources. And then what? What happens then?"

"You don't look like you're starving to death," Athas pointed toward the man's stomach. "You live in a mansion which probably uses lots of resources, but that's different?"

"I have earned it," Broaddrick insisted with a humored expression. "I have worked hard. I have contributed to our society. No one handed anything to me, but many of these bottom feeders wait for an inheritance or to win the lottery, but they do not want to work hard for what they want."

"But the average, middle class or lower class person has earned what they have too," Athas argued. "They struggle, but they've earned it."

"If they worked harder," Broaddrick reasoned. "They wouldn't struggle so much. That is what I am saying. Sometimes, we must make uncomfortable choices. Choices that go against the grain to obtain wealth. Charge a little more at your store, and go for the job with the money, even if you don't like it. There are always choices, but unfortunately, people are more interested in being *comfortable* than in having what they need. I see it all the time."

"I think they call that being happy," Athas reasoned. "When I was a social worker...."

"Ah, yes!" Broaddrick cut him off. "That is what I was waiting for, you to remind us, once again, that you have a history in social work, and I bet that work was much more fulfilling than what you do now, am I right? But yet, you are doing something that maybe does not make you happy, but it pays well. You will have a nice pension and be well off for the rest of your life. You didn't have children to overpopulate our world further, and unlike me, you are a lean man, so you only eat what you need to. See, this is what I mean, Mr. Athas. You have made sacrifices that benefit you and society as a whole. As opposed to continuing your social work, and what? How many people did you actually help? Remember, people must want to help themselves first, and let's face it, not many do. They want the magical solution, the psychic telling them they will marry rich, the easy option. You took the road less traveled and see where it brought you."

His argument caused Athas to recoil, and Jorge could see the anger building up in his eyes. They exchanged a look, but it was important he not show any alliance with Athas, even though the childless part of the conversation was a sore spot with the prime minister.

"He does make a point," Jorge explained to Athas, who looked as if his head was about to explode. "Sometimes, we must look at the greater good rather than what gives us happiness, and for how long do we have that happiness? I mean, really? Much of what they tell us we should want is overrated and painted in a way that is not true. This here is a good point."

"Yes," Broaddrick grew more comfortable as he glanced at Jorge. "This is what I mean. You know what I am talking about Mr. Hernandez. You might disagree with my methods, but the truth is that as much as you might not want to scare the sheep, sometimes you have to herd them together for their safety."

"Before the wolf creeps in," Jorge nodded as his eyes narrowed, and a sinister smile crept on his lips. "I do understand."

"So you drug them up?" Athas shot back. "What kind of..."

"In fairness," Broaddrick countered. "These pills do not harm. They calm the children by making them less reactive toward life. This allows them to focus better and be more productive members of society. Of course, they won't be for everyone. I'm sure, Mr. Hernandez, your children wouldn't be required to participate in this but merely give the impression they do. There are always exceptions to the rule, and it seems appropriate that this would be one of them."

Jorge nodded, noting that Athas continued to grow angrier.

"Don't tell me you're going along with this shit?" Athas snapped at Jorge. "Just because your kids…"

"Calm down, Athas," Jorge raised his hand, indicating that he relax. "I just think it is interesting to hear the man out. He has many valid points to consider."

"If you want to play God," Athas ranted. "Which is something you'd probably relate to."

"Ah, but I have never been compared to God,' Jorge reminded him, "the devil, yes, but never God."

To this, Roger Broaddrick laughed.

"And today, you wished to discuss this more with Margo Webber," Jorge continued. "Am I correct?"

"Yes, we were going to work out the final details together," Broaddrick nodded and grinned. "Is she running late?"

"No," Jorge grinned with him. "She's running *dead.*"

Broaddrick's expression dropped.

"So, I'm afraid she will not be making it today," Jorge spoke calmly as if they were merely discussing the weather. "You see, she talked like you, and it did not go well with Athas here."

Broaddrick appeared surprised as he glanced at the prime minister.

"It was quite messy, but we took care of it," Jorge continued. "You see, Athas, he works for *me.* But one of the luxuries of our deal is that when he is in a jam, I help him out. Yesterday, you could say, he was in a jam."

"Very messy," Athas added in a gruff voice.

"Not as messy as it would be if I did it," Jorge casually added. "But, you know, I come from the cartel. We tend to be a bit more brutal."

"I understand," Broaddrick grew visibly nervous. "What is it you want from me?"

"You've already done it."

"But, I do not understand."

"You just confessed, " Jorge replied. "It will be all over social media by the end of the day...I mean, with some parts at the end cut out, of course."

"Which parts," Roger Broaddrick automatically asked, but it was clear he knew the answer without them saying.

"This part," Jorge's voice rose as he abruptly reached for a weapon, pulled it out, and shot the man in the chest, causing Athas to flinch, but only momentarily before he looked away from the gasping man with a hand over his heart.

"I'm gonna have nightmares about this one," he confessed to Jorge, who appeared unfazed.

"No mess with a heart attack gun," Jorge reminded him. "I gotta use this one more often."

"I'm not talking about him dying," Athas replied as the man slumped over in the chair.

"The worst part," Jorge reminded him as he stood up. "Is there will be another one behind him."

"Everybody wants to rule the world," Athas spoke softly, his eyes vulnerable as he looked away.

"But only if you let them," Jorge reminded him. "Because first, you have to let them rule you."

Did you enjoy this book? Learn about other books in the Hernandez series at www.mimaonfire.com. Follow me on social media @mimaonfire.

Printed in the United States
Baker & Taylor Publisher Services

Printed in the United States
by Baker & Taylor Publisher Services